OF FEAR AND FAE
THE GODDESS'S DAUGHTER
BOOK II

WARD PARKER

Mad Mangrove Media

ISBN: 978-1-957158-23-5

Cover by TrifBookDesign

CONTENTS

CHAPTER 1

SOPHIE

A supernatural creature was inside the darkened building. It was aware of me, too, and my witchy senses were making the skin on the back of my neck prickle. I hoped the creature was Diego, the vampire who owned the building that housed the restaurant downstairs and the apartment above it.

But I couldn't be sure. The creature might be looking for Diego, intending to do him harm. In fact, there were traces of magic in the air; of what sort I couldn't tell.

A wooden sign with elaborate lettering announced "14 Granada Street," the address and name of the restaurant. I walked along the sidewalk in front of the brick building from the mid-1800s, pretending to be a random passerby. Assuming a random passerby would carry a crossbow and have a broadsword strapped to her back. But one could never be too careful nowadays.

I cut through the alley and peered into a window. It was too dark inside to make anything out. Whatever was in there didn't need light to see.

When I reached the parking lot in the rear of the building, my heart leaped at the sight of Diego's vintage Aston Martin parked at the far end of the small parking lot. But I remembered he often left it here and traveled by foot. Vampires can walk faster than the speed limit.

The hood of the car was cold, which told me he hadn't driven it within the hour. I walked to the rear of the building and peered into the kitchen window. The pilot light of the gas range provided just enough light to create scary shadows, but none of them moved. I checked the window of a private dining room but couldn't see through the curtains.

The official reason I needed to see Diego was to enlist his help in overthrowing the leadership of the Executive Council of the Supernatural Guilds of San Marcos. But the overriding reason I was here was to beg Diego's forgiveness. To throw myself on his mercy. He hadn't responded to my calls or texts, so I came here in person. I'd been giving him space, not contacting him, but my intuition told me he needed moral support.

My intuition told me this because I was an empath.

He needed moral support because his lover, a vampire named Lethia, was dead.

And I was the one who had killed her. She was ancient, powerful, and someone who deserved to be destroyed. My crossbow bolt, made from ash wood, entered her heart and ended her reign of terror.

She'd abused Diego and was feasting on him in front of me, about to take the last of his blood, before I intervened and saved him. Saved myself, too, because I would have been next.

I suppose I was searching for more than forgiveness, for something to erase the guilt eating my insides. That was the major downside of being an empath. I didn't just sense others' feelings. All emotions, mine included, were amplified to an almost unbearable degree.

Diego had wanted to leave her but still had love for her in his undead heart. My empathy reached out, sensing for that love, to see if he was here tonight. When you're an empath, your emotional fluency is so strong it reaches the level of a psychic power. With me, it included a medium's power to communicate with ghosts.

I just wished it helped me communicate better with a certain vampire.

I rang the buzzer beside the rear door and waited in vain for his voice to come over the intercom.

The rear door was locked. No surprise. I still had the key he had given me when I had needed a hideout, but I would not let myself in without an invitation.

"Diego? Are you in there?" I asked in a normal speaking voice. No need to shout at someone with vampire hearing.

I waited for a few moments before giving up.

A hand clamped around the back of my neck.

"SORRY, WE ARE CLOSED," DIEGO SAID AS HIS HAND RELAXED its grip, but lingered on my neck for a few seconds.

There was little affection in the lingering, though. It felt more like a protective gesture.

"I felt someone was home," I said.

"It's risky for you to be here."

"I don't think paranoid citizens will attack me."

"That's not what I meant." Diego turned his head to survey the parking lot and the historic homes backing up to it. "Come inside where we won't be seen."

He unlocked the back door, but instead of leading me upstairs to his apartment, he turned left and entered the rear of his restaurant.

"Would you like a glass of wine?" he asked.

"That would be nice."

We walked down a central hall to the front of the building and entered the bar and lounge. The restaurant was dark except for pale light from streetlamps filtering through window curtains. I felt my way to the bar and climbed upon a stool.

"Albariño?" he asked.

"Sure."

When he opened the refrigerator behind the bar, I was nearly blinded by its light. It reflected off the ebony skin of his hand as he withdrew the bottle. He poured me a glass of the white Spanish wine.

"Why did you come here?" he asked, remaining behind the bar as if I were a mere customer.

"I wanted to see how you were doing."

"I'm doing fine. Busy preparing the restaurant for the relaunch. There are so many difficulties, including a supplier who found out I'm a vampire and is blackmailing me."

"Sorry to hear that." I wanted to know how he was dealing with the loss of Lethia, but I sensed he didn't want to speak of such things. "I also wanted to talk with you about the Council. We need to do something about them."

"Indeed. They are another source of problems for me. Baldric in particular." I caught the gleam of a fang as he smiled bitterly. "He believes I destroyed Lethia. Apparently, he was even fonder of her than I had imagined. Imagine that. The faerie who was cuckolding me seeks to avenge the woman who betrayed me."

Guilt swept through me yet again. Not only had I taken Lethia from Diego, but I had left him looking guilty.

"You should tell him it wasn't you who destroyed her," I said.

"I haven't spoken with him directly about it. Ironically, my friends who told me about Baldric and Lethia believed I should have destroyed her, anyway."

I agreed but couldn't say so.

"The thing is," he continued, "I can't admit that a human destroyed her to save me. I would be the laughingstock of the entire Clan of the Eternal Night."

"What are you going to do?"

"Kill him, of course. You and I are of the same mind that he must be removed from the Executive Council. With him threatening to stake me, I'm left with no choice other than to fight."

Suddenly, every light in the establishment switched on. Background music blared. Even the blender behind the bar whirred loudly. I flinched on my barstool.

"Ah, I guess the time to fight is now," Diego said, not the least bit startled.

"I'd sensed magic, and now I know it's Fae," I said. "Your resident ghost, Acora, didn't do this. I'm going to put a protection spell on us."

"No. I don't want to hide behind a human. This is between Baldric and me."

Vampires are incredibly lethal. They have preternatural strength, speed, and senses, as well as the ability to mesmerize their prey. It's difficult to destroy them, and their wounds heal like magic, but vampires don't have the ability to use magic—not in the way human witches or Fae sorcerers do.

How was he going to fight Baldric if the faerie was launching this magical attack from afar?

The electricity went out, and the restaurant returned to

darkness. The silence was more total than before, when at least the HVAC system had blown cool air, and the refrigerator had hummed.

Diego, of course, could see fine and hear things I couldn't.

"What's that sound?" he asked with uncharacteristic anxiety.

"I can't—"

"Shhh! It sounds like thousands of tiny feet. Insect feet."

I didn't hear anything.

Diego gasped and frantically slapped his legs and torso.

"Spiders!" His voice was panicky. "I *hate* spiders!"

Vampires fear very few things. I'd never realized spiders were one of them.

My empathy told me that, no, this was not a universal vampire thing. Diego had a phobia of spiders.

Why was Baldric targeting Diego's phobia? To torture him before he killed him?

If the magic was being directed at Diego specifically, it meant Baldric probably didn't know I was here.

Which I could use to my advantage. If I could locate Baldric, I could launch a magical attack against him. *If* I could do it, that is, without his sensing my magic.

I cast a deconstruction spell that latched onto Baldric's magic. A deconstruction spell enables a magician to open the hood and examine the engine of a spell cast by someone else. I hoped to use it to follow Baldric's magic back to him. He wouldn't sense my efforts because I was probing his spell, not him.

The power and complexity of his spell were impressive. Its tendrils were embedded deep into Diego, throughout his mind and psyche.

The spell shifted imperceptibly.

Diego stopped slapping at the imaginary spiders and sank to

his knees on the floor. He covered his face with his hands and sobbed.

Not the kind of behavior I would expect from a vampire as stoic and elegant as he.

Waves of sorrow emanated from him like a storm tide.

"There is no reason to exist," he moaned.

"I hadn't realized you loved her so much," I said, placing a hand on his shoulder.

I quickly yanked my hand away as I felt the dark turn Baldric's spell had taken.

"No, it's not that. I see the complete futility of my existence," he said. "Enduring year after year, century after century, as an undead. Yes, there is no dread of dying from old age, but there is no hope of entering heaven."

No one agreed on whether vampires had souls or what happened to them when their existence was snuffed out. But I empathized with his bleak view of an existence taken for granted. Nothing seemed special, and boredom was tragic. It was why many vampires—Diego excluded—fell into bouts of decadent pleasure-seeking.

"Diego, you're brilliant and successful. You bring joy to others through your culinary genius."

"It means nothing."

"Sometimes, it's up to us to bring meaning to our existence. Savor the simple things, like the moonlight reflected on the ocean. Or the—"

"I don't want to hear your greeting-card poetry!"

He cried even harder. I think I'd made things worse.

"Don't you understand Baldric's magic is doing this to you? These aren't your true feelings. He's feeding them to you. This is classic Fae torture-magic. They used it on my mom, too."

"My feelings are true. And accurate. Every breath is a tedium in this mortal world. Everything that lives around me will die, while time grinds away at the landscape and the things humans have built. Everything is temporary, except for me."

I still had so much to learn about my empath powers, but I flooded him with all the comforting feelings I could manage.

Diego fell over and curled into the fetal position. My empath powers weren't working.

It was time to go on the offensive.

My deconstruction spell was still active, so I used it to trace Baldric's magic back to him. I couldn't tell where he was physically, but my spell found the point from where his magic emanated.

Once I had established the connection with him, I sent a blast of concentrated energy along the path to him. Energy designed to inflict pain. The kind of spell the faerie would use.

My body shuddered when my attack hit Baldric. His spell on Diego broke, and the vampire relaxed on the floor. In my eagerness to help Diego, I hadn't considered the mistake I was making.

Ah, Sophie, the voice of Baldric said in my head. *Your magic is impressive and quite painful. Unfortunately for you, I now know that you're with Diego.*

The ground shook as explosions wracked the building.

CHAPTER 2

SOPHIE

Dull popping sounds erupted all around me. The lights suddenly came on just in time to reveal the extensive wall-mounted wine racks gushing rivers of red and white as the bottles exploded.

"Yikes!" I exclaimed with my usual lack of eloquence.

"No, not the Rioja Gran Reserva!" Diego cried as he got to his feet.

Diego's restaurant was famous for its wine selection, which had now created a shallow lake throughout the lounge and the dining rooms as the hundreds of overpriced bottles were destroyed.

Next came all the liquor bottles on the shelves behind the bar. We had to duck to avoid the flying pieces of glass. The establishment was filled with the strong odor of wine-and-spirits punch.

Instead of simply obliterating the place, Baldric was taking his time, making Diego suffer. I mean, I was suffering, too, watching all the high-end booze be lost, and it wasn't costing me anything.

Diego dashed outside.

"Come here and show yourself!" he shouted into the night. "Face me in person, you coward!"

That's not the way it works in warfare. You don't trade your tactical advantage for your opponent's. I didn't bother reminding Diego about this because I knew he wouldn't listen.

The lamps above the restaurant's entrance exploded. The front windows followed suit, showering the empty street with glass.

I didn't care how macho Diego wanted to be; I quickly cast a protection spell that enclosed him and me in an invisible bubble before something horrible happened.

The windows of Diego's upstairs apartment exploded. He stood in the street raging, oblivious to the shards of glass falling upon him and bouncing off the protection bubble.

I smelled smoke. Thin wisps of it curled from the open front door. Diego glanced at me with alarm.

Dancing flames appeared in the doorway. I knew a spell that sucked the oxygen from a space. After I cast it, the smoke and flames abruptly disappeared.

It would be tempting to fist-bump Diego, but that would further enrage Baldric. Would the entire building now explode? If that happened, first responders would show up, and the sorcerer's fun would be curtailed.

A sudden massive force hit me like a freight train, knocking me off my feet and throwing me against the brick building. Diego hit the wall nearby. Encased in my spell's bubble, we harmlessly bounced off the wall.

"Are you protecting me with a spell?" Diego asked as he rose to his feet.

"I'm protecting both of us. It would be silly to allow that coward to kill us from afar."

Perhaps I spoke too soon. Tension filled me as Baldric attempted to deconstruct my protection spell. I pumped more energy into it.

We remained outside, where Baldric couldn't harm us by destroying the building. I felt vulnerable standing out here, but I reminded myself that my protection spell kept us safe from physical objects as well as magic.

Up to a point. As a Fae sorcerer, Baldric was more powerful than I. In fact, he had once been my magic tutor for a brief time. However, I figured that if he wanted to defeat my spell, he would need to be in visual contact with me.

He must have realized that too.

Why are you protecting this vampire? his voice asked in my head. *Do you fancy him?*

No, I responded in kind. *But he doesn't deserve to be destroyed.*

He destroyed the one I loved.

He did not. I destroyed her to save him. She was about to drain him to death. And she probably would have done the same with you once she tired of you.

My mother taught me to always tell the truth, but I had just signed my own death sentence.

Baldric did not reply. He did, however, appear on the scene, striding around the corner, approaching the restaurant.

Uh-oh.

"Release me from your spell," Diego said to me when he saw Baldric.

"You can walk out of the bubble. I'm keeping it around me, though."

Because I was going to need it bigtime.

Diego raced away from me like a kid let loose in a playground.

As fast as Diego moved, Baldric could see him coming. The Fae sorcerer crouched, bracing himself for impact. He carried a crooked staff that looked like a tree root and crackled with orange energy. I'd never seen him use a staff before, and he probably needed it for the long-distance spellcasting.

It turned out he had his own version of a protection spell. Diego collided with it and stopped short, unable to get his hands on the faerie. If he had, Baldric wouldn't have lived longer than a few seconds.

Baldric dropped his staff and pointed his hands, on outstretched arms, at Diego.

The vampire dropped to the street, writhing in pain.

I pulled my sword, Alfie (not exactly the best battle name), from its scabbard. Aiming the point at Baldric, I pumped it full of energy, and purple lightning shot from it.

The bolts bounced powerlessly off Baldric's protection sphere. I wasn't surprised, but I wanted to keep him off guard and distracted.

He pointed his hands at me. My protection spell prevented his magic from reaching me, but my spell weakened. I couldn't maintain it with enough strength to withstand his magic while simultaneously attacking him with my less-powerful magic.

I returned Alfie to its scabbard and loaded my crossbow with a bolt made of ash wood. Faeries were vulnerable to ash, and I'd discovered my bolts could penetrate their protection spells as well as penetrate them.

He sent a barrage of magic at me while I walked toward him.

Meanwhile, Diego, ignored now by Baldric, was sitting up, staring intently at the faerie. I guessed he was trying to mesmerize him. It was the one magical advantage Diego had over the sorcerer.

I needed to get closer to ensure my crossbow shot didn't miss. Yet, as I closed my distance from Baldric, his attack magic weakened my protection spell further. The blasts of pain he sent were seeping into my head.

Yeah, it was getting bad. I staggered.

"Baldric, we will settle these matters another time," Diego said, his words soothing. "Go home now."

Baldric turned to him with a confused expression. The pain in my head eased slightly, and I moved closer to the faerie.

"Go home," Diego repeated.

I had wondered if mesmerization could penetrate a protection spell. It looked like it could.

It was time. I aimed my crossbow at Baldric.

He'd been fighting the mesmerizing and seemed to snap out of it. Staring at my weapon, his eyes widened as he realized what kind of wood the bolt had been fashioned from.

I almost dropped the crossbow as a wall of pain slammed into my head. My vision turned gray, and dizziness overwhelmed me.

Diego had gotten to his feet. "Go home," he ordered Baldric.

Baldric must have realized he had lost the advantage. As I struggled to clear my vision and get my shot off, the sorcerer picked up his staff and sprinted away from us, turning the corner to disappear down a side street.

"It pains me to depend on your magic to survive," Diego said to me.

I laughed, despite the lingering effects of the pain.

"It was teamwork. Mutual dependence. We chased him off together."

He smiled with irony. "Perhaps that is the best way to fight."

THE ENCOUNTER DIEGO AND I HAD WITH BALDRIC SIMPLIFIED things greatly. No longer was there the question of how to topple the head of the Executive Council. Now, it was simply kill him or be killed by him.

Easier said than done. And I really didn't want to kill him. Ever since I blossomed as an empath, I'd found killing people to be too emotionally painful.

Diego returned to his restaurant to clean up, refusing my offer to help. After all, he reminded me, I had a day job. I would have to get up at the crack of dawn to help Mom prepare and serve breakfast for the guests of our bed-and-breakfast.

Yeah, as if I could fall asleep after the battle we'd just had. I trudged wearily up the stairs of the historic inn to my third-floor bedroom. I avoided the elevator when carrying weapons. It was an old, small elevator, which made me feel claustrophobic if guests got in it with me. And they always seemed uncomfortable when they noticed I was carrying a sword. Go figure.

My witch's familiar, a black cat named Cervantes, greeted me at the top of the stairs.

Hard day at the office? he asked me telepathically.

"Yeah," I replied aloud. "Don't ask."

He followed me to my room and jumped up on the bed while I showered and put on a T-shirt and sweatpants. When I crawled into bed, Cervantes curled up by my feet.

"Let me know if you sense any Fae magic brewing nearby," I said.

Have you made yourself another enemy?

"Yeah. Baldric. My former magic tutor. I killed his girlfriend."

The vampire Lethia?

"Yep."

I'm certain you had a good reason, but making an enemy out of a faerie sorcerer is not a path to dying of old age.

"I know. If only I had nine lives like cats."

Actually, I've had forty-three lives if you count all the cats my spirit has inhabited.

I might end up being reincarnated myself sooner than I'd like if Baldric had his way. Lovely thoughts like this raced through my head while I lay sleepless. But once my adrenaline rush waned, exhaustion overcame me, and I finally dropped off. I didn't even dream.

MY ALARM WAS LIKE A JUG OF COLD WATER BEING DUMPED ON my head. Mom was already at work in the kitchen when I dragged my sorry butt downstairs and poured a cup of coffee. It wasn't even dawn yet.

"How are you, Miss Sunshine?" Mom asked with her usual sarcasm.

"Tired. I got into a bit of a brawl last night."

Ever since I was a teen, I'd kept a lot of secrets from my mother. Teens are like that, but I was worse. After all, I had fallen in with a bad crowd and eventually got into trouble with drugs. But even after that, I shared little with Mom. She was blunt and practical, telling me truths I didn't want to hear.

But things changed when the magic gene activated in me. I became part of the supernatural community like Mom, and it was as if we were in a secret club together. When my empath powers came to life, these psychic abilities made me even more like Mom, who was a psychometrist.

We became closer, and I shared almost everything. It wasn't just beneficial for our relationship; it was a matter of survival.

I told her about last night—Diego, Baldric, and my confession to the faerie.

"Do you think you should go into hiding again?" she asked, concern etching her face.

"Look, Baldric could find me no matter where I go. If he tries an ostentatious magical attack, he's going to be another victim of the Great Unmasking. He'll be revealed as a supernatural, even though faeries seem to hold themselves above the rest of the supernaturals and believe they'll never be revealed."

"He could attack you secretly."

"Mom, I want to take him down. He should fear me as much as I fear him. Right? He, the governor, State Senator Poxton, and all the others who are using the Great Unmasking to gain power over us have to be stopped."

Mom frowned. "We'll talk about it later. Go set the tables, please."

Maybe sharing everything with Mom wasn't such a good idea after all.

I went to the dining room and spread tablecloths, lit the food warmers on the buffet table, brought out the plates and silverware. Then, I got the coffee pots brewing.

Trying to stay out of Mom's way, I made multiple trips from the kitchen, carrying chafing dishes of scrambled eggs, sausage, bacon, and potatoes. Then came the sliced bread for the self-service toasters, the fresh muffins, and, with great fanfare, Mom's famous scones.

The guests were filing in, couples and a solo traveler. We had one family with a kid staying here, but they hadn't come down yet. We were well below full occupancy.

You see, our reputation as a quaint historic inn that was

allegedly haunted had been tarnished, thanks to the Great Unmasking. The Esperanza Inn was now the subject of rumors about supernatural activities, witches, and unspecified demonic activity. We'd become associated with the new "others," the out-groups that it was okay to hate. Believe me, it wasn't good for business.

The room was half filled with guests happily eating, apparently unaware of our sordid reputation. There was a healthy buzz of conversation, even some laughter.

Mrs. Oxton, a regular guest and scone lover, took a seat near the buffet. We smiled at each other.

Mom strutted into the room, proudly bearing another tray of fresh scones.

And then she froze in the middle of the floor, in front of everyone.

Her "freezing," or "going away," occurred when she astral-traveled to visit Danu, the ancient earth-mother goddess who used her as a human vessel. Sometimes, it happened when she traveled to Ehrendil to visit the Elves.

It was scary and disconcerting to see her unmoving, seemingly in a catatonic state.

Usually, it lasted only a matter of seconds. This morning, it felt to me like an eternity. And she still hadn't come out of it. The room had fallen silent, and everyone was staring at her.

I calmly approached her and put my hand on her back.

"Mom," I whispered, "come out of it."

No response.

I tried to take the tray of scones, hoping to distract the scone-lovers in the room. But she had an iron grip on the tray.

I kept trying, tugging harder, unable to get—

The tray popped out of her hands with a jolt, and the scones went flying, bombarding Mrs. Oxton.

This was not going to help our wounded reputation. The bad online reviews floated through my imagination like a movie trailer.

"Can I pour coffee for anyone?" I asked.

No one answered.

"Should we call an ambulance?" a man offered.

"This happens all the time," I replied to him and the room in general. "It's a rare neurological condition. Perfectly harmless."

I frantically texted Cory to help me get Mom out of the room.

By the time he arrived, the guests had all left except for Mrs. Oxton, who was just finishing the last of the scones that had landed in her lap.

"She's never been gone this long before," I told him.

His face was grim as we picked Mom up and carried her to the kitchen.

"I guess it's time for her to get another MRI," he said.

"Maybe Danu's meeting just went long."

"If she doesn't snap out of it in a few seconds, I'm calling nine-one-one."

CHAPTER 3

DARLA

I stood ankle-deep in warm water beside a mangrove-covered shoreline. The waterway was wide, and the opposite shore had mangroves as well, but above them protruded condominium towers. The water was clear enough to reveal my bare feet on a sandy bottom.

Beside me was the bloated carcass of a manatee.

As the disorienting effects of my sudden appearance here wore off, I was wracked with sadness for the dead animal. And knowledge about the situation quickly filled my mind.

The manatee had starved to death.

The landscape told me I was far from home, in South Florida on the Indian River Lagoon, where manatees were normally abundant. But the seagrass upon which the sea cows fed was dying off precipitously, causing mass starvation.

As I wiped tears from my eyes, I noticed a bracelet made of daisies on my right wrist. I realized that this trip out of my body was not me, Darla, visiting Danu. It was me *as* Danu, a rare occurrence that was becoming less rare of late.

The rounded, blubbery backs of more manatees broke the surface nearby. These, fortunately, were still alive. Two adults and three calves stuck their whiskered snouts out of the water and made squeaking sounds at me. They were hungry, and they seemed to know who I was.

Their mother.

How was I supposed to help them? I'd heard of wildlife officials feeding heads of lettuce to starving herds. But the answer to my question came to me. It was simple and miraculous at the same time.

I, Danu, earth mother and guardian of the waters, held my arms out, palms facing the water. And the pure energy of life itself flowed from my solar plexus, through my chest and arms, filling the manatees with the nutrients they needed to survive and easing the hunger pangs in their bellies.

Tiny shoots of seagrass poked up from the sandy bottom of the lagoon. They grew at an accelerated pace into thick clumps of the wavy, weed-like plants.

The living creatures who had managed to survive in this stretch of the lagoon knew what I had done and swam here quickly. The shrimp, crabs, and tiny organisms whose habitat was seagrass moved into their new home.

The fish that fed on these smaller creatures arrived, followed by the larger fish that preyed upon them. Birds that hunted fish showed up, too.

More manatees appeared, as well as sea turtles that also consumed seagrass.

Joy filled me. Helping the starving sea cows was a pleasure. But never before had I experienced the ecstasy that came with this divine ability to create. I had to admit it was good for the ego, too.

Perhaps being the human vessel of a goddess wasn't such a burden, after all.

I couldn't fool myself, though. What I had done was merely put a bandage on the symptoms of the larger problems that were killing the seagrass and the creatures that depended upon it.

Fertilizer runoff was the biggest cause. Humans had created this problem, but not deliberately or maliciously. Still, they needed to be coaxed into stopping their assault on the earth.

I'd always suspected that this was why Danu, no longer worshipped and largely forgotten, wanted to return to the earth. To heal it. And to teach humans to love it again.

For the earth is their mother, as am I.

A sense of alarm came from the water. Suddenly, all the creatures who had returned to the rejuvenated ecosystem fled. Why? I wondered. What happened?

For as far as I could see, the surface of the water bubbled as if it were boiling. Yet it remained cool to my feet. Across the waterway, the tall condominiums were no longer visible. They weren't obscured by fog or anything—they simply no longer existed, as if I had gone back in time.

The bubbling intensified, and the bubbles grew larger, creating a steady drumming sound. The larger ones, bursting after rising to the surface, emitted the stink of sulfur and strange noises: moans, cries of suffering, the roars of unknown creatures.

My heart raced with fear. I didn't feel godlike anymore. I was merely middle-aged, mortal Darla standing in the Indian River when I should have been in my dining room serving breakfast.

As if the low rumbling of the boiling effect, the sulfur stench, and the cries coming from the burst bubbles weren't bad enough, a yellow, noxious mist drifted in, across the waterway, wrapping around my legs and sifting through the mangroves behind me. I could no longer see the opposite shore.

Fear gripped me, and I needed to escape. Behind me, the mangroves formed a dense wall, filled with the yellow mist, with no path through the trees' prop roots and the muck beneath them.

A piercing screech came from the waterway. I forced myself to turn back toward the bubbles. I wished I hadn't.

Two colossal eyeballs the size of beach balls rose from the mist-cloaked water. They were on eyestalks like the primitive eyes of crabs. When they rotated to fix upon me, my mind reeled, and my legs quivered as I fought to remain standing.

Remember, you are Danu, said a musical voice in my head that I recognized as the Goddess's. *You must not fear this entity. It is an elder god who ruled the emptiness that existed before the universe our God created.*

Why is it here? I asked.

It, and the other elder gods, never went away. They went into hibernation. They wish to destroy the world and everything God created so that they may rule again. The wickedness of humans and the Fae has given them permission to return.

Giant, crablike claws the size of cars emerged from the water. Instead of a crab's two claws, there were four of them. And they reached toward me.

You are Danu, she reminded me. *A goddess. You must stop this entity that does not belong in our world.*

How?

You have the power. You know you do.

The Goddess had the power to heal, to make the land fruitful and its creatures fertile. But there had been occasions in the past when she, while inhabiting me, had destroyed monsters that did not belong in our world—perversions and mutations that threatened the survival of her creatures.

An open claw thrust itself at me, and I barely danced away from it, splashing in the shallow water.

My fear faded as my sense of self disappeared, making me fully the Goddess again. Immediately, the familiar burning sensation grew in my solar plexus as her divine power amplified. The heat filled my entire body.

The claw tried again to grab me. I raised my hand as if to block it, but instead, a beam of white light shot from my hand and hit the claw.

It exploded into shards of shell and scraps of flesh.

An angry screech came from beneath the eye stalks.

A wave rose as the creature moved toward me underwater. The other three claws opened and swung at me simultaneously.

Hoping for the same result, I raised my hand again and blew apart the closest one. The remaining two came at me from opposite angles. I destroyed the one to my left, but crushing blows hit my back, chest, and right arm.

I had thought a goddess wouldn't feel pain. I sure as heck did.

The remaining claw lifted me from the water in its viselike grip, trying to crush me. The pain was searing, and I struggled to breathe as the creature squeezed my torso.

The logical part of my brain—Darla's brain—told me I wasn't in my actual body. I wasn't here physically at all; I had merely come here via astral travel.

To fight as the Goddess, I needed to shut down that part of my brain. My logic went silent as the giant claw held me aloft, shaking me and crushing me. I touched the claw with my left hand and sent the white energy into it.

Its grip weakened, but my pain doubled as my deadly beam of power that filled the claw touched me as well.

I looked down at the two eyes atop their stalks, watching me.

Those primitive organs revealed no emotion, but somehow they contained intelligence.

Pointing my free hand at them, I shot them with energy, one after the other.

The entity's screech was ear-splitting.

Its claw opened, and I dropped to the water with a splash. When my head emerged, I saw the eye stalks moving away from me, the entity's remaining claw nowhere to be seen.

The bubbling of the water and the eerie cries of suffering that had escaped them ceased.

I needed to finish off the creature. Could an ancient deity, who dwelled in the hearts and minds of humans, destroy this god who had existed long before humans?

Another beam of power left my hand and struck an eyestalk. Both eyes sank beneath the water.

I waded toward where they had submerged, and the water became deeper. Reminding myself that I was a goddess, I pushed onward as my head went underwater. I felt no need to breathe.

It was murky here. An enormous dark shape, like a crab-shaped submarine, glided away from me. I swam toward it, and as I got closer, I saw the creature was not truly crab-like. It moved on dozens of legs, and snake-like tentacles probed the lagoon's floor.

The three claws I destroyed had been restored, and the creature shifted, pointing all four claws at me.

You do not belong here, I said telepathically to the entity. *You belong in the emptiness beyond the universe where you have dwelled. This world was created by a different god, and I will not allow you to destroy it.*

I fired white beams of energy at the monster, one after another. Its squeals traveled back to me through the water and hit me like physical blows.

The entity retreated, and I swam after it, firing another energy beam, hoping to destroy it.

The enormous dark shape darted away from me with incredible speed for such a large being. I continued swimming forward, still with no need or desire to breathe. The elder god had seemingly left. Hopefully, it had returned to its sleeping place beyond the edge of the universe.

Movement—something gray—flashed far ahead of me. A large fish or shark was swimming toward me. No, it had more rounded contours than a fish.

Finally, I saw it: a baby manatee. It was ridiculously adorable. Were the creatures now returning to the seagrass beds I had created for them?

The chubby little manatee stopped just out of reach and floated weightlessly in front of me. That was when I noticed its eyes were yellow and glowing.

I shall return to kill you and your world, the god said in my head, in a strange accent it must have learned from a human centuries ago. *Your world is weak and dying, and I shall destroy it. I shall turn it into dust.*

The manatee disappeared, leaving me alone in the water. I rose to the surface and took a gulp of air. The air held the scent of the nutrient-rich saltwater and the faint, fishy tang of the creatures inhabiting it, as well as the perfume of the nearby trees, flowers, and plants.

I sensed movement around me as the fish, manatees, and sea turtles returned. The elder god was wrong. The earth was healthy and life on it was abundant.

I blinked and was suddenly standing again in the shallows. The condo towers had reappeared, towering over the mangroves on the opposite shore. I was back in the present, rather than the timeless era in which I had fought the entity.

The scents that came to me now were not as rich as the ones I had just enjoyed. And with them were the distant smells of car and boat exhaust, fertilizer in the water, and garbage on the land.

No, the earth wasn't dying quite yet. But neither was it healthy. It truly was vulnerable to a malevolent elder god.

Gods come and later fade away, the Goddess's voice said. *Newer gods must fight to keep the older ones from returning. That is what you must do with this elder god. His true name is Yavevi. Remember that and use it against him.*

My Darla persona had returned to me, and I had silly human questions for Danu.

Do the gods of the current religions today try to prevent you from coming back?

No, she replied. *I am not a threat to them. The gods that fight me are the human and Fae gods of greed and materialism. They are afraid of me.*

And then I was standing in the inn's kitchen, disoriented. My last memory of being in my body was when I was in the dining room.

"How did I get in here?" I asked.

"We carried you," replied Cory. "You made quite a spectacle of yourself, freezing in front of our guests. It was the longest you've ever stayed away."

"Were you with the Elves?" Sophie asked.

"No, I was with Danu. Actually, I *was* Danu. I learned that the Great Unmasking and the Unseelie Court's evil ambitions are the least of our problems."

"Don't tell me," Cory said. "I don't want to hear it."

"Tell me," said Sophie.

"There are elder gods who existed before the universe was created. They want to destroy the earth. I met one of them."

"Yikes!" Sophie exclaimed.

"Please don't tell me you're getting involved with stopping these gods," Cory pleaded.

I forced a smile. "Of course I'm getting involved. Whether I want to or not."

"But how?"

"I don't know. I guess Danu will show me."

CHAPTER 4

SOPHIE

I t's not nice to wish anyone dead, but that's how I felt when I saw Marge Moosebacher interviewed on our local TV news. The last I saw her, the president and co-founder of Moms Against Monsters was being attacked by a mob during a rally inspired by hate.

Yeah, I was to blame for her being attacked. She had driven the crowd to violence against supernaturals when my budding empath powers gave her the urge to shift into her natural faerie form.

The crowd saw her turn into an actual monster, like the very ones she had been railing against, and they did not take it kindly. When Mom and I left the event, I had believed Moosebacher was killed. It turned out that she survived her injuries but was stepping away from an active role with MAM.

I guess the stepping away part didn't last. Here she was on TV, inspiring fear in our little City of San Marcos.

"I was told by law enforcement that it was a coven of witches hidden in the crowd that attacked me."

"Liar!" I shouted at the kitchen TV.

Mom glanced at me, shrugged, and continued mixing flour and butter to make scones for breakfast. She had shown no regrets about what had happened to Moosebacher, but today she seemed disinterested.

"The witches attended your rally?" asked Meghan Whortle. The local reporter and influencer had helped spread the conspiracy theories that led to the Great Unmasking, uncovering the secret existence of supernaturals.

"The witches were there to incite violence and give our movement a bad name," replied Moosebacher, fingering her bright red hair. She was attractive in her human form, as was typical of faeries. "I was surprised they went so far as to attack me, but I shouldn't have been. Witches hate me for exposing their evil ways. They know I'm protecting families and their children from these foul monsters who use babies' blood in their Satanic rites."

Moosebacher knew I was a witch, but I wasn't sure if she realized I had been at the rally.

"You've healed so well, one can only imagine all the trauma you went through. I'm thankful you survived and recovered. I'm sure our viewers are, too, after all the good you've done in our community."

"What a load of bull pucky," I said. "Mothers Against Monsters is poisoning our community with fear and hate. Turning neighbors against each other."

Mom didn't reply. She was humming to herself, trying to keep her mood bright for when the guests came down to eat. I figured being the human vessel for a goddess made her feel above the pettiness of human affairs, but she was still in the muck of it, like the rest of us.

"Almost dying had a big effect on me," Moosebacher said.

"Of course," Whortle said with an exaggeratedly sad face.

"It's hardened my resolve to rid our community of the monsters who prey upon us. Today, I'm thrilled to announce Mothers Against Monsters is expanding our bounty program to reward citizens who do their parts in fighting supernatural creatures."

"How exciting! Tell us more."

"It's quite easy," Moosebacher said with a smug grin. "First, you must download our app, Monster Monitor. Then, all you need to do is take a photo of a suspected supernatural criminal and report them using the app. Everyone who uploads a report will receive free Mothers Against Monsters gear, like this MAM hat."

She held a white baseball cap with MAM embroidered on the front.

"I'd sure feel proud wearing one of those," Whortle said.

"Well, here you go!" Moosebacher handed her the hat. "And the bounties get better. If you document that you reported a supernatural criminal to the police, we'll send you a twenty-five-dollar gift card."

"How awesome! But I've heard the police have been over-whelmed by people reporting monsters."

"That's why the bounties get even better when you take enforcing the Supernatural Criminality Act into your own hands." Moosebacher grinned with fervor. "If you capture a supernatural and bring it to the police—and they arrest the monster—we'll send you a check for five thousand dollars!"

"Wow!"

"And if it's an especially dangerous monster, such as a were-wolf or vampire, the amount goes up to ten thousand dollars."

Whortle clapped her hands with glee.

"Now, we understand these creatures are difficult to control,"

Moosebacher continued. "Silver will help you constrain a were-wolf. Vampires are more of a problem, because crosses and such don't always work with them. If you decide to stake them, you must have video evidence of it. They'll turn into a pile of dust as soon as they are impaled, and dust is too expensive to analyze."

"What do you say to critics who say you're encouraging vigilantism?"

"I say, we sure are! I can't give any legal advice, and if you kill a monster, it will be up to you to prove it was really a monster. But the more of them taken off the streets, the better."

"This is horrible," I said. "I can't believe it's happening in San Marcos."

"And just about everywhere else in Florida," Mom said. "That's why the governor is leading by so much in the polls. Our fear is going to get her reelected."

Unless I revealed a secret: that the governor and a powerful state senator were faeries.

"I know what you're thinking," Mom said. "You'll be killed if you say what you know about Governor Witlessin and Senator Poxton. If they even suspect you know, your life is in danger."

"If I let the cat out of the bag, what's the purpose of killing me after the fact?"

"To stop you from going on TV with interviews like this." She pointed to the monitor. "The media aren't going to run with the story if you're killed immediately after telling them. They'll need you to testify about what you saw and heard in the Faerie Queene's palace. The media are too afraid of the governor to go out on a limb without your testimony."

It was a sobering thought. She was probably right.

"You can't talk about this to anyone," Mom said in a hushed voice.

I nodded.

Bella walked into the kitchen, making me instantly paranoid that she'd overheard something. Our only full-time housekeeper was twenty-something, pretty, and heavily inked with tattoos. She was also a normal human—the only one we trusted with knowledge of the supernatural goings-on at the inn. She'd worked here for years, and we considered her a member of the family.

"Mr. Jubbles is staying with us again," Mom said to Bella, who was pouring a cup of coffee. "He's in Room 302. Sophie will take care of his room each night."

"Great," I muttered.

Mom never said, though Bella understood, that Mr. Jubbles was a vampire. He'd been a guest here as a human when Lethia— yeah, the vampire I destroyed—turned him. He loved San Marcos so much he continued to visit and shop at the antique stores that stayed open after dark.

"You're allowing a vampire to stay here?" Bella asked, full of resentment.

"Of course," Mom replied. "He's a repeat guest."

"Who steals towels every time he comes."

"Not anymore."

"Oh, becoming a vampire got rid of his kleptomania?"

"Yes," I said to Bella. "Becoming immortal changes your perspective. You're less concerned with the small stuff."

"Does he ever leave you a tip for cleaning his room?" Bella asked.

"No," I replied. "Once a cheapskate, always a cheapskate."

"I don't think it's wise to have a vampire staying here. Not during this witch hunt." Bella looked at both of us defiantly.

"You're not a supernatural, dear," Mom said. "You have nothing to worry about."

"I'm sorry, but this inn has a reputation. It's haunted—you

even brag about that on your website. And Sophie is known as a witch."

"What do you mean by 'known'?" I asked. "Have you told anyone? Did someone find me in the Monster Monitor app?"

"No one mentioned the app. But last weekend, at a party, someone said you walk around town with a sword."

"I do not. Unless it's hidden in a duffel bag."

"I'm afraid I'll be accused of being a witch," Bella said. "That's the problem nowadays. Anyone can be called a witch and get arrested with no evidence. I mean, witches aren't obvious supernaturals like vampires."

"If you're so afraid of being called a witch, maybe you should lose the Goth look," I muttered.

"Sophie! That was uncalled for," Mom scolded.

"Sorry. I'm kind of Goth myself."

"And you *are* a witch," Bella said, glaring at me.

"Yeah. I was born with the magic gene. It doesn't make me better or worse than anyone else."

"It makes you illegal."

The kitchen was silent except for Mom sliding a baking sheet of scones into the oven.

"The new law is unjust," I said in a low voice.

"Yes, but it's the law."

"What are you getting at?" I asked. "Are you thinking of turning me in?"

Bella paused. "Of course not."

Her pause was too long for me.

"I told you I'm afraid of getting arrested myself," she went on. "This is serious. You're a witch. I got the app and saw you there."

"You got the app?" I was offended. "Why would you download that stupid crap?"

"It's trending in all the app stores."

"That's ridiculous."

"And I wanted to see if anyone I know is on there. It's a scary situation."

"No kidding," I said.

"I'm not on it, am I?" Mom asked.

"No," Bella replied. "The only psychic types I found were people who do it as a business. No one knows you're a psychometrist. But guests have noticed you're freezing. They could never imagine that you're possessed by a goddess, though. But any day, someone could accuse you of being a supernatural."

"Is Cory on the app?"

"No. Not at this time."

Right now, I was truly regretting that we'd been so open about our secrets with Bella. But like I said, we trusted her. She began working here part time when she was a college student and was now full time. She was like a family member.

It was inevitable that she would know some secrets, even if we hadn't told her things. There was that time, after all, when she came into work extra early and caught our resident vampire, Roderick, fangs extended, slipping into his crawlspace behind the fridge. There was no way to spin a lie about him.

"Bella, you sound like you're asking for permission to resign," Mom said.

"I love working here. All the historic charm. I don't mind the ghosts, even the mean lady who haunts 303. And I love you guys."

"You still love us, even though we're *criminals?*" I asked, not hiding my sarcasm.

A tear ran down Bella's pale face, and she wiped it away with a tattooed hand.

"Cheer up, love. You'll be fine," said an English-accented voice.

I looked up to find our gargoyle, Archibald, perched on the wall near the ceiling. Not the best timing for him to appear when Bella was experiencing supernatural regret.

"The Great Unmasking will eventually blow over," he continued. "Humans tend to go into hysterics about these things every couple of centuries, you know."

"And it doesn't end well for many people when that happens," I said.

"Keep your chins up, my fragile human friends. By sticking together, we'll weather the storm."

"Easy for you to say. You're immortal."

"Not true at all. Gargoyles can die. We can be pulverized to dust by the elements or by the wrecking ball. Old age can take our lives, leaving stone carvings that can no longer animate. Or, I suppose, a gargoyle can risk dying of a broken heart."

"Archibald, is there something going on in your social life we don't know about?" Mom asked.

"My heart is too enraptured to speak about it now. I'll tell you more another time."

I was about to pry more information from him when the doorbell rang. It was still too early for the front door to be unlocked to the public. The doorbell rang again. The visitor must be impatient.

"Since I'm the only one of us on the app, I'm not going to answer that," I said.

"I'll see who it is," Bella said, leaving the kitchen.

Mom gave me a worried look, and I slipped from the kitchen, too. I went to the parlor, where Archibald had returned to his fireplace mantel as an inanimate stone carving.

The empath in me was sending me feelings of suspicion and

distrust coming from several people waiting at the front door. I had a bad feeling about this. I cast a spell to heighten my senses, particularly my hearing.

The front door was at the opposite end of the hall from me, but I heard it click open as if I were right there.

"Can I help you?" Bella asked with fear in her voice.

"I'm Detective Siwicki with the San Marcos PD. May we come inside?"

"Good morning, Detective," Mom's voice said at the door. "It's quite early, and our guests are asleep. What can I do for you?"

"We've had several reports about your establishment and would like to take a quick look around."

"Reports regarding what, exactly?" Mom asked.

"Supernatural activity."

"Do you have a warrant?"

"As a matter of fact, I do. Here, you can read it if you want. We're coming inside now."

Footsteps of several individuals stomped into the foyer.

"Is your daughter on the premises?" the detective asked.

I had to get out of there. There was an exterior door to the parlor, which used to be the building's front door when this was a private home. It was never used nowadays, and I didn't think the cops would expect anyone to use it.

A quick peek out of the adjacent window told me no one was outside. So, I unlocked the door and—

It wouldn't budge. Years of humidity had swelled the wood. I struggled to pull it toward me, and the wood squealed. My hearing was still enhanced from my spell, so I couldn't tell if the police coming in the main entrance could hear the noise I was making.

I released the sense-enhancing spell and cast a different one that muffled sounds. Finally, I yanked the door open. Stepping out onto the sidewalk beside Hidalgo Avenue, I turned eastward and walked toward the burning ball of the sun rising over the Sangre River and the bay.

Just as a police car rolled up toward me.

I leaned against the wall and stretched my legs as if I were about to go jogging. My sweatpants and T-shirt outfit fit in well with that ruse.

The police car slowed to a stop, and the window slid down.

I cast a spell that obscured light waves and would make my face look obscured to anyone looking at me. And that's what the officer was doing, switching his gaze between me and his smartphone, as if he were comparing me with a profile in the Monster Monitor app.

At last, the police car drove off, and I exhaled my pent-up tension. There was no relaxing for me, though. I sensed chaotic emotions coming from inside the inn.

The strongest ones came from Mom. She was extremely frightened and threatened by the detective.

Something bad was going down.

CHAPTER 5

DARLA

"Sophie must have run out to buy a few things," I said. "We're short on butter."

"The grocery store and wholesale club aren't open at this hour," Siwicki said. He was young, with thick, heavily gelled black hair. His navy-blue suit was well-tailored, and his matching tie was narrow. The guy seemed a little too sharp to work in a small police department like ours. "Surely she wouldn't go to the convenience store."

"Breakfast must go on," I replied. "No matter how much we pay for the butter. Why do you want to speak with Sophie?"

"She was seen at a restaurant where a suspicious fire broke out. I wanted to ask her some questions about it."

"Are you sure it was her?"

He gave an insincere smile. "That's the funny thing. The witness recognized her from the Monster Monitor app. Are you aware she's listed there?"

"She told me a spiteful person wrongly reported her. Sophie

has nothing to do with the supernatural and plans to sue this person for defamation."

"I agree the app is more trouble than it's worth," Siwicki said, glancing around the kitchen. "Lots of false reports. But it helped the witness identify Sophie as being on the scene of the suspected arson."

Three uniformed officers, two men and a woman, stood in the hallway whispering to each other. They made me nervous.

Pinky, a skunk shifter who was our new cook, arrived for work. Her forehead was lined with worry because of our uninvited guests. She was followed by Cory, who belatedly arrived, curious about who was at the door.

"Detective Siwicki, this is my husband, Cory, and our chef, Pinky," I said. "Is there anything else I can help you with?" I hoped the police would leave.

"Yes, in fact. We'd like to take a more thorough look around to make sure your daughter isn't here. The inn is listed as her residence. What room does she live in?"

I hesitated. "Three-oh-five. And that's the only guest room you may enter. Your warrant didn't say you can barge into any rooms occupied by guests."

"Yes, of course. Ramirez, come upstairs with me. You guys, look around the common areas for anything of note."

"Gentlemen, I'll show you around," Cory said to the officers.

"I'm going with you," I said to Siwicki.

After the three of us crammed into the small antique elevator, I worried about what they would find in Sophie's room. I knew she had escaped the inn from the parlor, but her room was filled with incriminating items.

Her entire life I'd lectured her about keeping her room tidy, to no avail. This morning, she might very well pay the price for not putting things away.

"To be clear, Detective," I said as we exited the elevator on the third floor, "your warrant authorizes you to search Sophie's room for Sophie. You're not allowed to ransack her belongings."

He smirked. "Of course. She's not accused of any crime yet."

Yet, he said. I was sure if they wanted to, they could accuse her.

We walked past a narrow door before reaching Sophie's.

"What's this, a maid's closet?" Siwicki asked, yanking the door open without permission. "Ah, stairs to an attic." He shined a flashlight up the stairs to reveal an empty room at the top. "I think I'll get a search warrant for this another time."

Good luck searching the attic, I thought. The door and the attic didn't exist. They were part of a gateway—a portal of sorts created by an angel—and they appeared from time to time. If Siwicki walked up the stairs, he'd be transported to the In Between, which I wouldn't recommend to anyone. Believe me, I found out the hard way.

With trepidation, I unlocked Sophie's door and quickly surveyed the room. Had she left any magic gear lying around? The bed was unmade, piles of clothing were on the floor, but I didn't immediately see her sword, amulets, or anything of the like.

Siwicki pushed past me. I went inside, while Ramirez, the young female officer, stayed in the doorway.

Cervantes lay on the bed, eyeing the detective curiously.

Is Sophie in trouble? he asked me telepathically.

I'm not sure, I answered.

Ever since Sophie ended up in the app, she'd been careful to hide that she was a witch. Her small collection of spell books was no longer in her bookcase but hidden away somewhere. She didn't use a lot of potions, charms, and amulets. Those she did use appeared to have been hidden.

Unfortunately, she'd left her closet door open. Her sword was in a closed duffel bag on the floor in the back of the closet. But something else caught Siwicki's eye.

"Is that a crossbow bolt?" he asked.

"Where?" Sophie's crossbow was stored in a backpack, wedged behind the duffel bag with the sword. No one could tell a crossbow was in there.

"On the floor, there. A bolt, or quarrel, made of wood with a steel tip. It looks very unusual."

"Sophie hunts with a crossbow," I said with as much conviction as I could muster. She did hunt, after all, just not wild game. "She believes hunting with rifles isn't challenging enough."

"That doesn't look like the kind of bolt used for hunting."

"Remember, you're not here to search through her stuff."

He stepped away from the closet and looked as if he were about to leave the room, but dropped to the ground to look under the bed.

Cervantes hissed at him.

My stomach clenched as I worried about what Sophie had hidden under there.

"Detective, I could have assured you she's not hiding under there."

"I'm looking for supernatural contraband."

"Did you find any?"

"There's nothing but dirty clothes."

Siwicki's radio crackled.

"Detective? Um, we have something you should come look at," said a male voice.

My stomach clenched even more.

"What is it, Ford?" Siwicki spoke into the radio.

"Supernatural activity. Come to room two-oh-two."

Oh, boy. I knew what supernatural activity the officer was referring to and had no idea how Siwicki would handle it.

He and Ramirez left the room with me close behind.

"Hey, where's the attic door?" asked Siwicki. The gateway had, predictably, disappeared. "I thought it was right here. Whatever. No time for this."

We took the stairs down one floor. Not far along the hallway was 202, with its door held open with a rubber doorstop. A housekeeping cart parked outside told me Bella was cleaning inside, and the officers had walked by at the worst possible time.

Bella was working in the bathroom, indifferent to the supernatural activity going on.

The lyrics of Elvis Presley's "Jailhouse Rock" drifted from the room into the hallway, sung in perfect a cappella. It wasn't a recording; someone was singing it live.

Actually, not live. Dead. The singer was the ghost of an Elvis impersonator, Virgil Bungcroft, who had haunted the room's hot tub for decades.

Yes, we had a room with a hot tub, installed by a former owner in the 1970s. Yes, Virgil was one of our resident ghosts. And yes, he appeared in the daytime as well as at night, whenever musical inspiration hit him.

The two male officers stood just inside the doorway, staring slack-jawed at the hot tub, which was on a small platform at the foot of the bed. The water jets weren't running, but someone was sitting in the tub: a semi-transparent apparition of a naked man with huge sideburns. Virgil bore a striking resemblance to the King and must have made a good living as his impersonator. Unfortunately for those of us who beheld his nude body, his look was from the Fat Elvis period. But his rendition of "Jailhouse Rock"—undoubtably inspired by the police officers—sounded just like the young Elvis who had made the song a hit.

"What the?" Siwicki mumbled.

"He's good, huh?" said Cory, who was standing near the officers just inside the room.

"Mr. Bungcroft was a guest here while doing a week-long gig at a club in town back before we owned the inn," I explained to our law-enforcement visitors. "He died of a heart attack in the hot tub. And has been with us ever since."

"The ghost is illegal, correct?" Officer Ramirez asked Siwicki. "So, how do we arrest him?"

"Our idiot lawmakers were typically sloppy when they drafted the new law," Siwicki explained. "Supernatural activity is illegal, but I think they meant activity undertaken by *living* humans or monsters. The language was too vague."

"Handcuffs aren't gonna work on him," the younger male officer said.

"He did nothing wrong," I said. "He's just the manifestation of a spirit."

"He has a magnificent voice," said the older male officer.

"Enough!" Siwicki barked. "Finish your inspection of this building."

"We were finishing it when we came across Elvis here. We didn't find anything suspicious. Aside from having a hot tub in a historic structure."

"You can blame the previous owner," Cory said.

Siwicki stormed off and went downstairs. Everyone, including Cory and me, followed. The detective turned to me in the foyer. "When you speak to your daughter, tell her to contact me." He handed me his business card. "I want to talk to her about the fire at Fourteen Granada Street."

"Is all of this an excuse to arrest her because her name is in the app?"

"The police department does not endorse that app, and we

have nothing to do with it. And we don't appreciate all the dead-end leads Mothers Against Monsters threw in our lap."

He gestured for the three officers to exit the front door ahead of him. Just as he was leaving, he turned back to me. "Don't get me wrong. If I find any evidence that your daughter is practicing witchcraft, I will not hesitate to arrest her."

"Right."

"Have a nice day."

My anger allowed my mouth to run off. "You know, Detective Samson has already investigated our inn. There's no need for you to harass us."

Siwicki frowned. "What is that supposed to mean? This is not a territory that belongs to him."

I hoped my big mouth wouldn't get Samson in trouble. "Yes, I know. I only wanted to save you time and effort."

He wasn't buying that one bit. "Are you paying Samson protection money?"

"Of course not!" I feigned being offended.

"I can investigate anything I want."

"I understand, Detective."

"And I think I might have to make a return visit here soon."

I said nothing as he left and panicked when I saw what time it was. I raced into the kitchen and pulled a slightly overdone batch of scones from the oven.

"I was about to take that out," Pinky said. "I didn't want to interfere with your scones, but I was getting nervous."

"Pinky, it's not interfering. I have so many distractions lately that I'm putting you in charge of this kitchen."

"Really? That's awesome. I'm going to cook the eggs now because we're running behind schedule. Those cops were in my way."

Sophie, the police are gone, I called to Sophie telepathically. *So get your butt back here and help us serve breakfast.*

She didn't answer, but I wasn't worried, because the telepathic abilities she'd gained along with her empath powers weren't fully refined yet. I buried myself in the business of preparing breakfast and would try contacting her again a bit later.

But the freaking doorbell rang.

I was surprised to find Baldric at the door.

Baldric, the faerie who had tried to harm my daughter the other night.

"Good morning," he said with a big smile. "I come in peace."

Baldric was tall, slim, and gorgeous. He had a luxuriant head of black hair with no gray, Southern-European features, and a dimpled chin. He was also full of old-school charm.

I had to remind myself that his good looks were simply the human form he adopted. And that he was a powerful sorcerer who could kill me in an instant should he choose to do so.

"Sophie isn't here," I said.

"Please believe me. I'm not here to hurt her."

"And please believe *me*. She's not here."

"Do you mind if I wait for her? She won't return my calls."

"Is that such a surprise after you tried to kill her the other night?"

"I suppose not." He looked chagrined, as if this possibility was new to him. "I only want to mend fences, as you humans say. There's a lot of crazy politics going on now, and I've heard you're aware the Unseelie Court has designs on our territory again. I thought it best if Sophie and I were on the same side."

I wanted to say, but didn't, that he was the one playing treacherous politics, letting down the guilds, and associating with state politicians who were collaborating with the Fae enemy.

"You can see Sophie when she returns," I said, "but you'll have a chaperone keeping an eye on you."

"Hello, mate," Archibald said to Baldric. The gargoyle had appeared on the foyer wall above him.

"You can have a seat here until Sophie returns," I said. "I'm busy in the kitchen right now."

As I walked back to the kitchen, I sent a telepathic message to Sophie. *Do not come to the inn now. Baldric is here waiting for you. He says he means you no harm, but I don't trust him.*

Barely a second later, I heard the click of the front door unlocking.

"Oh, Baldric," Sophie's voice said. "Fancy meeting you here."

CHAPTER 6

SOPHIE

The faerie president of the Executive Council of the Guilds stood in our foyer, presumably not here to kill me—according to Mom's telepathic message I received too late. I should kill *him*. But I couldn't do that in my family's place of business. The most I could do was cast a protection spell, though it wouldn't necessarily save me.

I noticed Archibald was perched high on the wall above Baldric. The gargoyle watched him like an angry pit bull, exemplifying a gargoyle's unique mixture of scary, menacing, and weird.

"You don't need a protection spell," Baldric said, quirking an eyebrow. "I wouldn't harm you in your own home."

"Then why did you try to kill Diego in *his* home?"

"That was quite different. He is a vampire. You are a fellow practitioner of magic. You deserve professional courtesy, even though, frankly, you're only a human."

"We're not an inferior species."

"Now is not the time for an academic argument. I came here today to make a proposal. Can we speak somewhere private?"

I used my empath powers to assess Baldric's threat, but I didn't enhance them with magic because he would have sensed it. Baldric felt confident and egotistical. But he was also wary of how I would react to his proposal.

Deep inside, he still carried grief over Lethia's destruction. Dominating all these emotions was an underlying thirst for power. Just like a politician.

I hesitated, then led him down the hall to the parlor. We each took a seat in the two wingback chairs facing the fireplace.

"One of those gargoyles beneath the mantel is the same one that was in the hallway," Baldric said.

"Yes, Archibald. This is his regular hangout. Don't worry. He's fast asleep at the moment. He can't hear anything."

Which was a lie. Even when in stone form, Archibald knew everything that went on here. Whether he would wake up and protect me if I were attacked was the big question.

Baldric stared intently at me. I felt energy probing my mind despite the protection bubble, and I steeled my brain. As an empath, I'm as good at projecting emotion as I am detecting it in others. Using my magical energy was the only way I could effectively block his probing.

He smiled. "Ah, walling yourself off, are you? No matter. I learned what I needed, and it is no surprise to me. You distrust me and know I have dealings with Senator Poxton. That I'm collaborating with your enemy, as it were. Am I correct?"

I shrugged. "I'm a witch. Your politician buddy thinks I'm a criminal. Right?"

"What if I were to promise protection for you and your family?" he asked.

"What do you mean?"

"You'll be issued special documents from the governor's office that immunize you from arrest and prosecution for your magical activities. That includes your mother's divine powers."

"The papers won't protect us from vigilante mobs," I said, skeptical.

"You'll be free to use your magic to stop any citizens who attack you, because even if the magic reveals you to be a witch, you won't be arrested for it."

"Let's say I took your offer. What would I owe you in return?"

"Your support."

"I assume you don't mean emotional support."

He laughed mirthlessly. "Diego wants to remove me as Executive Council president, and I know you want the same thing. You must promise to stop undermining me and give me your full allegiance. In fact, you must convince the other malcontents in the guilds to support me as well. I believe you would be very persuasive."

"Be serious! I can't make up for your treachery. You're not protecting us from the government's witch hunt."

"Treachery is such a strong word." His face darkened.

"You've allied yourself with the people who want to kill, imprison, or banish us. And you have access to the membership rolls of every guild. We supernaturals are completely vulnerable to you if you decide to betray us."

"Convince me not to betray you, then. Support me and get the others to do so as well. The flip side to your argument is that I have access to and influence over the most powerful politicians and judges in the state. Which means I can protect the supernaturals of San Marcos, just like I promise to protect you and your family. The only supernaturals who would have anything to fear would be those who have refused to join a guild."

Two of whom I knew: Pinky and Roderick.

"I have a feeling your ambition is greater than to remain head of the Executive Council," I said.

"You are correct. In the next municipal election, I plan to run for mayor of San Marcos."

I stifled a laugh. "Really?"

"I'm a successful local businessman, well connected, blah blah. I'd do a much better job than our current mayor."

"It just doesn't seem like a job you'd want."

"I forgive you for not seeing the full picture," he said with a smug smile. "Do you understand why the governor and her allies passed the Supernatural Criminality Act?"

"Yeah. To divide the population and fill us with fear so she can be reelected and cement an overwhelming majority in the state legislature. In short, to make her and her party more powerful."

"You're smarter than I thought."

"The governor's motives are obvious," I said. I left out mention of her need to destroy the local supernatural population in order to make it easier for the Unseelie Court to invade and conquer our state and region. If my knowledge of the governor's plot with the Faerie Queene got out, I would be dead.

"What you're not seeing is that this is about more than state government. Our faction's dominance will extend to county and city governments. To the courts. To the media. It's all about ruling with total strength. Democracy is such a weak, messy system, you know. When there's one-party rule everywhere, governance is much more efficient."

I didn't agree, but kept my mouth shut.

"To sum it up," he continued, "I wish to rule this city—both the humans and supernaturals. If you and the supernaturals support me, I will protect you. You will help me solidify this support."

"I'm not sure how well I can do that. I'm not a politician."

"But you're an empath, are you not? It's the excuse you gave when you quit your job as an enforcer. Being an empath should mean you have the power to convince others."

"Not necessarily. I don't have much control over my abilities. I can feel others' emotions but can't really affect them." Downplaying my powers seemed like a wise idea.

"Orlena, the leader of your guild, will assist you with using magic to strengthen your empathy. I'll tell her to train you."

Bob, mage and former leader of the guild, had only been able to help me slightly. I had doubts Orlena could do better.

"More immediately," Baldric said, "I have heard that Diego is organizing a vote to remove me as leader of the Council. Your job is to derail his efforts."

"I've already found out I have little sway over him. He's very stubborn."

"You will try. Or else I'll assassinate him. And this time, I'll succeed. Even though you confessed to destroying Lethia, I blame Diego for causing it. Their ties were too deep and messy. He provoked her to drain him, and you were only trying to save him."

I nodded. Despite his words of forgiveness, I detected a simmering resentment toward me. But the urge to use me as his tool was greater.

"You see, killing him is easier to get away with than killing a human like you, even though you're a witch. I don't want a human's blood on my hands when running for mayor, after all."

He brayed with laughter. His sophisticated European vibe was totally ruined by his cartoon-villain guffaws.

"What happened to the Baldric I used to know?" I asked,

perhaps foolhardily. "I never saw this side of you when you tutored me."

He was silent. I worried he would lose his temper, but I sensed no new anger in him.

"I used to be content to run my business and lead my guild in this backwater city," he said. "But it's not enough anymore. To be frank, Lethia inspired me to want more. She was so greedy for power and wealth that I was embarrassed by my lack of ambition. Then I became friends with Ralph Poxton. He was just a client at first, and I serviced his sports cars. But we had additional things in common and hit it off."

Things in common, I thought, *such as being faeries.*

"I was a big donor to his election campaigns," Baldric went on, "and he shared with me a master plan that he, the governor, and others were creating. I found it kind of exciting."

"How could you, the leader of the city's supernatural guilds, be attracted to a plan that oppresses supernaturals?"

"Because Poxton's caucus could bring me power and money, like Lethia had always clamored for. I wondered why I should care about supernaturals who weren't Fae. I mean, humans don't all get along with each other. Why should supernaturals? Why should I consider vampires part of my team?"

"Because you were sleeping with one, maybe?"

"Ha! She had contempt for faeries and for vampires, too. For everyone and anyone who didn't provide something she needed."

"Why did you love her?"

"I didn't love her."

"You did," I said. "I know you did. And you were devastated by her loss."

"This is what I get for talking with an empath. Let's say I was smitten by her. She was beautiful, of course. And having existed for so many centuries gave her a goddess-like quality." He paused. "She had power in her. Not mere political power, but the genuine stuff. It was intoxicating. I must have gotten the addiction to it from her."

"Will being mayor bring you enough of the power and money you crave? We're a small city, after all."

"You don't understand how thoroughly our faction will rule this state, from the governor's mansion, to the courts, to the smallest school board. As mayor I'll control every contract, every purchase, every appointee. I'll make a mint."

"You mean, through bribes and skimming off the top?"

"Exactly." He smiled with self-satisfaction. There wasn't an iota of shame in him.

"I've heard reports the Faerie Queene has designs on Florida and the Southeastern states. As an indigenous faerie, how do you feel about the foreign Fae trying to conquer your territory after your faction executes this master plan?" I asked, unsure if he knew about the governor's attempt to forge a secret alliance with the Unseelie Court.

His face was blank. I couldn't tell if he knew about the plot.

"The foreign Fae infiltrated Florida centuries ago," he said. "Frankly, they're buffoons. They've tried to conquer us before and never succeeded. That I'm also a faerie is irrelevant. I consider them a foreign enemy."

I wasn't sure if I believed him.

"You've successfully distracted me from my reason for visiting," he said. "Will you accept my offer of protection in exchange for lobbying the supernatural guilds on my behalf?"

I had no intention of supporting him, but I didn't want him to know it. His offer could buy time for those of us who wanted to get rid of him. If the Executive Council could vote him out, Diego and I wouldn't have to kill him. First, I needed to assess how the guild members felt before I gave him an answer.

"Your offer is very appealing," I said, "but please allow me to see if it's even possible for me to influence the guilds."

"Don't sell yourself short. You're an empath, after all. With Orlena as your tutor, you'll become very powerful."

"I don't know. Diego could make things difficult. He's next in line to take over the Clan of the Eternal Night, and he's not exactly a big fan of yours. He also can block my empathy, at least until I strengthen it."

"Diego won't be a problem. He'll be a pile of dust when I'm finished with him."

"No, please don't," I said, revealing my affection toward Diego too much. "The vampires will never support you if you destroy him."

Baldric leaned back in his chair and smiled, studying me.

"Are you in love with Diego?" he asked.

"He's a friend of the family."

The probing sensation in my mind resumed, and I blocked it as well as I could. I also sensed magic coming my way as Baldric leaned toward me and stared into my eyes. His were slate gray, his teeth gleamed perfectly white, and a lock of his thick jet-black hair drooped over his forehead. He was giving me a dose of undiluted charm enhanced by magic.

Thank goodness my protection spell was still working. A fact he quickly noticed.

"All this time we've been chatting, and you didn't release your spell?"

"Girls need to be careful with powerful men."

He liked that response. "When will I get your answer about our deal?"

"Soon. I promise."

When I led Baldric from the parlor, Archibald's eyes animated and watched us leave.

Baldric had barely disappeared in his Maserati when a familiar-looking man with blond hair strolled up the sidewalk to our door. It was Leighnel, the Elven mage who had been imprisoned with Mom by the Fae, at the order of their Faerie Queene.

He smiled when I opened the door for him.

"I hope you're well, Sophie. Is your mother at home?" Beneath his smile was a strong feeling of urgency.

"Yes. I think she's in the kitchen. Follow me."

I had wanted to tell Mom about Baldric's offer, but that could wait. I sensed Leighnel had something big to tell her.

"Welcome to the Esperanza Inn," Mom said to him when we entered the kitchen. "It's nice to see you on my turf for once, instead of me being transported to Ehrendil with no warning."

"I was in the neighborhood, in a manner of speaking. But I'm afraid I must take you away again to something you must see. A scouting party of Fae from the Unseelie Court has been wiped out."

"By whom? The Elves?"

"No. By trees."

CHAPTER 7

DARLA

Instead of being in my kitchen, I found myself standing in a forest clearing, Leighnel beside me. We were surrounded by tall longleaf pines, innumerable, spreading out as far as I could see. Only the occasional saw palmetto broke up the uniformity of the pencil-straight trunks and branches with bushy clusters of needles.

There was supernatural energy in the clearing, but it was fading. The carpet of pine needles covering the ground was untouched, with no signs of creatures passing through.

"Fae were here?" I asked.

"They *are* here, beneath us, in a tunnel. They had collected a small amount of phytolucine, and the trees attacked them."

"Attacked?"

"With their roots. They crushed and strangled the faeries in the tunnel. We're essentially standing on their grave."

That creeped me out, both the grave and the fact that the Fae had successfully harvested phytolucine. They planned to use the mysterious substance, which was created by the trees' root systems, in their magic aimed at harming humans.

"Can you tell how much they collected?"

"Not enough to create their potion at scale," Leighnel replied. "But the fact they successfully collected any at all is disturbing. It means they're closer to developing the magic and deploying it against humans."

"If the phytolucine allegedly repels humans and faeries, how do the faeries collect and handle it?"

"My sensors identified it underground here, but I have no way of telling how it was harvested and transported. We still don't know what effect it will have when added to the Fae magic. Will it kill humans, or something worse?"

"Worse than death?"

"I meant harming another species. Like us."

"Are you, um, going to dig down there," I asked with dread, "and retrieve it from the, um, faeries?"

"Yes, but I won't make you watch me. I brought you here to see if you could communicate with the trees. It's not common that they kill faeries."

"I've seen it once," I said. "They did it to save me—Danu, really—from the Fae. The trees destroyed several tunnels. I'd given Danu credit for making them do it. What happened in this forest doesn't seem like something Danu would tell them to do."

"That's what we need to know—if the trees acted on their own."

"Okay, I'll do my thing and see what I can find out."

I didn't need to become Danu to get information from the trees. As a psychometrist, I could pick up their communications. I did, however, need some of the Goddess's magic to understand what the trees were conveying.

I sat on the ground at the base of a large pine just outside of the clearing's perimeter, where I hopefully wouldn't detect any memories of the Fae buried below the clearing. Leaning against the trunk, I placed my palms on the pine-needle-covered ground, cleared my mind, and opened my psychic senses.

The energy poured into my hands almost at once: thousands of electrical impulses and chemical transmissions flowing along the mycorrhizal network of fungi that connected the tree roots beneath the entire forest.

I didn't know what the trees were saying, but they were *pissed off.*

You didn't realize trees could get angry? Well, now you know. Think about that the next time you fire up the chainsaw.

Deep hostility flowed into my mind, and all I could figure out was that it was aimed at me because I was human. It was nothing like the kind of anger humans would feel: tinged with petulance, resentment, or self-pity. It was a fundamental revulsion against something that was harmful to plants and trees.

It was as if humans were a threat, just like gypsy moths, or even fire.

Danu, I called with my mind and soul. *I need you to help me understand the trees and tell them I am a friend.*

I waited for what seemed like several minutes, my hands still pressed upon the ground, the trees' agitated communications buzzing in my head. Finally, Danu spoke.

The trees are angry at both the humans and the Fae. The humans have been causing widespread death. Only a few miles from you, over 100 acres were destroyed so that humans could build where the forests once stood. And the Fae are killing them from below ground, severing their roots to make their tunnels and torturing them to extract a substance they seek.

What can I do to make peace with the forests? I asked.

You alone cannot repair what your species has done. This is one of the reasons I am returning to earth through you.

That left me dumbfounded. What was I supposed to do then? Just wait for Danu to take me over completely? I didn't want to be taken over. Why did she need me? Couldn't she just do her goddess work from wherever she's hanging out?

My connection with Danu abruptly ended, as if she had read my thoughts and was not amused, leaving me merely a human psychometrist trying in vain to communicate with trees.

I brushed off my hands and stood.

"Did you learn anything?" Leighnel asked.

I explained the meager information I had.

"We Elves have sensed a growing resentment in the forests and wetlands. It's been happening for centuries, ever since. . ."

His voice trailed off before he said the obvious: ever since human and Fae populations boomed.

"The Elves are so closely connected with nature," I said. "Can't your people help?"

"Help how? Yes, we have a symbiotic relationship with nature, but that doesn't mean we can repair the damage other species have caused. Only you and the Fae can do that. Or Danu, but she might do it in a way you wouldn't like."

I couldn't imagine Danu harming humans. Until I remembered that she had no compunction about destroying malevolent creatures that harmed the earth.

But humans weren't malevolent, right? That was one question I wasn't sure I wanted answered.

Leighnel suddenly tensed. "Someone is approaching," he whispered.

The ubiquitous background noise of the forest—birds calling, squirrels chittering, and insects buzzing—ceased. All was quiet except for the gentle sifting of a breeze through the trees.

Several individuals, he said to me telepathically. *Fae. We must disguise ourselves.*

Using his Elven magic, he transformed us into squirrels. It's a thing he did quite seamlessly, I have to say. It was a much faster and easier transformation than if I had been a squirrel shifter.

We scurried up the trunk of the tree I had been standing beside and squatted on a lower branch. Leighnel was staring toward our left, and so did I, though I couldn't see anything moving through the thick forest.

Finally, I heard something. Footsteps. They fell softly on the carpet of pine needles, but even I could detect them now.

Several individuals were approaching our clearing. Metallic clinks of tools or weapons were accompanied by slaps of leather.

Fear rose in me, even though I was just a squirrel. What if the faeries could tell I was really a human, and they picked me off with arrows?

Be not afraid, Leighnel said wordlessly. *They won't notice us.*

The sound of marching was much louder now. I caught glimpses of non-forest colors moving through the trees.

And then they entered the clearing.

Six male faeries, in their natural diminutive forms, passed by directly below me. Five were soldiers, and one was a sorcerer with a shaved head and red robes. He wasn't the one who had captured Mom and me in Palm Beach.

All six studied the ground intently. The sorcerer jabbered something in Fae and pointed to a spot near the center of the clearing. The soldiers took shovels that were strapped to their backs and began clearing away the pine needles. Next, they dug furiously in the sandy soil. They each worked on their own hole, rather than a single large one, as if they were unsure of the exact location they sought.

It was clear they were attempting to reach the collapsed

tunnel. I didn't know if they had any hope of finding their comrades alive, or if they simply wanted to retrieve the phytolucine they had collected.

After the faeries began digging, the sounds of the forest resumed. It was as if the birds, mammals, and insects had determined the faeries weren't a direct threat and that it was okay to return to business as usual.

But suddenly, the forest went silent again. The only sound was the wind through the trees and the crunching, scraping sounds of digging.

I glanced at Leighnel in squirrel form beside me.

Stay up here with me, he said in my head. *Do not go near the ground.*

I sensed a primal energy building inside the earth, a shift in air pressure. It was terrifying, as if an earthquake was about to strike.

And that's what it resembled at first. The branch on which we were huddling vibrated with increasing force as the entire tree trembled. I clutched the wood with my claws to hang on.

Then, the earth rumbled ominously. The faeries stopped digging and looked at each other with fear. The sorcerer jabbered at them angrily, ordering them to keep working. But even he was soon silent, glancing around with panic.

The first roots were small, sprouting from the soil like a time-lapse video of grass growing. As they rose from beneath the clearing, they grew thicker. When they reached about six feet tall, they waved like tentacles.

The first faerie to bolt clambered from the hole he'd dug and only ran a few feet before a root stopped him, wrapping around his leg like a vine. He howled and tried to tear it off.

The other faeries watched, frozen in shock, until the roots sought them out. They chopped at the tendrils with their shovels, but more and more roots rose from the earth and snaked around and up the faeries' legs and torsos.

The rumbling grew louder, turning into soft explosions as larger roots, as big as branches, broke free from the soil and moved jerkily toward the faeries, who were surrounded now by a mini forest of vertical roots that filled the entire clearing.

Red balls of fire shot skyward as if from a Roman candle. The sorcerer was using magic to fight back. A few larger roots caught fire, but that didn't stop them. Repeated screams echoed through the trees as the faeries were wrapped in roots, some of which were burning.

The sorcerer broke free from the roots encasing the soldiers. He appeared to have conjured a protection bubble around himself, preventing the roots from contacting his body. But as he stumbled toward the edge of the clearing, a mat of woven roots rose over and around him like a blanket, trapping him, pulling him to the ground.

He shrieked as the mat of roots thrust him, bubble and all, into the soil. With a muffled roar, the earth gave way, and the sorcerer disappeared beneath it.

Meanwhile, the soldiers had each become so wrapped in roots they looked like mummies. One by one, they were pulled into the soil, some feet-first, others head-first.

Their screams continued, even after their bodies disappeared, until they finally went silent.

The terrible rumbling noise grew softer as its source sank deeper below the ground. When it ceased, the only sound was a vibration of the branch we sat upon.

It was caused by my body trembling in fear.

I love trees, I said to Leighnel. *I'd always seen them as dumb but harmless. Virtuous, even, as they endured the weather and other forces of nature. But now they seem like monsters.*

Just as intelligent species like ours can become monsters when pushed far enough, Leighnel replied.

We sat on the branch for a while, making sure the roots wouldn't return. Finally, after the birds began to sing again, Leighnel scampered down the trunk to the ground. I followed reluctantly.

He transformed us back to our Elven and human forms.

I gingerly examined the destruction in the clearing. It looked like bombs had exploded. Deep holes descended into darkness, disturbed soil lay in random piles, and trenches curved through it all in random patterns.

There was no sign that Fae had ever been here, except for two shovels lying atop the dirt.

"Do you think the trees will attack humans, too?" I asked.

"I truly believe these faeries were killed because they harvested phytolucine. Why that would cause such a remarkable reaction, I cannot say. If trees ever seek revenge like this on humans, let's hope it's rare and without witnesses, because your species would wipe trees off the face of the earth."

"Let's hope they don't seek revenge at all."

Leighnel stared at me with concern etching his narrow, angular face. "You must convince Danu to bring peace to the forests," he said. "And we must prevent the Unseelie Court from obtaining more phytolucine. It will bring nothing but grief to all the Fae, both foreign and indigenous, as well as humans. And to the Elves, because we will be caught in the middle."

The next thing I knew, I was back in the inn's kitchen. Sophie was sitting on a stool at the island counter, deep in thought, her hands supporting her chin. Leighnel was standing beside me in the same spot as before we went away.

"You guys weren't gone very long," Sophie said.

"It was far too long." I described what I had witnessed.

"Jeez Louise, why does the entire world have to go to pieces all at once?"

"It's like the Chinese curse: 'may you live in interesting times.'"

"Yes, interesting," Sophie said, her mind wandering off.

"Sorry for taking you away so unexpectedly," Leighnel said, smiling at Sophie and me. "You two have a fruitful day."

After he left, Sophie said, "I have to decide whether to make a deal with the devil in order to protect myself and my family."

"What do you mean?"

"Do I join Baldric and the conniving local faeries who want to rule us all? If I don't, it could mean the end of us."

CHAPTER 8

SOPHIE

Orlena Managua, Arch Mage of the Magic Guild, greeted me at her door with a sour expression.

"Is this a bad time?" I asked, even though she had told me to come at this exact time.

"I told you two-thirty. So come in."

She disappeared into her house, leaving the front door open. I stepped inside, closed the door, and headed in the direction she had gone. Her house was historic, almost as old as the inn, and the layout had no rhyme or reason.

I smelled herbal tea and steered myself toward it, passing through a small room that looked like it had been an addition decades ago, and ended up in a lovely bright kitchen that had received many modern upgrades. It was much more fashionable than the kitchen at the inn.

"You want tea?" Orlena asked.

"Yes, please."

"Baldric told me you need to make your empath powers stronger," she stated as she poured me a cup of strange-smelling brew. "I said that's a job for a psychic, not a mage, but he said you'd already gone down the road of using magic to enhance your powers."

Orlena carried the tea to the kitchen table and gestured for me to sit down. She eased herself into a chair across from the tea.

"Yes. Bob helped me a little but could go only so far." I sat down and went to take a sip of tea, but sensed a spell in it, so I only pretended to drink. "My problem is I can't integrate magic with my empathy. I'm just using it to add energy to an ability I haven't learned how to control."

I told her about a couple of my successful deployments of my empath powers: convincing the troll to flee his home beneath the bridge and pushing Marge Moosebacher to reveal to the crowd her true faerie form.

"Why does Baldric care so much about your empath powers?" She squinted at me, as if she needed to be wearing the eyeglasses hanging from a lanyard around her neck. Orlena had straight brown hair going to gray, pulled in a tight ponytail. Her features were rounded—her eyes, nose, mouth, and cheeks, as well as her body. Her skin tone was light brown. I'd guess her age to be in the mid-fifties. I wasn't sure how closely allied she was with Baldric, and I think she was trying to assess the same of me.

I decided to be honest.

"He wants me to use my empath powers for persuasion," I replied. "To benefit him. He wants me to strengthen his support from the guilds. And he plans to run for mayor, so I suppose he'll need my help with that, too."

Orlena's demeanor was so flat that she gave no clues about what she was thinking. This was a case where my empath powers were easy to use. She was suspicious of me. Resentful of having to help me. Frightened of Baldric. And possibly frightened of me if I turned out to be loyal to him. My truthful answer increased her trust of me, though.

"How do you feel about providing these services to him?" Orlena asked.

"Not good. I don't want to help him."

I waited to hear how she'd respond, but she didn't.

"I came here because I'm interested in learning what you can teach me," I went on, "but I haven't given Baldric a final answer to his offer. He promised that if I persuade the guilds to support him, he'll protect my family and me. We're extremely vulnerable now." I laughed bitterly. "Even more so because of Baldric, right? He can turn us in."

Finally, I detected some warmth coming from my host.

She reached for my cup of tea and slid it away from me.

"You don't need this," she explained. "It causes honesty in people who are withholding information. Sometimes, too much honesty. I can tell you're telling me the truth."

"Thank you for not secretly enchanting me." My tone had a bit of an edge, but she ignored it.

"Baldric has leverage over me, too," she said. "And he's been using it to get his way. Such as making me give magic lessons."

This made me feel terrible until she cracked the first smile I'd seen on her face.

"If you're a suitable candidate," she added, "I'll gladly help you."

"Baldric has access to the Executive Council's records. All the names of the guild members. He could destroy us if he wanted to. And he's closely allied with the governor and Senator Poxton."

"I know. I have the same worries as you." She paused,

debating whether to continue. "No one should have the power to blackmail us like that."

"It sounds like you and I are of the same mind. What do we do about this situation?"

"Have you heard of Huey Long?"

"Sounds familiar."

"He was the governor of Louisiana during the 1930s and later became a US senator. He ruled the state with an iron fist. Some have called him America's first dictator. Governor Witlessin is copying Long's playbook."

"How so?"

"Using fear and hatred to rile up the population, making us turn to her to protect us and take away our fear. And capturing every aspect of government and society so that everyone is working for her. Punishing her critics so no one dares to challenge her. People like Baldric are her stooges."

I nodded.

"Baldric's only value to her—besides his campaign contributions—is that he can deliver supernaturals to be sacrificed on her altar. So, forget his promises. I guarantee he'll divulge the names on the guild membership rolls."

Orlena had opened up more than I expected. I wondered if my empath powers had encouraged her to do so, as I used them to instill in her my urge for us to be allies.

"How can we stop him?" I asked.

"Well, I can't in good conscience suggest what stopped Huey Long. A bullet stopped him. I don't want to go down that road."

I didn't want to, either, though my hands were already stained with blood. I'd used crossbow bolts instead of bullets on faeries and a vampire. But assassinating a public figure, even if she was a faerie, was totally out of bounds for me.

"I think we can help our community in a much simpler way,"

I said. "The Executive Council can vote to recall Baldric from office and keep him away from the membership rolls."

"What's keeping him from reporting you, me, the others on the Council, and any other member he can name?"

"We'll threaten him. If that doesn't work, we'll incapacitate him with magic." Note that I said "incapacitate" instead of "kill." I sincerely tried to avoid my initial urge, after he attacked Diego, to assassinate him.

"He's more powerful than you and I."

"We'll see about that," I said. "If all the mages, wizards, and witches team up, I think we can take him out."

She studied me, and that sly smile appeared again.

"You have a rather high opinion of your magical abilities," she said. "Allow me to test them. Do you know a protection spell?"

"Of course."

"Show me."

I concentrated on my internal energies and drew upon elemental energy, particularly that of water. In my core, I'm a water witch, so I made a magical connection with the nearby bay and took energy from its brackish water.

Trying to ignore Orlena staring at me, I wove together strands of energy while mentally reciting the spell's incantation. Soon, I was surrounded by a protection bubble.

"I wouldn't say you cast that spell with alacrity," Orlena said.

"I wanted to do it correctly because you're going to critique it."

"My first criticism is it took too long. If you're attacked, physically or with magic, you need protection instantly."

"I know, I know. I have been attacked more times than I want to count. And I've gotten my spell working in time to save myself."

Orlena frowned. "Release the spell and start over again. With alacrity."

I did as she requested, and in the middle of it, she sent a wave of force at me without warning. She didn't even blink an eye or move a muscle. I found myself on the floor, my chair knocked to the side.

"That wasn't fair," I complained.

"Life's not fair. Neither are your foes."

"My protection bubble was almost finished. Even if it had been, the magic you sent at me could have knocked me, inside the bubble, to the floor."

"Yes, that's the case with most protection spells. That's why they're not good enough. You must learn how to anchor your protection sphere—or bubble, as you call it—to a stationary surface, such as the floor. As it is now, you're safe in your bubble, but foes can knock it around like a balloon. How are you supposed to fight back if you're bouncing off walls?"

"I thought you were going to teach me to strengthen my empath powers," I said, sulking.

"I'll get around to that. In your Magic Guild registration, you listed yourself as favoring battle magic."

"Yeah." This embarrassed me. "I guess I have anger issues and like blowing stuff up."

Orlena smirked.

I added, "That's why the Council made me an enforcer."

"I was told you volunteered for that job."

"It doesn't matter. I don't want to do it anymore. Coming out as an empath has made hurting or intimidating people unpleasant."

"I should think so."

"What kind of magic do you specialize in?"

"Healing," Orlena said with pride. "To reach the level of

mage, you must be an expert in all forms of the craft. But healing has been my passion ever since I was a kitchen witch making potions to cure colds."

"What can you cure now?"

"Diseases. Serious wounds. But enough about me. Let's work on improving your protection spell. Empath or not, you're still going to use battle magic. It's too ingrained in you. So, we must be sure you're protected."

I shared with Orlena how I cast my spell. I was expecting her to make me change my incantation, but instead, she dissected the way I wove together strands of energy.

"The power of a spell comes from its most basic structure," she said. "The rest is window dressing. Now, your structure is competent, but you're skimping on the elemental energies."

"I'm naturally attuned to water," I replied. "That's why I harvest most of my elemental energy from it."

"That's fine, but you need more energy from the element of earth."

"Why?"

"It's quite simple, my dear. When you weave in strands of earth energy as you build your structure, it grounds you to the earth. In other words, you can attach your spell to the ground, the floor, the face of a cliff, whatever."

A surge of excitement ran through me. "That's brilliant."

"No, it's just basic spellcraft. Now, try it yourself. Remember, do this at the very beginning."

I followed Orlena's advice, building my spell as usual, but drawing in more earth energy and weaving it into the structure.

"Don't judge me on speed," I said after the spell was complete and I had cast it. "Because of the changes I had to make."

"No worries. Now I shall test it."

I braced myself as she sent a wave of force more powerful than before. This time, I wasn't knocked to the floor. My bubble was buffeted by the impact, and yeah, I felt it. Yet I wasn't hurt and remained in my chair.

"Excellent," Orlena said. "When you go home, practice this spell until you've shortened how long it takes to cast it."

"I'm on it."

"What else do you have up your sleeve?"

"I don't have my sword with me, but I use it to fire intense bursts of energy. Bolts of lightning, basically."

"If you rely on a prop for your magic, such as a wand, staff, or sword, you must always carry it with you in times like these."

"I know," I replied sheepishly. "It seemed rude to bring a weapon when visiting your home for the first time."

"You specialize in attack spells, but after the Great Unmasking, you need to think of it as defensive magic, too. You're no longer the hunter but the prey. If we're going to protect supernaturals, we have to stay alive." Orlena stood and walked to the stove. "I'm going to make us a pot of normal tea while you demonstrate more of your magic."

I did as she asked. At times, I felt like I was putting on a magic show for an audience. But I wasn't guessing which card she was hiding or making coins disappear. I levitated objects, created wind, produced a puddle of water on the flooring tiles. And I shot lightning from my fingers, but much weaker than from my sword, of course.

Orlena returned to the table and poured two cups of English breakfast tea—with no weird spices or magical ingredients.

"Your skills are good for someone of your experience level," she said, taking a sip. "I'll be happy to teach you more spells and give you additional pointers. But for now, we must work on your empath abilities."

"Thank you. Like I said, Bob did his best, but he doesn't know much about empaths."

"Bob knew little about empathy when he was human. He knows even less now that he's a vampire."

"Vampires aren't empathetic?" This bothered me. Was it because I wanted Diego to be empathetic—to me? "I used to read Bob's emotions."

"Perhaps, but I doubt he could sense yours."

"Don't vampires need empathy to mesmerize you?"

"No. They merely control your mind, which can indirectly trigger emotions. But they don't really care about those."

I remembered Diego blocking my attempts to sense his emotions.

"Vampires feel emotions," I insisted. "They can love."

"Of course. However, over the years, vampires become more selfish and self-absorbed. They care less and less about the emotions of others. But why are we talking about vampires?"

Because I couldn't stop myself from thinking about Diego.

"I don't know," I said.

"Let's talk about empathy and how you can integrate your magic with it."

"Please."

"First, I want you to kill me."

CHAPTER 9

SOPHIE

"You want me to do what?" I asked, gobsmacked.

"Kill me," Orlena replied.

"I don't want to kill you."

"I should hope not. But I shall make you."

Her lips moved almost imperceptibly as she cast a spell. As a mage, she could cast spells with much less effort than I, a mere witch.

Out of nowhere, I felt an urge to kill Orlena.

I mean, I still didn't *want* to kill her, but I had a desperate craving to strangle her while sending my destructive purple energy into her. It was like a drug crying out for you to take it when you wanted to stay clean and sober.

The impulse was powerful, and my hands rose from my lap on their own while I fought to keep them away from Orlena.

"What did you do to me?" I asked through gritted teeth.

"Oh, it's a spell I have that's akin to mesmerizing someone. It's a form of coercion. Comes in handy from time to time."

"Release the spell before I hurt you."

"See, I can make you hurt me despite your not wanting to. No matter how hard you fight it, I can pump more energy into it. But it has its downsides."

"Yeah, like being strangled by your magic student."

"If you truly, truly don't want to kill me, you won't do a good job at it."

"Doesn't matter. If you're dead, you're dead, no matter how sloppy I was."

My strength was giving way, and the impulse to attack her was winning. I involuntarily stood up and lurched toward her, barely stopping myself before my hands could reach her.

"And if my spell falters for some reason, you won't complete the job," Orlena calmly explained.

"Please release the spell."

"You see, there's an enormous difference between coercion and persuasion. I don't know if any magic exists that could make you truly want to kill me and keep that desire going. But you, as an empath, potentially have the power to do that."

"Don't make me kill you, please." I lurched closer to her, and she finally realized how close I was to succumbing to her command.

Orlena snapped her fingers, and the spell was released.

Shaking with exhaustion, I sat down again.

"When you used your empath powers on the troll and the faerie, you pushed them toward doing something they actually wanted to do deep down inside," Orlena said. "As an empath, with your psychic connection to emotions, you can actually make people *want* to do what *you* desire. Which is a lot more effective than coercing them."

"Even something bad, like killing you?"

"I don't believe you can make them want to do something against their own best interest or contrary to their nature, such as hurting themselves or someone they care about. But that still leaves you a great deal of latitude. How do you intend to use such powers?"

"Baldric wants me to make all the guild members support him. Forget that. I want to convince people to stop hating supernaturals," I said. "To break up mobs that are about to commit violence."

"Unfortunately, that's a tall order to get people to stop fearing, and thus hating, those who are different. And the pathology of mob behavior is complicated. Nevertheless, I believe it's possible."

"How?"

"The spell I used on you is quite effective in manipulating the limbic system of the brain. I will devise some alterations to the spell and teach it to you. If you cast it while channeling your empathy, you should have the power to change someone's emotions or instill new ones in them."

"I can break up a mob?"

"I believe so."

"And stop people from hating?"

"No, you can't remove hate from the world. People will always hate, unfortunately. However, on the individual level, you can persuade someone not to hate a particular type of person or creature for a while."

"That would be excellent!"

"I'll get to work and create a new recipe for the spell, just for you. Come back here in a couple of days to try it out."

"Thank you so much," I said, grinning. My smile quickly faded. "Before I go, what's the next step in dealing with Baldric?"

"I'll speak privately to the other members of the Executive Council about drafting a recall petition to fire Baldric. It doesn't sound very dramatic, but we must begin somewhere."

THAT EVENING, AFTER WINE HOUR AND SUNSET, I FOUND myself wandering across town to pop in on Diego. I didn't even bother texting or calling him because he hadn't been replying lately. Showing up in person was better anyway, so we could talk about matters that shouldn't be discussed on devices that could be hacked or tapped.

Diego wanted to kill Baldric. Orlena merely wanted to disassociate him from the guilds. To be honest, I thought Diego's solution was wiser because Baldric knew too much about the guilds and their members, which he could give to the authorities. Right? Many supernaturals could end up dead or imprisoned as a result.

I still couldn't bring myself to kill Baldric, though. I wanted nothing to do with it. Yeah, that made me a cowardly hypocrite. So I was willing to live with Orlena's solution rather than the more effective—and permanent—one.

When I arrived at 14 Granada Street, lights were on in the restaurant downstairs, but not in Diego's apartment on the floor above. I walked around back and was surprised to find three cars in the restaurant's parking lot besides Diego's. The establishment hadn't yet reopened, so the cars probably belonged to people, or vampires, helping him with renovations. Or maybe not; they were all luxury cars.

I decided to return to the front and enter the main door to see what was going on.

Before I could take two steps, the cold hand of a male vampire clamped over my mouth, and he lifted me with his other arm, carrying me through a back door into the kitchen.

"I caught this human prowling around outside," my captor said in a Spanish accent.

Diego, a female vampire I recognized named Helga, and a male with a well-manicured beard sat around a prep table.

Helga had been a close friend of Pedro, a former duke, or leader, of the Clan of the Eternal Night. After he was destroyed, Diego was next in line for the role. Until Lethia had come along and dominated everyone.

My captor set me down next to the table. I turned to examine him. He had an angular face with a pointy chin.

Diego stood. "This is Sophie of the Magic Guild. A good friend of mine. We can trust her."

"An enforcer," Helga said.

"Not anymore," I felt obligated to say.

"You've met Helga before," Diego said to me.

I nodded and gave her a little wave.

"This is Billy." He nodded to the bearded man. "And Eduardo," referring to my captor. "After me, Eduardo has been in San Marcos the longest, since the first colonial period before the English took Florida."

"Nice to meet you all," I said. "I apologize for intruding on your meeting."

"No need to apologize," Diego said. "We were just chatting. Most of the Clan assumed, with Lethia gone, that I would become the next duke. My friends have informed me there are others who seek the position."

"Aren't you next in line?" I asked.

Diego nodded. "But according to the rules, anyone can challenge me."

"Many members want this to be resolved with a Crucible," said Billy with a southern accent.

"A what?" I asked.

"Combat," he replied. "All those who seek to be the leader must fight hand-to-hand. And may the best vampire win."

"Are the losers destroyed?" I asked, horrified.

"It happens sometimes," Billy said with a dark smile.

I looked at Diego. He must have read my expression.

"In times like this, we can't continue without a duke," he said. "With the Great Unmasking, vampires are among those at the greatest risk. We need to fight the local faeries and their human stooges to change the course of this disaster. Especially before the Faerie Queene's armies invade. The Clan needs a strong leader, one who can get the Executive Council back on course and ensure all the guilds are united to face this threat."

"That's why we support you," Helga said.

She was tall with a shaved head and a beautiful face like a white marble statue.

"Isn't it counterproductive at this time to make your best vampires fight each other and possibly be destroyed?" I asked.

All four looked at me smugly, as if I were a silly child.

"This is the way it's done every century or so when there's a challenge," Diego said. "In a way, it's my fault. My relationship with Lethia made some in the Clan believe I'm weak."

"Nonsense," Eduardo said. "Your challengers are power-hungry and trying to get an advantage in this chaotic period we're in."

"We vampires must get used to fighting," Diego said. "We can't stand by passively while we're attacked. Like what happened today."

I looked at him questioningly.

"Sophie, I thought you were on top of all the news."

"I turned my phone off while I was being tutored in magic. Forgot to turn it back on."

"A vampire was captured today by vigilantes," Diego said.

"It's all over social media. He's the first one taken in the Great Unmasking. He was in town as a tourist, I believe. Now they want to stake him live on camera."

I turned on my phone, only to be met by several unread texts and voicemails from Mom and Cory. I only needed to see a couple of the messages to learn the bad news.

The vampire who had been caught was a guest at the Esperanza Inn. Mr. Jubbles. Poor, innocent Mr. Jubbles, who had only been a vampire for a year. He was abducted from an antique store that was open late.

I announced these details to the group.

"We had been planning a rescue attempt. I have no faith the Council will organize one," Diego said. "As a favor to you and your mother, we will expedite it."

"Please," I begged. "Mr. Jubbles is sweet and unable to fend for himself. Besides, we can't let these thugs execute him on camera."

"Of course not."

"Could we maybe begin tonight?"

Diego surveyed his fellow vampires. They all nodded in the affirmative.

"After I was turned," Eduardo said, "for my entire second life, I have been careful not to offend humans. I feed discreetly, never killing, always careful to leave no clues to my existence. Enough of that."

Diego frowned. "Eduardo. . ."

"Humans have declared war on us with the Great Unmasking. They're nothing but stupid livestock. Their only advantage is that they outnumber us. I refuse to worry about them anymore. We've been revealed. There's no reason to remain timid anymore."

"Please," Diego said, "I caution you—"

"For every vampire destroyed by these human cows, I will slaughter ten of their kind."

"Um, back to the outnumbering part," I said. "I don't think that's a wise strategy."

"I agree with Eduardo," drawled Billy. "We're predators. Heck, it's what we do. We prey. Now, the humans have made us their prey, and that's unacceptable."

"Vampires are more intelligent than humans," Diego said. "We are immortal, with preternatural powers, and will defeat them with our wisdom and our powers. We will *not* begin a bloodbath that turns a planet full of humans against vampires."

"They must stop persecuting supernaturals, then," Helga said. "They need to forget about us, to go back to believing we exist only in superstition. Humans can rationalize anything. Once we begin slaughtering them, they'll find a reason to blame it on something else."

"Guys," I said, "first let's rescue Mr. Jubbles. The fiery speeches can come afterward."

Diego agreed to use his friends' vampire senses to search for Mr. Jubbles. I called a computer geek friend to enlist him in searching for the IP address of the computer posting videos of Mr. Jubbles held captive.

On my walk home, while conducting searches on my phone, I saw a campaign commercial for the governor. It featured a poorly lit video of Mr. Jubbles, bald and overweight despite his lean diet of blood. His shiny scalp and jowls were emphasized with harsh highlights and opaque shadows as he sat on a bathroom floor, prodded with a crucifix until he snarled, revealing his fangs. Typography and a voiceover at the end of the video said:

"Re-elect Governor Witlessin. She'll protect you from fiends like this."

Yikes, things in San Marcos were spiraling out of control faster than I could grasp.

CHAPTER 10

DARLA

I paced back and forth in the inn's living room while Cory sat in a chair, his hands gripping the fronts of the armrests as if he were afraid he'd be flung off.

The living room was empty of guests at this late hour. They sometimes hung out in here to work on their laptops, add a few pieces to the jigsaw puzzle on the corner table, or relax with a glass during Wine Hour. Now it was like a war room.

Roderick leaned against the back of the sofa, offering unhelpful theories of how to find Mr. Jubbles. Archibald was perched on the wall beside a vintage oil painting of a monkey. With the frown on his impish face, he rather resembled the monkey. Now, if only Sophie would get here.

"Did you see this?" Sophie asked indignantly as she blew into the room like a hurricane. "The governor is using Mr. Jubbles in a campaign ad."

She thrust her phone in my face and played the commercial.

"That is so wrong," I said.

Cory came over to us, and she played it again.

"Your mother and I aren't very big on social media stuff, but there's already a lot of Mr. Jubbles out there," he said.

"We must find him before he's hurt," I said to no one in particular. "He's our guest. He put his trust in us to keep him safe."

"Technically, he wasn't abducted from here," Roderick said. "We have no responsibility for his safety when he's out and about."

I glared at him. "It's our freaking fault he was turned in the first place. Lethia came here seeking me. She drained and turned him right here."

"In the pantry," Roderick said. "While he was stealing cocktail peanuts in the middle of the night instead of being safely locked in his room."

"It happened here, so I consider it our responsibility."

Roderick harrumphed. "Do not forget that I helped him with his transition to vampire, which his maker should have done."

"As a vampire, don't you have special ways of locating those of your kind?" Sophie asked him.

"Well, I suppose," he sputtered. "It's been said we do. However, I am not part of a nest or the Clan of the Eternal Night. I'm not bound to any vampires. A free agent is what I am."

Sophie huffed, then walked into a hallway to make a phone call.

The doorbell rang, and I rushed into the foyer to let Samson in.

"Thanks for coming," I said, giving him a quick hug.

He had bags under his eyes and his normally tidy beard needed trimming. There were more gray hairs among the brown than before.

"I don't know how much help I can be," Samson said. "The department has been totally swamped by reports of supernaturals. Most are false, like people trying to harm an enemy by accusing them of being a vampire or werewolf. Mothers Against Monsters is encouraging vigilantes by offering bounties. They're making Florida totally lawless. But whoever abducted your guest should have reported him to us."

"What would the police have done to Mr. Jubbles?" I asked.

Samson hesitated. "The procedures are in flux at this point in time. Normally, we would put him in a special wing of the county jail until prosecutors tried him for being a supernatural. But now, the state is getting involved. The governor is ordering local agencies to turn over supernatural prisoners to the Florida Department of Law Enforcement, which is taking custody of them."

"That sounds ominous. What are they doing with them?"

"The FDLE is setting up camps to hold the prisoners. I don't know what they're going to do to them."

The grim expression on his face said he expected the worst.

"That could be my family ending up in those camps. It could happen to you, too, Michael."

As a werewolf, Samson was very aware of the danger to his life and career should his secret be revealed.

"I offered to help you as a friend," he said. "Not as a police detective. The police would be of no help to Mr. Jubbles, even if we rescued him from the vigilantes."

Sophie joined us in the foyer.

"I called a friend who's in IT," she said. "He'll try to trace the IP address of the original computer that posted the video of Mr. Jubbles. It's going to be difficult, though, because it's been reposted so many times on different social-media platforms."

"If he can't do it, tell him to call me," Samson said. "We can subpoena the information from the social-media companies."

"Is there time for that?" I asked.

"Only if the vigilantes are in no hurry to stake Mr. Jubbles. Let's hope they're intoxicated by their videos going viral and will want to drag it out for as long as possible. In the meantime, do you know where he was abducted?"

"One of the few antique stores that stay open late—the ones on Antique Row closest to restaurants. I don't know which. He's mentioned he loves shopping at the Elephant in the Room."

"I'll talk to them and the others. Hopefully, there's security-camera footage and witnesses."

Samson left, and minutes later, Diego showed up. Somehow, his presence made me feel a little more confident, I guess because he was an old friend from the Memory Guild and a more competent vampire than Roderick.

"Can you let me into your guest's room?" he asked. "I need to memorize his scent so I can search for it."

"Like a hound dog?" I asked. Sophie visibly cringed at my tactlessness.

"Yes, indeed," Diego replied without being offended. "Scent is a useful tool to help me identify him. When I'm close enough to a vampire's location, I can feel their presence. We vampires use that ability to alert us of others' hunting territories and if a vampire is encroaching on ours. When I get closer, scent will tell me if the vampire I sense is he, without having to confirm it visually."

"Come with me," I said, leading Diego to the stairs and up to room 302, followed by Sophie.

I let us in with the master key card I carry. The room was a mess, even though Sophie had made the bed and tidied up after Mr. Jubbles had gone out on the night he was abducted. Clusters of shopping bags and various antiques were scattered on the floor and atop the furniture. Mr. Jubbles had been a heavy drinker when he was a human. Now, it appeared, antiques were his addiction.

Diego moved slowly through the room. Sophie and I tried to stay out of his way. If I hadn't known what Diego was doing, I would have thought he was simply visually searching for clues. He didn't thrust his nose into the bedsheets and the clothing in the closet like a hound dog would. Only by looking at Diego closely could I see his nostrils flaring as he inhaled the scents.

"Thank you," he said. "I have a decent olfactory portrait of him now. It's time to hit the streets."

"I'm going with you," Sophie said.

"So am I," I said. When Sophie gave me the side-eye, I added, "I'm the innkeeper. I feel responsible for his safety."

We went downstairs, and I explained to Cory what we were doing and told him to keep his phone close.

Diego's Aston Martin was parked at the curb, and we piled in. Sophie had put her duffel bag, with her sword inside, in the trunk. Her crossbow sat in her lap.

"I hope you're not planning on using those weapons," I said. "I assume Mr. Jubbles is being held by humans. If you kill one, that's murder."

"I'm not planning on killing any humans. But the way things are, I can't go anywhere unarmed," she said with a tone. "Neither should you."

The vintage engine rumbled to life and sped off, the tires dancing upon the cobblestones.

"Where are we going?" Sophie asked.

"I know the locations of the vampire nests and the residences of most of the solitary vampires," Diego replied. "I'm going to avoid those areas and cover the rest of the city until my senses locate him."

This strategy seemed dubious, but I had more faith in it than the human alternatives.

At this late hour, our tiny city was largely asleep, with only the 24-hour convenience store and diner open. No one spoke as we rolled slowly through the streets of Old Town, and then the relatively newer neighborhoods that surrounded it, including the college that Sophie had attended.

Diego suddenly perked up. "Vampire ahead."

We went through an intersection, and Diego stared to the left. I couldn't see anyone.

"No. False alarm," Diego said. "It's a female in the shadows next to the closed dry-cleaning shop. She's waiting to ambush prey. A late-night dog walker, perhaps."

Soon, we ended up in the neighborhood where my mother lived, which was filled with Victorian homes.

"I'm sensing a vampire nearby," Diego said, turning from the avenue into the side streets.

"This is close to the antique shops where Mr. Jubbles was shopping," I said.

Diego didn't answer. He was lost in concentration. Our route seemed random, moving along tree-lined residential blocks going north, then east, south, and east again. The smell of saltwater and mudflats drifted into the open windows as we got closer to the bay.

Finally, Diego pulled up in front of a house with no lights on inside or out.

"Stay here," he commanded as his lithe frame sprang from the car. He disappeared into the shadows.

Sophie wound up her crossbow's string.

"I warned you about shooting humans," I whispered.

She shushed me. A vampire in the house could easily hear us.

I jumped when Diego appeared beside the car and got back inside.

"It's not Mr. Jubbles," he said. "I scented a different vampire inside. The homeowner, I believe."

He started the car, and we left the neighborhood, continuing our patrol northward.

"I truly hope Mr. Jubbles is not in the suburbs," Diego said. "We'd have to cover so much ground. And then there are all those new subdivisions sprouting up in the countryside."

"They could have taken him anywhere," I said, frustrated.

"The earliest posting of the video was around nine o'clock on the night he was captured," Sophie said. "They couldn't have taken him too far. You know, let's head back toward downtown and check out that seedy neighborhood to the west—the cheap motels and apartments there."

"Good idea," Diego said.

Sophie beamed at his praise. It made me wonder if she was developing a crush on the vampire. I wasn't sure I liked the possibility of having a vampire as a son-in-law.

Diego made a U-turn and drove south toward the center of town. Then, we took a main thoroughfare west, crossing the railroad tracks, and entered a section of fading retail stores and old office buildings. Up ahead were two dilapidated hotels where tourists with the smallest budgets, and local lowlifes, stayed.

Diego inhaled sharply and pulled into the parking lot of a two-story motel with a neon sign featuring an alligator.

"Definitely a vampire here," he said. "One who's in distress."

He parked as far away from the building as possible.

"Stay in the car, and I really mean it," he said with a warning stare at Sophie.

Diego disappeared and only seconds later returned, standing

outside the driver's door. He was texting, his face illuminated by his phone screen.

"He's in a room on the second floor," Diego told us, leaning in through the driver's-side open window. "I scented him. Three humans are in there now."

Sophie reached over beneath the dashboard for the lever that opened the trunk, leaped out of the car, and removed her duffel bag.

"I told you not to attack humans!" I said to her.

"I'm hoping I won't have to. Nothing is more persuasive than the shiny blade of a broadsword."

We both glanced around, realizing that Diego wasn't beside the car anymore. Sophie took off running, with me right behind, thudding up the exterior steps and sprinting down the open breezeway outside the rooms.

Diego stood beside a door halfway down where a plastic do-not-disturb sign hung from the handle. He put his finger to his lips when we approached. We stopped running and tiptoed. The sensation of magic made my skin tingle. Sophie must have cast a spell.

"I can hear a human talking," she whispered. "He's making another video."

"Let us handle this," Diego said.

"Us?" I asked.

Suddenly, three vampires appeared at the door: two men and a woman with a shaved head whom I vaguely recognized. Diego must have texted them. It was remarkable how quickly they had arrived. That was vampirism for you.

Diego put his arms around Sophie and me and led us down the breezeway, away from the room.

"You guys can't be here for this," he whispered.

"Why not?" Sophie asked. "I want to help."

"I don't care if and how well the humans are armed," he replied. "They don't stand a chance against four vampires. But most important, you can't witness what's going to happen. You don't want to be legally exposed like that."

"Are you going to kill them?" I wanted to know.

"We don't plan to, but there's going to be violence. You do not want to be witnesses. I don't want you to be."

He led us to the stairs and followed us down.

"We already know some bad stuff is going to go down," Sophie said.

"If you leave the premises now, you'll have plausible deniability. You can honestly say you came here with me, and you left without seeing what happened. Here." He handed Sophie the keys to his car. "Drive to the inn now. I'll pick up my car later."

Sophie and I nodded dumbly and got into the car. Diego ran back up the stairs. I was worried about the raid that would ensue and was eager to grant Diego what he wanted. Sophie, well, was another story.

"I'm not leaving," she said.

"Yes, we both are. Start the car."

"I don't know how to drive a stick shift."

"I do. Trade seats with me."

As I got into the driver's seat, I watched Sophie carefully, worried that she'd run away and go upstairs. But she got into the passenger seat. I started the engine.

"Wait just a moment before you start driving," Sophie said. "I'm trying to make an empathetic connection with Diego to see if I can tell what he and his friends are doing."

We sat there with the engine purring and my heart beating like a pneumatic hammer. I wanted to get out of here before the poop hit the fan.

Sophie was in a meditative state with her eyes closed. Magic emanated from her and gave me goosebumps.

Her eyes shot open.

"Omigod," she gasped. "I've made this incredibly vivid connection with him! It's like I'm seeing the world through his senses."

Just then, a *boom* came from upstairs. It sounded like the door to the room had blown open.

Yes, the poop was being flung from the fan blades.

CHAPTER 11

SOPHIE

Diego kicked the door with the bottom of his foot, and it flew inward as though it were made of cardboard. His three vampire friends rushed inside to face three men who were startled but ready to fight.

Through Diego's eyes, I saw the humans, dressed in quasi-military uniforms. Two pulled handguns from their belts, and one reached for an assault rifle lying on the bed. He didn't make it.

He went flying across the room and smashed into a wall, knocking a framed print of an alligator onto his head.

Because I was seeing things through Diego's consciousness, I could make out everything that happened, even though it was at the vampire hyper-speed that normally was a blur to me.

The other two humans had their pistols wrested from their hands with the sound of breaking bones. Helga and Billy smacked the humans with open hands, knocking them unconscious without cracking their skulls. The men dropped like logs to the floor.

Leaping over them, Diego headed for the bathroom while Eduardo grabbed the human who had crashed into the wall.

Diego stepped into the small, sad motel bathroom and whipped open the shower curtain. Mr. Jubbles sat in the tub, bound with steel cables. A Communion wafer was stuck to his head, surrounded by a ring of burned flesh.

"G-get me out of here," Mr. Jubbles said.

Diego picked up the elderly vampire and threw him over his shoulder. When he returned to the bedroom, he saw the three humans lying face down on the room's dirty carpeting, their hands bound by plastic zip ties.

"Pull the van up below the balcony," he said to Billy. "Be prepared to mesmerize any witnesses."

Diego placed Mr. Jubbles in a sitting position on the bed and ripped the Communion wafer from his forehead.

"Ow! That hurt."

"Your strength should return soon," Diego told him. "Hold still."

With two hands, he severed the steel cables and unwrapped them from Mr. Jubbles.

"Hungry," the old vampire moaned.

"You can feed when we get you to safety."

Diego stepped out onto the breezeway, looking left and right. No one was visible. One floor below, a white van was parked. Billy stood outside it, looking up at him.

Returning to the room, Diego picked up Mr. Jubbles and tossed him over the breezeway railing. Billy easily caught him and put him in the back of the van.

The other vampires had reached the parking lot, and they caught the three humans as Diego dropped them one by one.

Where are they taking the humans? I wondered.

Diego returned to the room and propped the detached door back into the doorway as best he could. When he turned to head to the stairs, a nearby guest-room door opened, and a woman peeked out.

"You have seen nothing and remember nothing," Diego said, mesmerizing the human. Her door closed.

Diego sped down the stairs and hopped into the passenger seat of the van. He turned to Billy behind the wheel.

"Take us to the safe house first so we can unload the hostages. Then, we'll drop Mr. Jubbles off at the inn where he's staying."

Hostages! Yikes! This could get hairy.

At that moment, it seemed Diego noticed my piggybacking his consciousness. My connection to his senses abruptly ended.

"Mom," I said as she drove the Aston Martin, grinding the gears with every shift. "The good news is Mr. Jubbles has been rescued, and no one was killed."

"Is there bad news?"

"The vampires took the three humans as hostages."

Mom blew out a deep breath between closed lips. "What are the vampires thinking?"

"They would have preferred to kill the humans, so this is not as bad. I guess the hostages are their leverage against further abuse of vampires."

"It's only going to lead to a crackdown."

"Yep. I'm praying that Diego knows what he's doing. Though nowadays, it seems like no one does."

WE WERE AT THE INN ONLY LONG ENOUGH TO UPDATE CORY before the vampire van showed up. This was the result of Mom's erratic driving of Diego's car and the vampires' preternatural speed at conducting the raid and depositing their hostages in the safe house.

Diego led a very shaken-up Mr. Jubbles into the foyer. All guests were long asleep, but if anyone saw the homecoming, they would have assumed it was an elderly gentleman assisted by a medical aide.

Mr. Jubbles looked stunned, but calm, with a smudge of blood on his chin. He also had a round burn mark on his forehead from the communion wafer. It appeared to be healing, but not as quickly as a normal wound.

"We helped the old guy feed on one of his captors," Diego explained. "Let's get him to his room for some much-needed rest."

Diego, Mom, Mr. Jubbles, and I crammed into the tiny elevator and helped the vampire to his room and onto his bed. At the moment, he seemed like a frail senior, not an immortal creature. When it came to surviving emotional trauma, humans and supernaturals were pretty much the same.

We took the stairs down, and I asked Diego how the raid went, pretending not to know.

He looked at me suspiciously. "It went well. No one was hurt, except for some bruising on the humans and a couple of broken hands."

"What did you do with them?"

He didn't answer me until we arrived in the kitchen, where Cory, Roderick, and Archibald were waiting.

"I'll be candid," Diego said, "since you'll all hear about it soon enough. We took three humans hostage tonight. My companions wanted to kill them out of revenge, but I convinced them to compromise."

"Hostages?" Cory asked. "Isn't that going to cause a bunch of trouble for vampires—and all of us?"

"Absolutely," Diego said with a bitter smile. "Could the trouble it causes be any worse than the trouble we're in? Those psychotic Mothers Against Monsters are offering bounties to encourage citizens to kill or capture supernaturals. Many state politicians support that. It's time to send a message that we won't be passive while humans persecute us."

"Hear, hear!" Roderick exclaimed.

"Are you willing to fight with us?" Diego asked him.

"Well, um, I do support you, of course."

"You're just as endangered as any vampire. You might as well go all in."

"Well, you see, I'm not a member of your guild, because of an old dispute about outstanding dues," Roderick sputtered. "So. . ."

"If you want someone to rescue you when you're abducted and face staking on live video, you'd better join us."

Roderick nodded, swallowed, and smiled weakly. He slipped a finger beneath his starched collar as if it were too tight.

"Very good, brother." Diego slapped him on the back, and Roderick flinched. "I'll make arrangements to reinstate you into the Clan of the Eternal Night."

"What are you going to do with your hostages?" Mom asked Diego.

"We'll keep things quiet for now. They're wearing uniforms that suggest they're part of an extremist militia, so I want to interrogate them to see what we're up against. Then, if a majority of Clan members agree, we'll put out a statement demanding that vampires be left alone and threatening the hostages if we're harmed."

"I miss the days before the Great Unmasking," I said, "when vampires could do their thing without fear of detection."

"The horse is out of the barn," Diego replied. "The videos of Mr. Jubbles being abused with religious icons, and him baring his fangs—there's just no going back from that."

"I had hoped we supernaturals could fight for equal rights and understanding."

"Sophie, Sophie," he said condescendingly. "There's too much hatred and fear of us. We must fight back before we will be treated fairly."

"First, promise me you'll help unseat Baldric from the Executive Council and make sure he doesn't release the membership lists. We need to keep the guilds united before we fight back. Orlena is with us, too."

"I had planned to kill him."

"Let's handle this in a civilized way," I pleaded. "We can't be barbaric like the haters."

He quirked an eyebrow. "Your empath side has truly taken over. If you insist, I won't kill him. Not yet. If I become the new duke of the Clan, I'll have the clout to influence the other guilds to turn against him."

Dawn was approaching, so our kitchen conference had to break up. Before he left, Diego took me aside and asked, "What did you do to get inside my head back at the motel?"

"What do you mean?" I feigned ignorance.

"You know very well. I felt you watching me. Were you using magic on me?"

"No, I didn't," I replied. "Honestly. Before we left the motel, I tried to make an empathetic connection with you so I could feel your emotions and get an idea of how well the raid was going. But something odd happened. I connected not just with your emotions, but your senses, too. I experienced everything you did."

He was angry. "I would never have allowed that. I feel violated."

"It wasn't intentional. And, Diego, you *did* allow it. There's no way I could have connected with you like that if you hadn't allowed me to, even if you did it subconsciously."

He stared at me quizzically, anger fading. "Why would I allow you to do that?"

I wanted to say it must mean there was a special connection between us. But I was afraid how he'd react.

"I don't know," I mumbled.

"I'm afraid there will be much warfare ahead of us, between supernaturals and hateful humans, and between us and the Fae. I suppose such a connection will come in handy if the two of us are going to be allies in these wars."

"Yes," I said, brightening. "Of course we will be."

It dawned on me, not for the first time, that I wished we might become more than allies.

We stepped outside. The van had left, and I handed Diego his car keys. The air was comfortably cool yet moist, with the scent of saltwater and gardenia. To the east, a purple glow was on the horizon, heralding the coming dawn.

Diego stepped toward me, and my heartbeat picked up. But he only placed his hand on my shoulder. "Be careful and stay strong," he said.

"Thank you for rescuing our guest," was all I could think to say.

"It was my duty. We supernaturals must stick together. No matter how different we may be from each other, the Almighty has made us all special."

He climbed into his car.

"Very special," he added with a last glance at me.

When I returned to the inn and headed for the stairs, Archibald's voice came from the kitchen.

"Goodnight, love. Something tells me you've become smitten."

"Goodnight," I replied. "And what does a gargoyle know about being smitten?"

Surprisingly, I was about to find out.

CHAPTER 12

SOPHIE

I awoke to someone making gooey love talk. At first, I thought I was hearing the TV in the room next door playing a romance film too loudly. But no, the voices came from the inn's courtyard.

You see, I'd been keeping my window open at night. Being on the third floor, I wasn't at risk from human intruders, though faeries in their natural forms could fly inside. But I felt the benefits of being able to listen for danger outweighed the risk of flying faeries.

Occasionally, drunk guests by the tiny swimming pool woke me up. Which was what I assumed was happening now.

"How could I have lived for nearly a thousand years without you?" asked a man with an English accent. The voice sounded familiar.

"Life can be cruel before it brings happiness," said a different man with an American accent. He sounded like he was gargling.

"Can't you live here with me?" asked the first voice.

"I would love to, but they would miss me at the hotel."

"You look even better in this fountain than in theirs."

I finally recognized the English accent, jumped out of bed, and ran downstairs. I crept to the French doors in the dining room and looked out into the courtyard.

Accent lights in the fountain's basin illuminated two individuals. One was Archibald, perched beside the fountain on the coquina-stone wall at the rear of the courtyard.

The other individual was also a gargoyle, mounted on the rear of the water feature. He had a lion's head, and the fountain's water poured from his open mouth.

The problem was, our fountain didn't have a gargoyle.

I stepped outside.

"Ah, Sophie," Archibald said cheerily. "Come and meet my new friend, Jerry."

"Hi, Jerry," I said, moving closer to them.

"Jerry is a true gargoyle, because he spouts water," Archibald said. "I'm technically called a grotesque, because I'm merely ornamental, but I hate the word grotesque."

"You are too handsome to be called grotesque," Jerry gurgled.

"Jerry lives at the fountain in the Alhambra Hotel. That's where I met him," Archibald explained.

"You wouldn't believe how many times a day I'm pelted with coins that people toss into the pool of the fountain," Jerry complained.

"Our fountain suits you much better," Archibald said. "You make it look stunning."

"You're such a flirt, Archibald."

"Actually, you look pretty good in this fountain, Jerry," I said. "It's almost as if it were designed around you."

"See, love, I told you!"

"And your water isn't chlorinated," Jerry said. "Tastes much better."

"We can't use chlorine because we have koi in the basin below you," I explained.

"Can Jerry live here?" Archibald asked.

"I don't see why not. As long as we're not accused of stealing him from the hotel. And if you guys don't talk loudly like this at night. You woke me up."

"Sorry," Jerry gurgled.

"Um, are you two. . . an item?"

"I would blush," Archibald said, "if I weren't made of sandstone."

"I didn't realize gargoyles had partners."

"No sentient creature wants to be alone," Archibald said.

"Except for sphinxes," Jerry said. "They're total loners."

"Oh," I said. "I learn something every day. It will be comforting to have someone monitoring this side of the hotel. If you, Archibald, could guard the main entrance. When you're not chatting with Jerry, that is."

I sensed I had overstayed my welcome, so I said goodnight and returned to my room.

The gargoyle conversation continued, so I closed my window to fall asleep.

THE NEXT MORNING, I RECEIVED A TEXT FROM ORLENA:

I've spoken to the leaders of all the guilds, except the vampires, because they're still leaderless.

Diego will be the next leader, I replied. *He supports our goal.*

Excellent. Everyone supports us, except the Undead Flesh Eaters. But they'll come around.

Good.

I'm almost finished with your "recipe." Come by tomorrow.

I will. Thank you!

After breakfast service, Mom sent me to the wholesale club to buy more bulk flour and other supplies. Most of our food came from local farmers, but we still needed to buy paper napkins, plastic wrap, and other items in bulk. Like tater tots. You can't skimp on tater tots.

As I drove Cory's SUV into the store's gigantic parking lot, a line of rental trucks caught my eye. I wondered why they were there. I soon got my answer.

The rear doors of the trucks opened, and men climbed out of the one parked nearest the store. They appeared to be wearing military-style uniforms.

The same kind worn by the men who had kidnapped Mr. Jubbles.

I stopped before entering the store and took pictures with my phone. What were these guys doing there? There were about twenty of them, with more still inside the trucks. I expected they had weapons in there, too.

They could be there to rescue their comrades, but there had been no news yet of the hostages who were taken. These new guys could be in San Marcos for the same reason as Mr. Jubbles' abductors: to hunt supernaturals.

I felt sick to my stomach and texted Diego to tell him what I'd seen.

No, we haven't released information about the hostages yet, he replied. *And they haven't been missing long enough to raise such an alarm. I think the men you saw are here to hunt us. The question is, who sent them here? MAM? Baldric? State politicians?*

I didn't know. Every city in Florida was hunting supernaturals. San Marcos had one of the largest populations of them. So, these extra militiamen had been told to come here.

It made me wonder if the governor, MAM, and the indigenous faeries had special plans for San Marcos.

I tried to put the thoughts behind me and focus on my shopping list. Pushing my oversized cart through the oversized store, I collected oversized packages of the things we needed, as well as things we didn't. After all, who could resist the giant plastic tub of honey-roasted peanuts? Even if Mom didn't want to serve them at Wine Hour, I could snack on them. Over the next several months.

And look—my favorite cereal. The box was so large I could fill several bathtubs with it. But it was such a cost-effective price!

Before I got too excessive, I forced myself to steer the cart toward the checkout lanes. That's when I heard the shouting.

I emerged from the cereal aisle and saw the commotion near the freezer cases. A dozen militia members converged on a biker dude and tackled him.

I couldn't believe they were attacking someone in public like that.

Having landed on the floor, the biker screamed obscenities and tried to escape. Half the militia members held him down while the others punched and kicked him. I abandoned my cart and ran over.

"Leave him alone!" I shouted and pulled out my phone to call 911.

The biker was a familiar type: beefy, with a big gut and huge white beard. He wore a leather vest and a US Navy veteran's hat, which was quickly knocked from his head.

Other shoppers also appeared to be calling the police, and some tried to help the victim, but the militia thugs pushed them away.

"He's a werewolf," one attacker explained. "We're making a civilian arrest."

Everything was happening so quickly, I couldn't concentrate on casting a spell. I had to, though. Putting the militiamen in a sleep spell would create unanswered questions, but I had to try.

As the biker struggled, the crowd of attackers shifted, and one bumped into me. Possibly on purpose.

My spell fell apart. Rather than trying again, I went for empathy. I focused feelings of calm and benevolence on the most brutal of the attackers, a guy with a shaved head covered in tattoos.

A skinny young store employee, probably a manager, arrived at the melee.

"Stop," he said. "You can't—"

"Yes, we can," shouted an attacker. "We're authorized by the governor."

I cast magic to strengthen my emotions and filled my target with them. This was the only way I knew how to do this until Orlena taught me her new spell.

My target backed away. But then others took his place, kicking the victim on the floor. I simply didn't have the ability to affect a large group at once.

The biker howled in distress and then went quiet. The militiamen pulled him to his feet and carried him, half conscious, through the store and into the parking lot.

Everyone in the store stood stunned and frightened. Many looked ashamed, like I was. But how do you stop a dozen vicious men carrying weapons? Perhaps some customers carried weapons, but it was too risky to fire them. And they had been told the innocent victim was actually a monster.

But the biker wasn't a werewolf. I didn't sense the supernatural in him. The militia guys were just stereotyping him.

I was the only one in that store with powers that could have saved him. But I had failed.

WHEN I RETURNED HOME, STILL MARINATING IN SHAME, I pulled the SUV into a space next to the main door that was reserved for guests checking in. I carried a giant box of napkins to the door and was surprised to find Baldric blocking my way.

"Good morning, Sophie," he said with a fake smile above his cute, dimpled chin.

"Oh, hello. What brings you here today?" The carton of napkins wasn't heavy, but I placed it on the ground as my palms began to sweat.

"I'm checking in on you. Have you come to a decision on the generous offer I gave you?"

"Yes." I had no choice but to lie. "I will do my best to convince the guilds to support you."

Being dishonest was the only way I could buy time for doing the opposite of what I promised: to help Orlena rally the guilds to depose Baldric. I had been raised to treasure honesty, and lying made me feel dirty. Getting pulled into power struggles gave me no other choice.

"Have you met with Orlena to learn how to amplify your empath powers?" He seemed really concerned about this.

"Yes," I said. "I'm making great progress."

"Good. I'm happy to hear that. I need your help now more than ever. There's been quite a bit of scheming going on behind my back. Do you know anything about it?"

"No," I lied.

"It seems some of our guild leaders are more interested in their own ambitions than in what's good for the supernaturals of our city."

"Um, really?"

"I'm afraid so." He studied me. "You might make a good leader of your guild someday."

"I'm just a witch. It would take years to rise to the level of mage. But Orlena is a good teacher."

Baldric smiled in a creepy, self-satisfied way. "You've learned all you need from her for now. Perhaps you should resume your lessons from Bob."

An icy sensation filled my gut. "Why?"

"Orlena is one of the schemers. I wouldn't trust her anymore." Baldric picked up the box of napkins and gave it to me. "I'll check in on you again soon about your lobbying efforts," he said with an intense stare. "And let me know if anyone resists."

He walked away and turned the corner onto Hidalgo Avenue.

I had a terrible feeling. Dropping the box, I pulled my phone from my pocket and called Orlena.

No answer.

I texted her to contact me as soon as possible. After I brought the supplies into the inn and put them away, I tried calling her again. Still no answer.

The bad feeling inside me was growing. I had to speak to Orlena. I left Cory's SUV where it was and hurried to my car, parked further down the street.

Orlena's house wasn't far away. If she wasn't there, I would drive all over town to find her if need be. When I pulled up, her car was in her driveway. The car's presence made me even more concerned when she didn't answer the doorbell or my loud knocking.

I tried the handle and found it unlocked, so I let myself in.

"Orlena?" I called. "Are you here?"

There was the possibility she had gone for a walk, but I doubted she would have left her door unlocked. This was a safe neighborhood, but tourists frequently wandered through it, and who knew what kooks could pop up in her living room.

"Orlena?"

I moved through the various common rooms with no sign of her. The living room had a good view of the small backyard, and she wasn't out there.

When I approached the bedrooms, I caught the coppery scent of blood, and my heart raced.

On her bedroom floor, at the foot of her bed, lay Orlena.

CHAPTER 13

SOPHIE

O rlena was crumpled on the floor, face down, blood leaking from her ears. She had no visible wounds or injuries. A paramedic might assume she'd suffered a brain bleed. But I sensed lingering magic. Fae magic.

I felt her neck for a pulse. I was surprised to find one, faint though.

I called 911 and frantically begged for them to hurry. The operator asked me if there were signs of head trauma. I said no. I wished I could tell her Orlena was the victim of a magic attack, but said it was probably a cerebral aneurysm.

The operator promised an ambulance would arrive soon.

Baldric had done this to Orlena. He'd come close to confessing to it when he had spoken to me outside the inn. He tried to kill her because he found out she was organizing the guild leaders to resist him. Somehow, she'd survived without his realizing it.

Did Orlena save herself with her own healing magic before she completely lost consciousness?

It would be only a matter of time before Baldric found out that my agreeing to his demands was a lie. Would I end up like Orlena?

As disrespectful as it seemed, I had to find the spell Orlena had written down for me before the police and paramedics arrived. I didn't have a key to the house and couldn't come back to search at my leisure.

She had created the spell to help me fight the oppression and injustice that had seized our communities. To help me defeat Baldric and his allies. To cast her spell would be to honor Orlena, in case she didn't survive.

There was a desk in the living room. I searched the drawers and leafed through a notebook lying on the desk. I went through her daily planner that was on the kitchen counter.

Bookcases filled one wall in the living room, and I saw grimoires on the top shelf. I flipped through those, hoping to find a loose sheet of paper with the spell on it, but no such luck.

Then, I got more invasive, opening every drawer and cabinet I could find in her home.

Where was the darn spell? Why did she hide it so thoroughly? It's not as if it had nuclear codes in it. It was basically just a recipe for casting the spell.

A recipe was what she'd called it.

And there was a shelf in the kitchen with recipe books on it.

Desperately, I went through every book until I grabbed one about Caribbean cooking. When I pulled it from the shelf, a piece of notebook paper slipped out and dropped onto the counter.

It was the spell she had customized for me. I folded it and slipped it into my back pocket. I needed to cast it as soon as possible, but it would have to wait until tonight.

Now, all I could do was wait for the first responders to show up.

And begin praying for a woman I didn't know well, but who could be my mentor and friend.

It was at times like this that I wished I'd studied healing magic instead of attack magic. But I suppose I'd rather win a fight than try to heal myself after I'd lost.

THE SPELL INSTRUCTIONS ORLENA HAD WRITTEN FOR ME ALSO came with an actual recipe that required a measuring spoon. A witch like me, of lower ability and power than Orlena, needed magical assistance in the form of an amulet to boost the main spell. Normally, these were small sacks filled with various dried natural ingredients. This one, though, was a liquid, not to be drunk as a potion but to be kept in a watertight vial and worn.

The amulet was meant to enhance my emotions magically, to make them as powerful as possible before sending them into other people. I was touched to see that Orlena was recognizing my strength as a water witch with this potion made of sea water, fresh water from a stream, and wine, plus a few drops of my tears and blood.

The recipe also called for other ingredients that were quite interesting. Rather than specify herbs or materials from animals and insects, as most magic spells did, it called for ingredients of my choosing.

Namely, seven samples of items that evoked powerful emotions in me.

I chose pine needles that reminded me of the live Christmas trees we had when I was a kid. Cervantes donated a couple of hairs because of the love I felt when stroking his fur. I added a drop of skin lotion that made me feel pretty. Then came a squirt of the hair gel favored by my biological father, who Mom had divorced years ago. Its scent reminded me of him and how he had made me feel special.

Into the magic brew went a small piece of the dust jacket of a book of fairy tales from my grandmother, because reading it had filled me with wonder. From a broken piece of a staff owned by my late wizard magic tutor came a tiny splinter of wood, because learning magic had made me feel inspired and proud. And, of course, a few crumbs of Mom's scones, the smell of which when baking has always made me feel content, secure, and loved.

After the ingredients were soaked in a vial, I followed the instructions for a spell to activate them. I attached a leather cord, measured so the vial would rest against my chest by my heart.

On the back side of the recipe, Orlena had written instructions for the primary spell that would enable me to instill my emotions in others. She had told me that my attempts at doing this before were merely encouraging individuals to act on emotions they already had. This spell, however, should be able to make them feel how I wanted them to feel, assuming the emotions didn't cause them to harm themselves or be completely out of character.

The instructions outlined how to gather and channel my psychic energies, create the intended emotions in myself, strengthen them with the amulet, and send them into another individual. There was an incantation that must be chanted during the procedure. I struggled to memorize it.

It wasn't until two days later that I had practiced the spell enough to feel ready to try it on someone. I went down to the kitchen before breakfast, the amulet hanging beneath my blouse and resting against my heart. Mom and Pinky were there.

Pinky was whisking a bowl of eggs prior to scrambling them. Mom was at the table doing paperwork of some sort. Pinky had worked hard over a period of months to earn Mom's trust in her to prepare our signature breakfasts. That kind of trust from a tough cookie like Mom was something a mere spell like mine couldn't create.

Both women were in good spirits. Since the Great Unmasking, we'd learned that concentrating on daily routines was crucial to avoid the anxiety and depression caused by the constant danger to supernaturals like us.

Someday, we might fall victim to the attacks, but all we could do for now was to be careful and try not to go crazy.

Pinky happily hummed the tune of a recent hit song as she worked. She would be my first experimental subject.

I stepped into a corner, out of the view of the two women, and went through the steps I had memorized. Focusing on the back of Pinky's head, I silently recited the incantation, felt the intended emotion rise in me as the magic came to a boil, and sent it at Pinky. I waited.

Soon, her humming ceased. She continued her work, now stirring the eggs in the skillet, but her motions were less fluid, jerkier. I walked around her and opened a cabinet, pretending to search for something while I watched her.

Her face had turned red. She sniffled. And then, like the emptying of a rain cloud, she broke into tears.

"What's the matter, dear?" Mom asked.

"I don't know," Pinky said through gulps of breath. "I just feel so sad. Something must have triggered me."

My spell still active, I sent another burst of magic at her, ferrying a different emotion.

Pinky stepped away from the stove, dried her eyes and blew her nose with a tissue. Then she smiled as she washed her hands at the sink.

"Funny, but my case of weepies is all gone now," she announced. "I feel totally normal again."

She returned her attention to the eggs and resumed humming.

A moment later, she looked at me suspiciously. Shifters can't sense magic like Mom and I can, so Pinky merely shrugged and went back to work.

Mom, on the other hand, stared at me with a knowing expression.

Did you do that? she asked telepathically.

Yep. Trying out a new spell that Orlena created for me before she was attacked.

A little while later, I tested the spell again, this time on people I didn't know.

The dining room was filling with guests—fewer than usual, thanks to rumors that our inn was run by supernaturals, but what could we do? Anyway, I noticed an elderly couple eating at a table. The man and woman weren't talking. In fact, they ignored each other, and their body language signaled emotional distance. My empath's sensitivity told me their relationship was cold and indifferent.

So, I fired up the spell again while observing my test subjects.

The man said something to his spouse, and she replied. Their conversation began picking up, both of them smiling and chuckling. Before I knew it, they were holding hands. Then they leaned closer and exchanged a quick kiss.

Throughout the rest of their meal, they gazed at each other like smitten teenagers.

Mission accomplished.

I was pleased that the spell had worked and that I could affect more than one person. But a married couple was much easier than a crowd of strangers. Time to go look for one.

Fortunately, there were no murderous mobs wandering San Marcos at the moment. The next time I encountered one, I couldn't merely test my spell; I had to make it work.

I wandered to the tourist areas of town, but all the people I saw were focused on different things. There were no crowds unified in purpose or circumstance. I made a mom, dad, and their two young kids become really excited watching the historic mill wheel turning in Old Town, but I couldn't achieve mass emotion in any of the throngs of tourists.

It was time to clean up after breakfast, so I headed back to the inn, passing a Catholic school in my neighborhood. A bunch of young boys and girls in school uniforms played soccer in the adjacent field.

This could be an interesting test, I thought.

I approached the fence and watched the game, looking like a proud parent to anyone who noticed me. The nun on the field supervising the game was having difficulty getting the kids to play properly. It was like herding cats. And the perfect challenge for me.

Lacking the understanding of the role of each position, the mass of little kids simply chased the ball wherever it went. Finally, a Black girl with pigtails scored a goal. The goalie, a towheaded white boy, looked devastated.

I focused on him. In a matter of seconds, he smiled. And soon, he was laughing hysterically.

I turned my focus to the rest of the kids. Sure, laughter is contagious, but it helps to use powerful empathetic magic. All the kids began giggling and laughing.

As the emotion of amusement spread through them, they laughed so hard they dropped to the ground, kicking and squirming with hilarity.

I chuckled to myself. But the pièce de résistance was when the middle-aged nun cracked a smile before guffawing with abandon.

My work was complete. I released the spell as I walked away, but the laughter continued because it just felt too good to stop.

WHEN I ASKED TO SPEAK WITH BALDRIC AT HIS AUTO-REPAIR shop, the lady at the front desk said he was unavailable. As I'd done before, I simply stormed past her desk and through the door into the repair bays. My emotion spell was all queued up and ready to go, so I didn't want it to go to waste.

This time, the receptionist had wised up. She sent a mechanic to stop me, a guy who looked like he would gladly use a socket wrench on someone's eyeballs. He was much bigger than me and blocked my path across the large open space, pushing me backward with his chest.

Being human, he was no match for my sleep spell. He sat down on a hydraulic lift, then curled into the fetal position, snoring.

I walked past a couple of Italian sports cars being worked on but saw no sign of Baldric. At the far end of the space was a door marked "Private." That's where I headed.

The door was unlocked. I stepped into a small office where Baldric sat behind a desk opposite none other than State Senator Ralph Poxton, with his helmet of brown-dyed hair sprayed into place.

The senator looked at me, confused. Baldric glared at me. "You can't just barge in here like that. It's rude," he scolded.

"Sorry if I hurt your fee-fees. I need to know what happened to Orlena."

"It's okay," Poxton said, getting up from his chair. "I've got to head to another meeting."

He squeezed past me out the door, my skin tingling with the magic he had used to shift to his human form. Normal humans, though, would never have guessed he was a faerie.

"Close the door," Baldric said to me. "I know nothing about what happened to—"

"You attacked her. Don't even bother denying it."

I filled my heart and mind with the urge to unburden myself of the truth—and sent it directly into Baldric.

"Are you using magic on me?" he asked with a sneer.

"Why did you hurt her?"

He seemed to struggle briefly, then relaxed. "I had to. She was plotting against me. You said, 'hurt.' Is she still alive?"

"You told me to convince all the guild leaders to support you. I hadn't even had the chance yet to work on her."

"It was too late. She'd been busy spreading mistrust about me."

"You shouldn't have done it. She's a wise woman and a powerful mage whom you need on your side. As unlikely as that would be."

I shouldn't have said that last part.

"See," Baldric said. "You admit she was a hopeless case. And she survived, didn't she?"

"She's in critical condition and might not make it. How are you going to win over the other guild leaders after attacking Orlena—especially if she dies?"

"Most of them are in the bag already. Except for a few.

Orlena was one of the holdouts, but it turned out to be too late for her. Maybe you can convince Diego, so I won't be forced to destroy him."

I knew that wouldn't happen, but I kept my mouth shut.

"Are you such buddies with Orlena that I need to worry about your loyalty too?" he asked.

"What about *your* loyalty? I get the feeling that you're only loyal to other faeries, like Poxton."

Oops.

"What did you say?" Baldric stood and loomed over me. "Poxton is not a faerie."

"Slip of the tongue," I said.

The problem was, I had filled myself with the need to confess the truth in order to insert it magically into Poxton. What's the expression—hoist with my own petard?

"Go do your job and get Diego to support me," Baldric said. "Same with the other guild leaders. Report back to me by the end of the week. Now, get out of here."

I left the repair shop in a hurry, worried about what kind of trouble my slip of the tongue would cause.

CHAPTER 14

DARLA

"What made you so frisky tonight?" I murmured to Cory, who had awakened me with kisses.

"I had a nightmare that I lost you," he said, ramping up the kiss intensity.

"Lost me?"

"Yes. I don't want to talk about it. I'm just happy that you're here, and I want to immerse myself in Darla."

By this point, I was wide awake, and our kissing was having quite an effect on me. I was more than ready for total immersion.

That's why I was really annoyed to suddenly find myself in a familiar primeval forest, standing beside the pool in the creek beneath the waterfall.

Danu had summoned me at the most inopportune time. Cory must be beyond upset.

But where was Danu? The Goddess hadn't emerged from behind the waterfall like she usually did.

I felt compelled to wade into the pool created by the waterfall. It was as if the water was tugging at me. Oh, was I fully Danu in tonight's astral visit? I realized I was naked, as Danu always was when I visited her. Of course, I had been naked in bed before I was yanked out of it.

I resisted the urge to enter the water. Nope, not going to do it. I was Darla, not Danu.

The constant roar of the waterfall was playing tricks on my ears. I thought I heard words formed.

Mother. Mother of waters. Mother of all the earth and the creatures upon it.

That's not me. You're mistaking me for someone else.

The wind rustling the leaves of the forest seemed to say, *You are Danu.*

I am not. I am Darla, a middle-aged innkeeper with some psychic gifts, but I am most assuredly not a goddess.

You are Danu, said the wind in the trees.

Danu, sang the birds in the branches.

Buzz, said the bumble bee flying past my head. It obviously didn't have an opinion.

Without realizing it, I had stepped into the water. Its coolness didn't bother me as I waded into the deeper part of the pool. My feet stepped upon smooth stones and silky sand.

Mother, cried the water tumbling from the cliff above.

A feeling of serenity filled me, along with a love for everything in the landscape around me. Responsibility, too. The duty to care for everything on the earth.

A tiny pinch of rebellion rose in me, like stepping on a sharp stone beneath the water.

"Take this cup from me," I said aloud. "I don't want to be a goddess. I want to keep my life."

No one appeared. No one was listening to me.

"I'm serious. I want out. Stop hijacking my brain. Stop taking me away from my family. Don't steal my life from me."

Up to this point, I had accepted Danu's presence in my life because I didn't have a choice. At first, it was a strange novelty, such as having seedlings sprout up everywhere in my home. It became kind of cool to have the power to heal, and being consumed by the melodies of ancient songs that soothed all those who heard them.

When I was a little girl, I fantasized about being a princess. As a woman who was getting older and seeming to lose my agency in the world, why wouldn't I be pleased about becoming a goddess?

Before long, though, it had stopped being amusing. The moments when I "froze" and "went away" frightened my family. Being thrust into conflict with the Fae was something I could do without.

Finding the cyst on my brain really freaked me out, even if it had been benign. Was it there because of Danu?

Sometimes, I wished all these Danu things were only hallucinations caused by the cyst. But the doctor said that was unlikely. The cyst could cause minor seizures, not hallucinations.

Yes, it was hard to imagine hallucinating that feeling in my gut of the divine power growing, then flowing from me to heal. And sometimes, to destroy.

Witches like Cory and Sophie, no doubt, would relish that feeling of power. But I did not.

I just wanted my life back.

Pushing through the waterfall came Danu. And I felt like myself again, naked, cold, and out of place here.

"You must not resist me," she said aloud in ordinary English, but with a strange accent. "What is happening to you is preordained."

"I don't want it."

"You are the reincarnation of my demigod son, the Dagda. His spirit chose you to provide a vessel for me so I could return to the world."

"Right, so *you* can return. You don't need me."

"The earth is ill. I wish to save it before it dies. But I can't. My power is limited because I am a forgotten goddess. Through you, I will return, and my power will grow."

"What will happen to me?" I asked.

"You will become me."

"But what does that mean? What will become of this body?" I slapped my hip. "Will it die so I can go off to wherever goddesses live?"

"We shall see," she said with a serene expression that made me annoyed.

"What do you mean? Don't you know?"

"I do not. When I first cared for the earth, gods and goddesses walked the land like humans when we wanted to. The world, and humans, have changed so much that I don't know how best to manifest myself."

"You're a goddess. You should know everything."

"The world is such a wonder, even I can't know everything."

"That's no excuse. You should have done your homework before you started jerking me around. I'm done with this."

"You have only begun," she said, her serene expression gone. "You must stop the Fae from manipulating the forests. And you must protect the earth from the elder gods."

I made a goddess angry. Great job, Darla.

"I saw a forest kill a bunch of faeries," I said. "The trees could do that on their own?"

"I empowered them."

"Then what do you need me for if you have trees doing your bidding?"

"That's not a natural action for trees. It was in response to an emergency on earth and can't be sustained. Their actions came solely from my power, and I empowered them through you. Because of your physical presence in the world, I can affect the world. I can't do so from here."

"I've been meaning to ask you where 'here' is."

"All this," she said, spreading her arms, "is memory. The collective memory of humans and, especially, those who worshipped me."

"That's mind-blowing. Too bad I don't understand what it means. And I still want to resign from my position of goddess's human vessel."

"It's too late. Your transformation has already begun. You must prepare to take on your powers and responsibilities."

With that, she disappeared. And I was left alone, standing naked in the pool beneath the waterfall. In this world that existed only in the ancient memories of others.

I walked toward the waterfall. I don't know why, I simply felt like I had to. The closer to it I got, as more and more spray from the cascading water sprinkled my skin, the more exuberant I felt.

My hair felt different. I touched it and discovered the stems and blossoms of flowers woven into it.

My petulance from being manipulated by Danu disappeared as I walked into the full force of the waterfall. My sense of self dissolved, too.

I was Danu, mother of the earth, and I had much work to do to heal it. But where could I begin?

I pushed through the water into the darkness behind the

falls, where there was a pitch-black cave. I knew I was supposed to enter it, but I was not ready.

My eyes opened to find Cory frowning at me in the light from our bedside clock radio. He was lying beside me, his head propped up on his hand, and I remembered what we were about to do when I went away.

"Sorry," I said. "How long was I gone?"

"A few minutes," he replied, his eyes sad. "You disappear for longer periods now. I was wondering if I should call an ambulance."

"Again, I'm sorry." I lifted my head and kissed him. "Blame Danu. I tried to quit being her plaything, but she wouldn't accept my resignation."

Cory lowered his head to his pillow and sighed.

"I wish we could get you away from her," he said. "I wonder if there's any magic that can defeat a goddess."

"I doubt it. And I do believe the earth needs her help. I only wish she would find someone else to use as a vessel. But she said I was preordained to this role, because I'm her son reincarnated."

"Do you really believe that?"

"Kind of." I remembered the strange dreams I'd had of riding a horse named Cael across the Irish countryside. "But I don't want to talk about this anymore. Let's go back to sleep."

"Back to sleep? Really?"

"No, let's go back to what we were doing before I went away."

I kissed him ravenously.

And then alarms on both our phones went off.

Our security system doesn't have a klaxon-like burglar alarm that blares throughout the building. You can't have that when there are guests sleeping inside. Only the fire alarm makes noise like that.

"It looks like someone picked the lock on the main door," Cory said, showing me his phone with security video of a man entering the inn.

"I'm calling the police," I said, retrieving my phone from my jeans, which were draped over a chair.

"I can't believe it," he said. "He just shifted. Better not call the cops after all."

He replayed the video, showing the man shifting not into a wolf, but a dog. A bloodhound.

"He's going upstairs," I said.

"Let's go catch the dog."

"Catch it how?"

"I've learned an immobility spell. I'll try that."

We threw on clothes and rushed across the courtyard into the main building. Running up the stairs, we made a quick tour of the second floor. All the guest-room doors were closed and there was no sign of the dog.

My heart froze when we arrived on the third floor. Sophie's door was ajar. We moved quietly along the carpeted floor toward her room. Seeing that the antique door had been busted open, I peered inside the room.

The dog, larger than any I'd ever seen, stood atop Sophie's bed. His muzzle was buried in her pillows as he sniffed so loudly it sounded industrial.

Sophie was not in her bed, nor anywhere to be seen.

The dog looked up and regarded us with unnatural yellow eyes.

Cory was as surprised as I. His lips moved as he cast his immobility spell.

We both jumped at a loud *THWACK* on the wall above the bed. A crossbow bolt was lodged there, having narrowly missed the dog.

Cory didn't cast his spell fast enough. The dog leaped, sailing past us into the hall. The thuds of his galloping feet disappeared down the stairs.

"I can't believe I missed that . . . thing," Sophie said, exiting her closet where she'd been hiding. "I saw it coming up here on the security app, and it was not a real dog."

"He's a shifter," I said.

"What the heck was he doing?" Cory asked, shaken. "Why was he sniffing Sophie's pillows? You'd think he would have smelled her in the closet."

"My protection spell must have masked my scent," Sophie said.

"He was getting Sophie's scent from the pillows so he can track her down," I guessed. "I'm calling Samson. He's really knowledgeable about shifters."

Samson didn't answer, and I didn't blame him because it was 3:30 a.m. My family and I were too rattled to go back to sleep, so we sat in the kitchen drinking coffee, speculating about the shifter, and complaining about life after the Great Unmasking.

Shortly after 5:00 a.m., Samson returned my call. I put him on speaker.

"Are you okay?" he asked in a sleepy voice. "Your voicemail doesn't make any sense."

I explained about the bloodhound shifter and what he had done.

Samson was silent.

"Michael, are you still there?"

"Yeah," he replied. "I think your visitor was a guy named Wilfred who's new to the Shifter Guild. It bothers me that he was interested in Sophie. It must mean he's gone rogue and is working for Baldric. Sophie learned Baldric almost killed Orlena, so maybe he wants to keep tabs on Sophie."

That's not all Sophie learned, I thought. *She knows that the governor and Senator Poxton are faeries.*

"Baldric doesn't need to search for me," Sophie said. "That dog wanted my scent for a specific reason."

"Yeah," said the detective. "That also bothers me. You see, Wilfred is a dream scenter."

"A what?"

"It's kind of like how Darla uses her psychometry to read people's memories. Dream scenters always shift into animals with excellent senses of smell, like dogs, wolves, bears, rats. They use your scent to read your memories and dreams. I'm guessing Baldric sent Wilfred here to find out if Sophie knew or saw something."

Sophie turned pale.

"Today, I'll speak with Rufus, the Alpha of our guild," Samson went on. "I'll ask him if he knows what Wilfred is up to. But for all I know, Rufus might be betraying his guild like Baldric is."

We thanked Samson. After ending the call, I asked Sophie why she looked so frightened.

"Yesterday, I let it slip to Baldric that I knew Poxton is a faerie. I said I misspoke, but the damage was done."

My heart sank. "Oh, no."

"Yeah. The dream scenter must have been here to verify what I know about Poxton. And he surely found out that I know about the governor, too."

"Sophie, you could be in great danger," Cory said.

"That's putting it mildly."

CHAPTER 15

SOPHIE

"Yes, go into hiding," Diego said over the phone after I told him about the dream scenter. "You're welcome to stay at my place. I can protect you."

"Thank you," I said, relieved. I also liked the thought of him wanting to protect me.

"There's one slight wrinkle," Diego added. "Yena is living here now. After Lethia was destroyed, Yena was cared for by the servants, but they all quit. And the house wasn't Lethia's—she had simply seized it from Pedro, and it's going to his heirs."

Yena was the toddler-age daughter of Lethia. The two lost their human lives in an epidemic thousands of years ago, and a demon resurrected them as vampires. Mom told me that Yena had the imperiousness of having existed for millennia, but the brain and maturity level of a two-and-a-half-year-old.

I'd only seen the child once. From what I'd heard, she was a monster—cute, but a nightmare.

"Oh," I said. "I wouldn't want to intrude while you're being a dad."

"You wouldn't be intruding. Yena might even bond with you. Why don't you stop by tonight and properly meet her?"

I couldn't say no—right? —and ended up at Diego's door with my duffel bag full of weapons that I was forced to carry with me everywhere, now that it was open season for Sophie.

"Welcome!" Diego said, giving me a quick kiss on the cheek that stirred my blood despite its brevity. "Come in, come in. Yena, meet my friend."

I entered his apartment and left my duffel bag by the door. My eyes swept the gorgeous decor in the living and dining rooms without seeing Yena.

"Yena, meet Sophie."

"Where is she?" I asked.

"Right here."

I was searching my brain for any facts about vampires being able to become invisible, when the sofa lurched violently upward. There was a blur of movement and a hideous shriek, and a creature landed on my shoulders, clawing at my head.

"Yena, get down!" Diego scolded. "That's no way to greet company."

He wrested the creature off me, which came with the loss of several of my hairs, and held her, struggling to free herself, at arm's length.

The creature was a little girl with long, straight red hair, green eyes, and a pale complexion fitting for a vampire. Her lips were unnaturally red, and her fangs were extended.

She snarled and stared at me with demonic fury.

"Retract your fangs," Diego told her. "That's not polite. You will *not* feed on Sophie."

Despite his command, I had little confidence that I would make it out of here without losing blood.

Yena retracted her fangs but still stared at me as if I were meat.

"Let me get her a sippy cup of blood," Diego said.

"Don't leave me alone with her."

He chuckled. "I'm bringing her to the kitchen. Come along."

Diego placed her on the quartz countertop while he took an IV bag of whole blood from the refrigerator. He warmed it in the microwave before pouring it into a plastic spill-proof kiddie cup.

He handed it to her, and she drank from it using both hands. She seemed to have forgotten about me for the moment.

"Does she feed on humans?" I asked.

"That's a big no-no," Diego replied. "I feed her with blood purchased from a blood bank. Because the demon who created her took her from her mother after they were turned, Yena was never properly trained to hunt. I'm told the demon fed her captured humans, but she never learned to stalk and mesmerize prey. And I'm not going to teach her. She's simply too young in body age."

"Good. It wouldn't be safe for her—or the population of San Marcos. Especially nowadays."

"Yes. We vampires are keeping a low profile. I'm sorry, what a terrible host I am. Would you like some wine?"

"Just a water, please."

He took a bottle of expensive spring water from the fridge, and I shrieked as pain flared in my arm.

Yena had leaped at me, sunk her teeth into my forearm, and jumped to the floor. She sat on the tiles, watching how I'd react.

"Good gracious! Naughty girl!" Diego scolded. "I'm sorry, Sophie. Come with me to the bathroom."

He held my arm and led me to the guest bath, where he cleaned the puncture wounds with alcohol and then applied a white cream from an unlabeled tube. There was something slightly erotic about his rubbing the cream into my skin. The feeling quickly dissipated when I remembered what the wounds were from.

"This is a special antibacterial ointment that counteracts the effects of vampire saliva."

Vampire saliva is known for reducing pain and being an anti-coagulant to aid feeding. When it dries, though, it speeds healing to help the victim recover for the next feeding.

While you'd think I'd want the anesthesia and healing effects, vampire saliva also makes victims crave being bitten again.

"I'm going to put her down for a nap so we can talk strategy," Diego said.

He put a small bandage over the wounds, and I went to the living room and sat on the couch. Snarls and sounds of struggle trailed from the kitchen to the guest bedroom.

"I'm so sorry," Diego said, joining me on the couch. "Remember, she spent thousands of years inside a cave in the In Between, where the demon had hidden her from Lethia. She's usually calmer. You'll see, when she gets to know you."

Being an empath could sometimes be a burden, but it was helpful in awkward situations. I sensed the truth—that Diego didn't want me to stay here now that he'd been saddled with Yena. His protective feelings toward me were real, though.

"I think it's not a good idea for me to stay here," I said. "I don't know who will come after me, Baldric or forces from the state, but it will be too risky for you and Yena."

"Did Yena frighten you off?" he asked with an ironic smile.

"I'm serious. They could show up here, guns blazing. I haven't explained to you how deeply I'm in trouble."

I recounted the story about discovering that the governor

and Senator Poxton were faeries. The dream scenter had most likely confirmed to Baldric after my verbal slip-up that I knew their secret.

"I'd told no one except Mom and Cory, because I knew how dangerous this knowledge is."

Diego winced. "And now *I* know. Where will you go?"

"I'm not sure yet. Probably cheap motels. Maybe I'll have to leave Florida."

"If it's true that they found out you know about the governor and Poxton, there's no need to keep quiet anymore. You should use their identity to our advantage and get it out there in the media and the internet."

"That's why they will try to kill me."

"We won't let them kill you," Diego said with fervor. "Instead, we'll demolish their credibility. Everyone in Florida will find out that their government leaders are imposters, criminals, too, under the same law they passed to oppress others. The governor and many of her cronies in the statehouse will lose in the upcoming elections, and those not up for election this year will be forced to resign."

You wouldn't think a centuries-old guy would be naïve, but there you go.

"The governor and her faction pretty much control all the media in our state," I said. "They've intimidated all the TV stations and newspapers to tow the party line, and their rich friends have bought the ones that didn't."

"Social media is more important than traditional media. Word will spread that our governor is a faerie."

"I don't know. People are too sealed in their ideological bubbles."

"News that extraordinary will reach them," he insisted.

"The governor's supporters will believe it's fake."

"Aren't you a pessimist."

I laughed at his exasperation. Normally, Diego came across as too stoic to show such an emotion.

"Everything you suggested is correct," I said. "We will get the word out that our state is being led by imposters. But that information is not enough in itself to make this regime fall and to stop the persecution of supernaturals."

"Then what do you suggest, since you apparently have it all figured out?"

"Revolution," I replied.

"What are you talking about?"

"We must kick them out of power ourselves. Remember, the Unseelie Court wants to conquer us. Right? The governor and her cronies will let them do it, if they can share power with the Queene. We can't let them do that. The supernaturals should rise up and stop them."

"Or," Diego said, "we can create friction between the Unseelie Court and the indigenous faeries. Pit them against each other."

"I like that idea. Too bad I don't know how to go about doing it."

"We'll discover how as we move forward."

"You sound like we have the luxury of time. I guess *you* do." I chuckled. "And Fae live much longer than humans. I don't have enough patience. Especially when my life could be snuffed out at any moment."

"Don't speak like that." Diego placed a hand on my shoulder to reassure me. What it did was make my face flush. "I'm on your side, and soon the entire Clan of the Eternal Night will be, too. And I think you should become the leader of the Magic Guild."

"I'm too young and inexperienced for that, but thank you.

And I can't do much of anything if the governor comes after me because of what I know."

"Whoever comes after you, I will kill," Diego said with utmost seriousness.

Yena yowled from the bedroom like an angry mountain lion.

"Excuse me." Diego headed for the hallway. "She wants her monster doll."

THEY DIDN'T WASTE ANY TIME BEFORE THEY CAME AFTER ME.

I went directly from Diego's apartment to the inn and packed lightly so I could travel easily. It hadn't been long since I last did this when I was hiding from Lethia's wrath. This time, I wasn't even sure whom I needed to flee from.

I was in my room, stuffing clothes into a backpack, when the burglar alarm alert went off on my phone. The video feed showed the man who had shifted into the dream-scenting dog had returned and was opening the main door. I guess the locksmith hadn't come yet to change the lock, or this guy was just too good at picking them.

While he held the door open, several men carrying pistols and assault rifles filed inside. They wore the uniforms of the paramilitary militia that had abducted Mr. Jubbles. Their arrival here was more evidence that the governor and her cronies were directing them.

Baldric followed them inside. He must be the commander of tonight's mission to kill or capture me.

At least now I knew who I was up against. Namely, just about everyone.

Mom called to me telepathically, warning me of what I already knew: these goons were coming for me.

I checked the feed from the camera above the stairs. The militiamen were heading upstairs, leaving a few stationed on the ground floor. Baldric was nowhere to be seen.

Heart pounding, I strapped my sword to my back, put on my backpack over it, and slung the duffel bag with my crossbow over my shoulder.

At times like this, I wished I had a gun, but there was no way I would fire it inside our inn where guests slept. I also decided not to use my crossbow. Killing faeries and vampires was one thing; dead humans would cross the line legally.

Though deep down inside, I knew it might come to that soon.

Tonight, my sword and my magic would be my weapons to wound, but not to kill.

First, I cast a protection spell around myself. I needed to move freely, so I didn't anchor the bubble to the ground the way Orlena had taught me. It was also closer to my body, because I planned on escaping through my window. This meant it might not stop bullets.

Next, I crept into the hall and cast a protection barrier across the stairway to prevent the soldiers from reaching my floor.

Okay, time to get out of here.

I had two bundles of rope in my duffel bag. I tied the end of one to the foot of my bed and ran the rope out my window. It dangled a few feet short of the courtyard, but that was okay.

I climbed on the windowsill and psyched myself up to rappel down the exterior wall. That I'd never done something like this before couldn't stop me.

I'd barely made it out of my window when a bullet struck the stucco of the exterior wall near me. The gun must have had a suppressor because I hadn't heard it.

Yikes! I flew back inside my window and took cover.

What was I supposed to do next? Obviously, the soldiers were shooting to kill. They weren't here to capture me.

I glanced out of my door to the left. Soldiers stood at the invisible barrier of my protection screen at the top of the stairs. One man saw me and fired his handgun, the silenced weapon making a sharp spurting sound. The bullet ricocheted off the screen, forcing the soldiers to duck.

I couldn't resist firing back through the barrier, which my protection spells allowed. Pumping as much energy as I could spare into Alfie, I sent bolts of purple lightning at the soldiers on the stairs. One screamed and fell over the banister. The others took cover and fired back at me.

A single bullet made it through the protection barrier and lodged in the wall near me. I had put too much energy into my attack magic, leaving the barrier weaker. I needed to get out of there.

The window at the far end of the hall caught my eye. It overlooked the alley on the side of the inn. The alley might have been left unguarded, and Mom's scooter was parked out there.

I untied the rope used in the unsuccessful escape from my room's window and pulled it back inside. The hallway was still empty. The only object near the window that I could tie the rope to was the handle of the last door in the hall. I took a deep breath, then dashed down the hall toward the door handle.

But as I neared the befuddled soldiers on the stairs, I saw Baldric had joined them. He made motions with his hand, indicating he was dismantling my protection barrier.

The soldiers would trap me in the hall before I could escape through the window.

I put on the brakes and ran the other way. I would lock myself in my room, even if there was no escape, and fight for as long as I could, with every weapon I had, no qualms about killing humans.

If I was going to die, I'd rather do it in my own room. I would have preferred to die there in my sleep, but no such luck.

Before I reached my room, I noticed the attic door was open a crack. Of course, we didn't have an attic. Mom had warned me that if I saw a door there, it was actually a gateway that would take me to the In Between. I did not, she had stressed, want to go there.

In that brief moment, with my death imminent, going to the In Between didn't seem like such a bad idea.

With the thuds of boots running toward me, I darted through the door that didn't really exist, up unfinished wooden stairs that didn't exist, and into a vertical field of shimmering air with darkness on the other side.

Nausea swept over me as I stepped through the gateway.

CHAPTER 16

DARLA

Again, Cory and I were awakened by the burglar alarm on our phones. Again, the dream-scenting shifter had picked the lock on the main door. We had ordered a new, more secure key-card lock, but it hadn't been installed yet. Why had this guy returned? What was he sniffing for?

I got my answer when the security camera showed a seemingly endless line of men in military-style uniforms filing into the inn. I swiped through the different video feeds, and exterior cameras picked up additional men stationed outside.

Baldric arrived. And reality struck me all at once.

"They're coming for Sophie," I said to Cory, who stood behind me, looking over my shoulder at my screen.

I tried to send her a warning telepathically.

Baldric and a bunch of goons with guns are here. I think they're coming for you.

She didn't reply, and I repeated the message.

On it, she finally replied. *Please try to distract them.*

Cory had already run inside the inn and confronted the men. His angry shouts echoed out into the courtyard.

Be careful, Cory, I said telepathically, though I doubted he heard me.

I called the police, then crossed the courtyard to the inn, trying to formulate a plan. I couldn't fight back with magic like Sophie, and it would be foolish to use our handgun against the heavily armed men.

Lights were coming on in the guest rooms that faced the courtyard. Our already-reduced occupancy levels, thanks to the Great Unmasking, would probably drop to zero after this raid.

Sophie's light was on. I wondered if she was still in her room or had escaped the inn somehow.

A man armed with an assault rifle appeared in the doorway to the main building before I reached it.

"Sorry, ma'am, you can't go inside now," he said in a heavy southern accent.

"I'm the owner of this inn."

"Sorry. We're conducting an operation. You can go inside when it's complete."

"Who the heck are you guys?" I demanded. "You have no right to be here."

"We're the Boogaloo Brigade, here on a government-authorized mission."

"Booga-*what?*"

"We're a militia, ma'am. Dedicated patriots trying to keep our community safe from supernaturals."

"There aren't any supernaturals here."

A rope flew from Sophie's window, straightened, and smacked against the stucco exterior wall. Sophie appeared in the window, preparing to climb down.

The soldier ran past me and fired his rifle at Sophie.

"Stop shooting!" I shouted.

Fortunately, he missed. Sophie jumped back inside.

"What are you doing?" I screamed. "That's my dau—that's my guest!"

"Ma'am, go back into your cottage, or you're going to be hurt."

A dark figure raced across the courtyard from the shadows and tackled the soldier. The attacker was on top of him, growling, as the soldier struggled and gave a cut-off scream.

The struggle ended. Slurping sounds ensued.

I grimaced. The attacker was a vampire. Could it be Roderick? I didn't think he had the guts to attack a man like that.

The vampire finished his meal, then stood facing me. I was terrified. The vampires in town knew who I was, and that I was a member of a supernatural guild. But with all the chaos nowadays, I wouldn't be surprised if there were rogue vampires out there.

He stepped toward me, and ambient light from the inn caught his face.

"Mr. Jubbles!" I said. "I never expected to see you out here."

"There are intruders in the inn," he replied. "And I was hungry for a snack."

"Is he still alive?"

Jubbles shook his head no and giggled.

"You shouldn't have done it on our property. And you'd better not turn him," I said in a warning voice.

"He will stay dead. This man was one of the ones who kidnapped me. He got what he deserved."

Before I could become angry, gunshots rang inside the inn. I ran into the building with no plan, just motherly fear for my daughter.

I saw no one at first. The hallway from the courtyard was

empty. So were the living and dining rooms. The kitchen, too. I passed through the foyer and saw a guard stationed outside the safety-glass main door.

A handful of soldiers stood at the foot of the stairs, two of whom were holding Cory. Everyone was looking up the stairs.

The place smelled of discharged guns and the ozone scent of Sophie's attack magic. I approached the stairs, but a soldier gestured for me to stop.

A shout came from the second floor, followed by the pounding of several feet going up the stairs to the third. The men down here ran up after them, leaving the two guys holding Cory.

Cory looked at me sadly.

I think she escaped, I said to him telepathically, and he seemed to understand.

With no one to stop me, I ran upstairs.

Men were going in and out of Sophie's room. One peered out the window at the end of the hall, and the rest milled about.

Baldric strode from Sophie's room, wearing a big scowl.

"I thought I saw her going through a door here," a soldier in the hallway said, pointing to an empty wall near the bedroom. "But there's no door here now."

The attic door. Sophie had fled through a gateway. I even sensed a trace of the supernatural power left behind. She was most likely in the In Between.

"We need to search the other bedrooms," Baldric said to me. "Let us in, or we'll break down the doors."

"They're unoccupied on the third floor, except for this one." I pointed to 303. "There's a couple from Maryland staying here who are probably frightened to death from all the gunfire. And three-oh-two has a guest, but he's out and about tonight," I said, referring to Mr. Jubbles' room.

"Let me in three-oh-three. I'll cast a sleep spell on your guests, and I'll be quick."

I let him in with my master key card and felt a rush of magic. He was true to his word and soon exited—with me following him every step of the way to protect my sleeping guests. I prayed they were unaware of the intrusion, although they had surely heard all the commotion before they were enchanted.

"Let us in the other rooms," Baldric ordered, his hand on the handle of 302.

"Tell me why you're searching for Sophie."

"She violated an agreement."

"What agreement?"

"I can't say. Now, let me into this room. You said the occupant isn't here."

I tried to search his mind, but he had sealed it off. He knew I was telepathic.

"Are you conducting the search for your own reasons, or were you ordered to do so?" I asked. "Like by the governor's office?"

I was pretty sure either the governor or Senator Poxton, or both, were behind this.

"That is none of your business," Baldric replied, trying to control his temper, his knuckles white as his hand squeezed the handle.

"This inn belongs to my family. And you're not law enforcement. You can't trespass on my property and try to abduct my daughter."

"Soon, this city will be run by me and ruled by me. And I'll be able to do anything I want. Best not to get on my bad side. Open this door before we break it down!" He rattled the handle.

It was clear I couldn't drag out this encounter any further. I unlocked the door and, thankfully, Baldric didn't seem to sense any vampiric energy in Mr. Jubbles' antique-filled room. Then I unlocked the doors of the vacant rooms on that floor. Baldric and his thugs quickly realized Sophie was not to be found. We went through the same routine on the second floor, with Baldric enchanting the few guests in the occupied rooms before searching them.

When he was finished, Baldric approached me in the hallway. He had changed his demeanor to one of charm, smiling over his dimpled chin.

"I know you're angry with me," he said, "but we guild members must work closely together as allies. Your guild's leader, Dr. Noordlun, has been cooperative."

"I agree. We should be allies. Against those who are persecuting us. But you appear to be allied with them."

His face darkened as some of his fake charm disappeared. "I'm doing what I can to protect us. If it weren't for me, the police would have shut down your inn by now."

Samson had never mentioned Baldric intervening, but he didn't know everything going on with his superiors in the police.

"You can repay me by helping me," he continued. "I know that the vampire who was all over social media after being abducted was a guest here. Which means you were breaking the law by hosting him. But that's neither here nor there. Some local vampires rescued him and took his abductors hostage, my sources tell me. Those hostages are members of the militia that's here with me tonight."

"Couldn't have happened to a better bunch of fellows."

He ignored my snark. "The militia has connections in very high places. I need your help in locating the hostages. I know that you're friends with Diego Fernandez and other vampires. Use your connections."

Before I could think of an answer, a militiaman called from

the stairs. "Baldric, please come downstairs. We found O'Neil dead outside."

Baldric's brow furrowed, and he turned away, heading down the stairs.

It was at this perfect moment that the police finally decided to show up. They normally dragged their feet when they got a call from this address. They knew about our supernatural reputation, so why would they want to help when we were being invaded by thugs?

The problem was, I had called them before Mr. Jubbles killed the thug. This was not going to look good.

It seemed like I was the last person to arrive in the courtyard. Two uniformed officers walked up to the crime scene as Baldric and a bunch of militiamen stood there staring at the body that was obviously dead. Having most of your neck removed will do that to you.

The militiamen slunk away after the police arrived. Cory, no longer restrained, put an arm around me.

"Any witnesses need to remain here until the detective arrives," said a female officer, whom I knew all too well. "Mrs. Chesswick, is this like the twentieth dead body found on your property? I've lost count by now."

"You exaggerate," I said.

"Not by much. The victim is wearing a uniform like these other guys. Is this some kind of militia?"

"Deputized by the Florida Department of Law Enforcement," Baldric said. "To help investigate supernaturals."

"That seems fishy to me," said the officer, whom I disliked but knew to be an honest cop.

I had hoped the detective assigned to this would be Samson, so I was not happy to see Siwicki saunter into the courtyard. He squatted next to the corpse.

"The body looks like it's been drained of blood. The medical examiner will tell us for certain, but I would say a vampire did this. And if that's the case," he said as he stood up, "this inn is going to be shut down."

"You can't do that!" Cory said.

"Under the provisions of the Supernatural Criminality Act, we sure can."

"The vampire who did this wasn't a guest here," I lied. "Any vampire can jump over the courtyard wall from the street."

Siwicki looked askance at me. "I assume you have security cameras on your property?"

"Um, yes."

"We'll look at the videos and see where the vampire came from."

"If he came onto the property in an area covered by cameras."

"Of course. I'll want to see the video immediately." Siwicki added with a sneer, "Wouldn't want anyone to delete it."

A crime-scene team arrived and broke up the party. Before Siwicki even interviewed the man who found the body, he asked me again to see the security footage.

I unlocked my phone and opened the app. "See, this is the man who picked the lock on the main door. And see, he's letting in the militia guys."

I hadn't seen any of the video after that, because I'd been too busy running around.

Siwicki continued scrubbing forward through the footage. From the two cameras in the courtyard, there was no sign of a vampire jumping over the wall. We saw Cory running from the cottage and entering the inn. The militiaman appearing in the doorway and blocking my entrance.

The other courtyard camera showed the rope dangling down

the inn's wall and the militiaman running over and firing upward. Sophie climbing out of the window was not in the camera's view frame.

Then, the militiaman was attacked and fell out of frame, so you couldn't see the actual murder. The first camera showed me running into the inn. Shortly afterward, a bald man slipped inside, but you couldn't see his face.

"That's the murderer, I would wager," Siwicki said.

Then, he scrubbed backward in time, before we'd been awakened by the burglar alarm. There was nothing going on in the courtyard until. . .

Mr. Jubbles walked out of the inn and disappeared into the shadows.

"Hey, that guy looks familiar!" Siwicki announced. "I'd recognize him anywhere after he was plastered all over social media. That's the vampire who was kidnapped and then rescued. He's a guest here, isn't he? How long has he been here?"

I didn't answer, but Siwicki knew he had me.

"Not answering? We'll just subpoena your records. And according to the footage, you were out here when the victim was murdered by the vampire. You witnessed it, didn't you?"

"I think I should have a lawyer here before I answer any questions," I said.

AFTER SIWICKI AND THE OFFICERS DETERMINED THE VAMPIRE was not in the inn (thank you for leaving, Mr. Jubbles), the body was removed, the crime scene was secured, and everyone left.

It was nearly dawn. I had an appointment with the detective later in the morning to have a "little chat," my lawyer in tow. They wouldn't arrest me for witnessing the murder, but I didn't know if I could be for knowingly booking a room to a vampire. I'd have to argue that I wasn't aware he was a vampire.

Sure, he was pale, Detective, but I didn't see any fangs.

Awkward. I'd have to practice my delivery.

I took a shower, but had a little time before breakfast preparation began. So, I went upstairs to the third floor to examine the door handle Baldric had touched while demanding to enter the room. With luck, he had left his thoughts upon it, and I could read them with my psychometry.

Sure enough, the brass handle was full of Baldric's psychic energy. I held my hand as close to the metal as I could without touching it so I could test for Baldric's memories without going into a trance.

Into my mind drifted my conversation with him while he held the handle, waiting for me to unlock the door. Unfortunately, we were talking the entire time he held the handle, so he wouldn't have had any long trains of thought.

I placed my fingers on the metal and felt Baldric's psychic energy flow into me. Ah, here was a little snippet of memory that I—

—can't trust Sophie to be my advocate. I had no choice. I had to tell Governor Witlessin and Poxton that Sophie knows they are faeries. Dangerous knowledge ... Why won't this stupid human open the door? . . The governor was furious. She's making me use this moronic militia to kill Sophie ... Open this door before we break it down! . . Will the Faerie Queene honor her promise to make me viceroy of Florida and the region if I deliver San Marcos to her as the first city to fall? Much better than being a mayor—

—His last memory was turning the handle and realizing it was unlocked.

I had hit the jackpot. Baldric confirmed what I had guessed, that Sophie's verbal slip had led him to report Sophie's knowledge, which caused the governor to order her murder.

Not her arrest, her murder. Now I was the one with dangerous information that could cause the governor to lose reelection. Too bad I learned it through psychic means, and no one would believe me.

The last little nugget of Baldric's memories was very interesting. In the Queene's palace, Sophie had overhead the governor floating the idea of her being the Queene's viceroy if Florida were conquered by the Unseelie Court. Yet the Queene had offered Baldric the same title if he delivered San Marcos to the Fae.

I assumed that meant San Marcos would be like a beachhead —the Unseelie Court's first conquered city, perhaps leading to a domino effect of other cities falling.

Baldric's chances of being elected mayor of San Marcos were excellent thanks to the governor's powerful political machine. But with the Queene's secret deal, he would end up running the entire Southeast simply by oppressing the city's supernaturals, undermining the city's security, and helping the Queene.

My knowledge of these deals weighed on me. How could I save San Marcos and my fellow supernaturals? If Sophie were there, she'd tell me to fight with every weapon I had.

I didn't have her magical abilities, but I had weapons that no one would expect.

CHAPTER 17

SOPHIE

W alking through the gateway felt like blindly stepping from an elevator that had stopped several inches above the floor. I fell hard, but the grassy ground was soft.

And grass was all I could see around me: rolling hills of it, emerald green and kind of fake-looking. The grass was of uniform height: longer than the grass in your yard, but not as tall as in a wild meadow.

I didn't know which way to walk or what I was even hoping to find. All I had wanted was to escape Baldric and the militia. Well, I could check off that box, but I didn't know what the next one was.

Could I ever go home again? Governor Witlessin and Senator Poxton now knew that I had learned they were faeries. They couldn't allow me to live because their political careers would be over if the populace found out that they were among the very creatures they were persecuting for political gain.

You can't rile up voters by insisting that supernatural creatures are dangerous and evil when you are supernatural yourself.

Just like Marge Moosebacher had almost been killed by the mob she had incited when she shifted to her natural faerie form in front of them.

She had lucked out, though. She had shifted back to human form before her attackers killed her. Thanks to all the confusion during the incident, no witnesses could say for certain she had been a faerie. No photos of her in her natural form surfaced.

Marge was successfully rehabilitated as the passionate human leader of Mothers Against Monsters. I, on the other hand, was now an exile.

I began walking through the green terrain. The grass underfoot was unnaturally green, and there were no weeds or stones. Not even any insects.

I had to find shelter, food, and water. The only things I had were my backpack, duffel bag, and weapons. Thankfully, they had stayed with me when I passed into this strange realm.

In which compass direction was I headed? It was then that I noticed there was no sun. The sky was white, with a tinge of blue, bright enough to bathe the landscape in normal daylight, but it was artificial, looking like a giant electric dome.

Mom and Cory had been to the In Between, but I never had. I'd traveled through a gateway once, but it had taken me elsewhere on earth, not here.

From what Mom had told me, gateways were actually angels, low in the angelic hierarchy. They could take you just about anywhere, even to different eras of time.

But they mostly brought people here—the souls of dead people, that is. The In Between was a separate plane of existence in between worlds, but mostly in between heaven and the bad place down below. It was a sort of purgatory for the unfortunate souls waiting to be judged whether they'd be sent upstairs or downstairs.

For a reason no one knows, living humans and other highly intelligent creatures could also go there, but only stay for a few months at the most before they suffered molecular damage. A trip back to earth would heal the damage, and they could return there.

Why would they want to return? Because the In Between was a refuge for the persecuted. Mom said she'd met a witch here from Salem during the witch trials, a defrocked monk who had practiced magic, and various nonconformists from different periods of history.

I supposed I belonged here now, since I was no longer safe on earth. Well, maybe I could live off the grid in my planet's last wilderness areas, assuming I wasn't killed the moment I was transported back home. The In Between was the ultimate off-the-grid hiding spot.

Most of the people there were witches, Mom had told me, or were supported by witches, because magic was necessary to create food and water. Everything found in the landscape was fake, an illusion.

Too bad I didn't know any magic spells to create food and water out of thin air.

Distant thunder came from behind me. No, it wasn't thunder, but was deep and rumbling. Rhythmic. And it was coming closer, from just over the rolling hills. It was almost a beating of the air, but not like from helicopters. No, it was like giant wings flapping.

Rising from behind the rounded horizon were three dragons flying in my direction. I didn't think they were fake. No, these were real.

With colossal leathery wings, hind legs stretched horizontally behind them, and forelegs tucked against their chests, they created shadows on the grass like airliners flying low.

I dropped to the ground and lay flat. There was no place to hide.

The dragons drifted lower and flew directly over me, studying me. After they passed, they made a lazy circle and returned to me.

But my fear evaporated. My empath abilities detected the dragons' feelings toward me.

Benevolent curiosity.

They knew I was a witch—a good, not evil, one. They sensed my supernatural nature, which made me akin to them, at least compared to the typical human who might have ended up as dinner for the dragons.

Briefly, as they passed overhead, I made eye contact with one of them whose head crest was partially missing with signs of scarring. A feeling of warmth spread through me from the gaze of his yellow eye with its vertical pupil.

The dragons continued on their original path. Soon, they were far enough away that they looked like simple birds flying across the sky.

Dragons! Mom had told me they existed. They'd been driven from the earth by humans and Fae, but thankfully not been made extinct. The In Between was their refuge, I guessed.

We had that in common. But I couldn't consider this a refuge until I found sustenance, my growling stomach reminded me.

I kept walking up rounded hills and down them. There were hills that seemed slightly higher than the others, and I would eagerly climb them, hoping when I reached the top, I would be able to see different landscape features in the distance, maybe even signs of humans. But no such luck.

It felt as if I'd been there for hours, but there was no sun progressing across the sky to indicate time. My watch and phone were completely dead. I'd never expected to find cellphone service there, but I didn't realize the batteries would be drained. I hoped the devices weren't fried.

My heart leaped when I saw a bird fly overhead. It was large and resembled an eagle. Other than the dragons, that was the first living creature I'd seen there. It circled high above me.

It was time to use some magic, a projection spell. I would try to attach my consciousness to the bird, so I could better survey the landscape. It wouldn't be like making a psychic connection with the bird the way I'd done with Diego during the rescue of Mr. Jubbles. This spell was more akin to attaching a camera to the bird.

I gathered my internal energies, but quickly realized there were no elemental energies here to supplement mine. I was an elemental witch—I needed that energy.

Using every drop of my own energy, I struggled to cast the spell. I sent my consciousness up to the bird, but it wouldn't stick. My magic simply wasn't working there.

Yet it was enough to enrage the eagle.

The bird dove at me. As it dropped in altitude, I realized it wasn't an eagle. It was like some mythological chimera—the beaked head and wings of an eagle, with the body of a leopard.

It plummeted toward me, leaving me no time to cock my crossbow. I pulled Alfie from its scabbard, still strapped to my back, and held the sword pointing upward so the creature would impale itself.

It didn't. When it was just above me, it jerked sideways, missing my sword. The creature was much larger than I'd thought—twice the size of me.

Wings flapping furiously, it flew at me from behind.

I spun around and slashed at the creature, but it avoided my sword again. It hovered just out of reach, then attacked again, its beak wide open, large enough to swallow my head.

But it didn't use its beak. A leopard paw batted my sword, knocking it from my hand.

I dove to the ground and grabbed the sword, rolling to face the creature. A paw slashed at my face, drawing blood, while its beating wings kept me from rising.

I lunged, driving Alfie straight into the creature's chest.

And nothing happened. The eagle-leopard pushed its paws against my sword until it was free of the blade. The wound didn't bleed at all, and the creature seemed utterly unaffected.

It attacked again, the paws grasping me by my upper arms, preventing me from using my sword. The open beak came for my throat.

A sharp whistle came from nearby, startling the creature. The eagle head turned to look behind it and screeched in anger.

"Get out of here!" a woman shouted.

The creature released me, and I fell backward onto the grass. Yet the monster still hovered over me, wings beating.

"Okay, if you insist," said the woman, who looked like a 1980s punk rocker with a bleached-blonde Mohawk haircut and leather jacket.

She swung a wooden staff at the creature, and it exploded in blood and feathers. The creature disappeared, and so did the blood and feathers. It was like it had never existed.

I panted, still holding my sword, and sat up.

"You must be new here," the woman said. "The monsters always find the newbies quickly. We think the monsters were put here to keep explorers away. This place was really intended just for souls in limbo until we refugees showed up."

She extended a hand and helped me to my feet. Frowning, she touched my wounded cheek, and I felt magic flowing into it.

"All patched up," she said.

"Thank you. And thank you for saving me from that thing."

"No prob. Nice sword you've got. But conventional weapons are useless with these monsters. You need magic to defeat them. As you can see, they're not real flesh-and-blood animals. They're magical."

"Are there many of them?"

"Yeah. And in all sorts of shapes and sizes. You can't go anywhere in the In Between without a magical staff or similar weapon." She sized me up. "I'm Fran. Who are you?"

"Sophie. I didn't plan on coming here, but I was escaping from people trying to kill me."

Fran laughed. "That's the case for a lot of us. I had the FBI coming after me, along with a bunch of holy rollers. A lesbian feminist activist who's also a witch? Not a good recipe for survival in Alabama."

I considered her outdated look. "What year did you come here?"

"1985. And when I return there to regenerate my health, it's always that year. I would have preferred sometime in the future when things would be better."

"They don't get better," I said with a laugh.

The emotions I felt in her were warm and caring, so I relaxed even more, feeling safe at last.

"I sense magic in you," she said. "Are you a witch, too?"

"Yes, I am. That's part of the reason I'm in trouble back home."

"As it always is with we people of the craft. Do you need help to find a gateway to return home?"

"I can't go home right now, unless I'm dropped off in another city. Ideally, another state. Our governor, among many, wants to kill me."

"One thing you've got to remember is time passes differently here than at home. You can spend a day here, while only a minute passes back home. If you're hoping to wait until your enemies lose interest in you, you're going to be here for a very long time. Let's go speak with Celric. He'll have wise counsel."

"Is he your leader?"

"We don't have leaders here," Fran replied. "We all do our own thing and support each other. I'm sharing a campsite with Celric and others during my current stay here."

I followed her in a straight line through the homogeneous green countryside. She seemed to know exactly where she was going.

"Were you out for a hike when you spotted me?" I asked.

"I was on patrol. We watch for people who have arrived here accidentally, and try to prevent them from being killed by monsters."

"Oh." What a grim reality. "How many humans live in the In Between?"

"Like I said, we don't live here permanently. And I couldn't answer that question. Each time I stay here, I come across only a few people, never more than a dozen. I assume there are more in other parts of the In Between, but no one goes on long journeys. It's too dangerous. No one even knows how big this place is. It looks like it's endless and all the same, but each time I come here, it's different."

We climbed a gentle hill, and when we came down the other side, I saw three tents in the distance in a small flat area between hills.

"It's only Celric, Wally, and me in this camp," Fran said. "I have other friends in the In Between, but I haven't seen them during this visit."

"Do Fae or Elves ever come here?"

"I've never seen any. They have different religions than humans. Maybe that's why."

As we approached the campsite, I noticed the campfire had no fire or smoke, but a pot floated above it with steam coming out. The tents were squarish and appeared to be made of canvas, but I saw no signs of tent poles.

Fran must have noticed the quizzical look on my face.

"The fire is magical. So are the tents. They're just an illusion to create privacy. We don't need real tents to protect us from the weather because there is no weather."

Two men emerged from their "tents." One was obviously a medieval monk, wearing a habit, his white hair cut in a tonsure. He had a strange gold medallion on a leather cord around his neck and carried a staff similar to Fran's. He seemed ancient in age, yet brimming with power and vitality, much of that coming from magic.

"Everybody, meet our new arrival, Sophie. She's a witch. Sophie, this is Celric," Fran said. "He's a monk and a mage. The mage part is why he was driven from his monastery. And this is Wally." She gestured to a younger man in thick eyeglasses, wearing a short-sleeved dress shirt and a narrow tie with a tie clip. "He's the man who invented timeshares, which is why he was driven away from earth. He learned magic here in the In Between from Celric."

Wally smiled beneath a pencil-thin mustache. "I also can translate when you speak to Celric. He's not so good with modern English. He speaks Middle English, the language of Chaucer."

"Who?" I asked.

"Only a famous poet. You know, *The Canterbury Tales?*"

"No."

He sighed. "What brings you to the In Between?"

"Escaping people who want to kill me."

Celric said something I didn't understand. It sounded like

French mixed with German. I recognized only a few familiar English words.

"Celric says he met your mother," Wally translated. "She came to the In Between many times. On the last visit, she took a vampire child back to earth."

Yeah, it was Mom who had reunited Yena with Lethia a couple of years ago. Mom had done it as a peace offering, to convince Lethia to end her deadly rampage through San Marcos. It had worked at the time, but it hadn't changed Lethia's personality one bit. And now, thanks to my destroying her, Diego was stuck with her daughter.

"Wow," I said, "it sure is a small alternative plane of existence."

Wally didn't bother translating that.

Celric spoke again.

"He says he sensed a pagan goddess in your mother. What has become of her?"

"Mom is fine, but the Goddess is still in her," I replied.

Celric was getting animated now and said something in a worried voice.

"He says there's an evil force trying to invade the In Between," Wally translated. "Not a demon, but more powerful. An ancient, forgotten god. You must tell your mother. Celric is a Christian, obviously, but he has seen and experienced magic and power that are not part of our belief system. He believes your mother, as Danu, has the strength to fight this dangerous god."

"Tell him I will pass along the message to her. Thank you. In the meantime, will I be allowed to stay here for my safety?"

"Yes." Wally translated Celric's response. "You must learn more magic in order to do so. And you must return to earth frequently."

"Why?"

"To fight the evil ones who oppress others. All of us here have suffered oppression, but never has it been as bad as this. You must fight and defeat it."

"Little ol' me?"

Celric didn't reply.

CHAPTER 18

SOPHIE

My hosts and I shared dinner that night. I mean, it wasn't really night, because the In Between remained illuminated by the enigmatic white sky, and no one had timepieces that worked. I called it dinner because it felt as if an entire day had passed, and I was ravenously hungry.

Our meal reminded me of a vegetarian dinner back home, except it was made with magic rather than plants. The pasta was pretty good. If you can make decent spaghetti from zucchini, you can make it from anything, even magic. There were protein patties that Wally browned in a magically made skillet over the magically created fire. And there were raw carrots that tasted like the real thing.

Fran created a magical fake tent for me, and I went to bed soon after our meal. Believe it or not, it was the best sleep I'd had in a long time because I felt truly safe, protected by the three magicians. Even when I snuck out of my fake tent and went behind a small hill for privacy to take a real pee on the fake grass, I felt safe. A fake candle burning in Celric's tent told me he was awake and watchful, able to respond quickly if I cried out.

When I awoke, in what I assumed was a new day, Wally and Fran were sipping from mugs by the campfire.

"Want some coffee?" Fran asked. "I'm a coffee snob, so I tried to imitate it as best I could."

I nodded, and like a stage magician performing sleight-of-hand tricks, she produced a mug filled with hot coffee from nowhere.

"What do you guys do to pass the time here?" I asked.

"Practice our magic," Wally said. "The rules are different here. If you can get a spell to work here, it'll work even better on earth."

"Celric also prays a lot," Fran said, pointing to the monk kneeling on the grass just beyond the campsite.

I sipped the strong coffee, feeling antsy. How long would I need to stay there, especially if time went by more slowly than on earth?

"Do you guys ever plan on returning to earth for good, instead of just brief visits?" I asked.

"Whenever we go home, we're back in the same bad situation that we needed to escape," Wally replied. "Celric says that one day, a gateway will take us to a different year where we'll be safe. The gateway will decide when we're ready and where we'll go. Gateways are a kind of angel, you know."

"Yeah," I said. "My mom discovered that."

Celric spoke, standing behind me. I hadn't noticed him joining us.

"He says your mother needs you," Wally explained.

"I know," I said, ashamed to have run away.

"Celric says that after much prayer, he realizes you are rare among those of us who are oppressed. You actually have the power to fight and possibly defeat your oppressors. It is your duty to do so immediately."

Celric spoke again. I recognized the words, "Tuatha De Danann."

Wally continued translating. "He says he feels the divine in you and believes you are one of the Tuatha De Danann sung about by the druids and described in a manuscript he found in his monastery. If he is correct, you are destined to achieve great things. Now is your time to begin."

"It sounds like you're on your way home," Fran said. "I'll take you to find a gateway."

If my hosts were telling me it was time to go, my little vacation in the In Between was over.

I said goodbye to the others and followed Fran over the gently rolling hills.

"I've been here long enough to be pretty good at finding gateways," she said.

"My mom can summon them wherever she is."

"Wow. Yeah, Celric said she's a goddess."

"Sort of. She's the human vessel of Danu, but we're afraid she'll actually become her someday soon. It's hard to explain."

"You protect her during her metamorphosis?"

"That's a good way to put it."

A forest was suddenly in front of us. For a moment, I thought it was an optical illusion.

"Watch out for creatures," Fran said, entering the dark woods. "Lots of them are in here."

She didn't follow a path, but there was no undergrowth, so it was easy to walk between the trees. Suddenly, she stopped and shook her staff above her head.

I followed her stare and saw the giant squirrel perched on a tree trunk nearby. It was about the size of a bear and looked just as mean.

"The squirrels won't attack unless they can surprise you," Fran explained.

I was nervous walking farther into the forest, leaving the squirrel to our rear where he could sneak up on us. But soon, the forest ended at the shore of an enormous lake that stretched to the horizon, trees surrounding it for as far as I could see.

"Now where do we go?" I asked.

"We'll follow the shoreline. I sense a gateway nearby."

The shoreline was a narrow belt of smooth brown sand, firm enough to make walking easy. Unlike a real lake, there was nothing from nature washed up onto the shore, and the waters were completely still. We went in a counterclockwise direction, the lake to our left and the forest to our right.

Fran stopped suddenly, brandishing her staff, staring out into the lake.

"A creature?" I asked.

"There are dangerous fish in here, but something else is out there now. I sense that it's different from anything I've encountered in the In Between."

I sensed something, too. Magic unlike anything I'd ever felt before. It creeped me out.

Far from shore, objects broke the surface. There were two of them. They didn't protrude from the water enough for me to tell what they were, but they created a wake as they swam.

Straight toward us.

Fran pointed her staff at them, tensing for the attack.

The objects stopped moving and rose higher from the water. They were two primitive eyes atop eye stalks, like you'd see on a crab.

"Giant crab?" I whispered. I was nervous, worried that Fran

couldn't protect us. Somehow, I knew the creature wasn't like the giant squirrel or the eagle-leopard.

"It's not from the In Between," Fran said in a shaky voice. "It's powerful and evil and doesn't belong here. I think it's the elder god Celric was talking about."

It must be the one Mom had fought. It wasn't only trying to invade the earth, but also an alternate plane of existence created by a belief system this entity had no place in.

"I don't think it's strong enough to attack us," Fran said. "Not now, but maybe in the future."

The eyes disappeared beneath the surface.

"Celric will be disturbed to hear about this. You must tell your mother."

I nodded, and we continued walking, glancing nervously at the lake every few steps.

Before long, we came upon a vertical disk of shimmering air, about eight feet tall, suspended at the edge of the trees to our right.

"Your ride is here," said Fran said. "Just walk into it without hesitating."

"Thank you so much for your help. It was nice meeting you."

"Good luck back on earth, and stay safe. I expect I'll see you here again someday."

"I hope that elder god doesn't show up here again."

I gave her a little wave and strode purposefully toward the gateway. Nausea griped my gut just before I stepped through it—

And found myself on a dark, narrow staircase. A sliver of light came from a slightly open door below me, so I descended the stairs and peeked through the opening.

As I expected, this was the non-existent attic door near my room. There were no sounds, so I opened the door. I saw no one in the hallway.

My bedroom door was open. The room was a wreck, as if it had been hastily searched, but no one was around.

Voices came from below my open window. Carefully, I moved to the window, placing myself where I could see out without being seen from the courtyard.

Down below were two police officers, a handful of the militiamen, Mom, and Cory. There was also a dead body.

I had to get out of here before I was seen.

My backup rope was still in my duffel bag, so I tried my aborted plan to tie the rope to a door handle and rappel down to the alley from the window at the end of the hall.

And it worked. I made it down the side of the inn and landed uninjured.

Mom's motor scooter was parked out there. I retrieved the key she always hid in a crevice between the inn's stone wall and a window frame and rolled the scooter silently along the alley to Hidalgo Avenue and east for half a block. Only there, out of earshot of the courtyard, did I climb onto the scooter and start the engine.

I couldn't call Mom. I didn't know if the cops and others were still around—and wasn't sure if I could get my phone to work again—so I sent a simple telepathic message.

Went to the In Between. Back on earth. Snuck out of the inn.

Be careful, Mom replied in my head. *Get in touch when you can.*

I drove on the bumpy cobblestone street, off into the night.

Away from my home and family, uncertain if I'd ever be able to return.

AFTER MULTIPLE TRIES, MY PHONE FINALLY POWERED ON, BUT it wasn't getting a signal. I hoped it wasn't permanently fried from traveling to an alternate plane of existence. Unable to call anyone, I was unwilling to show up at any of my casual friends' doors at this late hour. I didn't want to put them at risk, either. I was radioactive, with everyone, it seemed, wanting to kill me.

I needed to find a hotel that would accept cash, so I headed for the seedy part of town. The motel where Mr. Jubbles had been held captive was a likely place to start.

After I checked in with a male desk clerk who eyed me like he thought I was a prostitute, I got back on the scooter and drove randomly around the city. The depressing motel room was more than I could bear now.

But I ached with the need to speak with someone who could calm my fears. I took a detour to Diego's place.

Just then, I heard Mom's words in my head.

Baldric has gone behind the governor's back and made a secret agreement with the Faerie Queene. He promised to deliver San Marcos to her. The first city to fall. In return, she'll make him viceroy of Florida and the Southeast.

The cars parked behind the restaurant looked familiar. I knocked on the locked rear door. Diego opened it. He looked stunned when he saw me, before a big smile brightened his face.

"I'm so glad you're okay," he said, hugging me tight, which immediately warmed me up inside. "Our vampire spies told me that Baldric tried to kill you."

"He came to the inn with a little army of paramilitary extremists. They report to the governor, I think. With a stroke of luck, I escaped to the In Between and returned to the inn when I was able to sneak away. It looked like someone had been killed."

"Oh, yes. We're quite aware of that. In fact, it's a bit of a crisis. You might as well come in."

I followed him inside, to the restaurant's private dining room in the rear. The three vampires, Helga, Billy, and Eduardo, were there. Surprisingly, so was Mr. Jubbles.

Tension filled the room. Mr. Jubbles sat at the end of the table, fear straining his jowly face. The other vampires were in chairs pulled close to him, as if they had been interrogating him. Diego sat at the opposite end of the table, and I remained in the doorway.

"Your inn's guest has put us in a pickle," Billy said to me.

"Were you the one who killed that man at the inn?" I asked.

Mr. Jubbles nodded, his jowls jiggling. His bald head was shiny with sweat, even though vampires rarely perspired.

"I was hungry," he said defensively. "And the man I fed on was one of my kidnappers. That rat tortured me. That's why I couldn't stop feeding and drained him. It was emotional eating, that's all."

"When we took the human hostages, we did it to protect ourselves," Diego said to the room. "We sent a message to the regime that if they left us alone, they'd eventually get the hostages back unharmed. But now we've killed a human right in front of their faces."

"I was hungry," Mr. Jubbles whined again. "I saw that man prowling around and recognized him. But I didn't know there were lots of them there."

"The regime is going to come at us with brutal force," Eduardo said.

"It's gonna be vampire-hunting season," Billy added.

Helga said, "We must go on the offensive."

Diego nodded. "I've had secret meetings with Rufus. His says his wolves and other shifters will fight with us. The other guilds haven't committed yet." He glanced at me. "The Magic Guild is currently leaderless, but we have at least one witch who will fight with us. Correct, Sophie?"

I nodded. It looked like I was going to do more than hide in a motel room.

"We can pick off those militia members one by one when the opportunities present themselves," Diego went on. "What I worry about is how involved law enforcement will be. I'd rather not fight them."

"Well, I don't think it's local law enforcement we have to worry about," I said. "Or even the governor."

Everyone turned to look at me. Diego raised a quizzical eyebrow.

"My mother contacted me. She must have used her psychometry to find out that Baldric has done an end run around the governor. He cut a deal with the Faerie Queene to deliver San Marcos to her as the first city to fall. His reward will be to rule over the whole region after the Unseelie Court conquers Florida and the rest of the Southeast."

"How can Baldric deliver our city to the Unseelie Court?" Eduardo asked.

"Perhaps this is why he wants the guilds to support him," Diego suggested. "We supernaturals will be his soldiers to weaken the city and its infrastructure, leaving it vulnerable to the Queene's forces. We need to learn if this truly is his plan."

"I thought you wanted to kill Baldric," Helga said.

"I do. I must wait, though. In the meantime, we'll fight the militia and spy on Baldric."

"Your theory sounds right," I said. "He wants to subjugate supernaturals. And kill me."

"Why kill you?" Helga asked.

"I betrayed the deal I made with him to convince the guilds to support him."

Diego knew, but I couldn't reveal to the others, that Baldric had been ordered to kill me because I knew the governor's secret identity. I couldn't risk having more people know and putting them in danger.

"Well, friends, we are entering a state of war," Diego said.

"We want you to lead us," said Helga. "But the rest of the vampires won't follow you yet."

"You must earn your title of duke by winning the Crucible," Billy added.

"Ah, yes, the Crucible." Diego frowned. "Seems like a waste of effort, and possibly good vampires. But we must follow tradition."

"What happened to simply voting on a leader?" I asked.

Everyone laughed.

"Humans are so naïve," Eduardo said.

Great, I thought. Diego had to risk being destroyed. I might lose him, and our city might lose everything.

CHAPTER 19

DARLA

When I showed up for my morning interview, Detective
Siwicki didn't bring me to one of those cramped, dingy
interrogation rooms with a two-way mirror, like you see in the
cop movies. No, he invited my lawyer and me to a cramped,
dingy, windowless conference room with a long table.

So, I was one step above a suspected criminal.

My attorney, Louie Choco, was not a criminal defense attorney. I'd used him once before to defend the inn against a friv-
olous personal-injury lawsuit: a drunk guest who thought it
would be fun to dive headfirst into our tiny four-foot-deep pool.
But Louie was the only attorney I knew and could get with no
notice.

"Okay, one more time," Siwicki said wearily. "You didn't see
the vampire until he attacked the victim?"

"That is correct," I said. "Like we wrote in the statement we
gave you."

"I prefer to hear it from you. And, you say, you didn't recognize the attacker?"

"Correct. I thought it was your garden-variety mugger. Until I heard the growling and slurping sounds. I realized then that the attacker might not be human."

Louie looked like he was going to get sick. He undid the top button of his too-tight dress shirt.

"At what point did you realize the attacker was your registered guest?"

"After he was finished with . . . what he was doing. That's when I discovered it was Mr. Jubbles and that he was a vampire."

I had to hedge the truth here. I couldn't admit that I knew Mr. Jubbles was a vampire when I gave him a room.

Sure enough, Siwicki asked me if I knew he was a vampire when he booked his room.

"Not at all," I replied. "Mr. Jubbles was a repeat guest. He never showed any signs of being a vampire. On this visit, I noticed he didn't go out during the daytime, but I thought he wasn't feeling well."

The questioning went on and on, with much repetition, until Siwicki had finally had enough.

"Okay." He closed his notebook and looked at Louie. "Please make sure your client is available to testify soon." He turned his gaze to me. "The Supernatural Criminality Act requires me to report this incident to the Florida Department of Business and Professional Regulation. It's entirely their decision whether to revoke your hotel license."

"I understand."

"If they revoke it, you'll need to appeal it with them. And they'll conduct inspections to make sure you don't have any guests at your inn."

"We won't be able to survive without the income," I said, trying not to whine.

"That's what you get for doing business with monsters. And harboring witches."

"My daughter's not a witch. I don't care what the stupid app says."

I was tempted to unload more frustrations on him but bit my tongue and left the station with Louie, who still looked like he was going to throw up.

When I got home, I explained the situation to Cory.

"Are they going to put us out of business?" he asked. "It's like we're in a banana republic."

"I know. There's nothing we can do now but wait to hear from the DBPR. In the meantime, we have an inn to run and guests to serve."

"We're only at thirty percent capacity. All the raids and drama have given us a reputation as a freak show."

"Well, we are going to maintain our reputation for cleanliness, quality, historic charm, and excellent service. Go fix that leak in two-oh-four."

THE INSPECTOR DIDN'T LOOK LIKE A GOVERNMENT bureaucrat. He looked like a has-been actor. You see this type a lot in Florida: a former model or television actor who retired to the Sunshine State, then, his retirement savings coming up short, auditioned for roles in local TV commercials for health insurance companies. In this guy's case, his new role was for the state.

His aging skin had a fake tan—I couldn't tell if it was from tanning booths or makeup. It didn't hide his considerable cosmetic surgery. His thick head of dark-brown hair didn't have signs of gray and appeared to be a toupee.

"I am Frederick Flossman," he announced dramatically when he approached me at the check-in desk—which was only a small table in the rear of the foyer. "I am an inspector for the Florida Department of Business and Professional Regulation."

"Darla Chesswick. What can I do for you?"

"I've been assigned to ascertain your facility's degree of supernatural infractions."

"Look, we were reported because, unbeknownst to us, one of our guests turned out to be a vampire. It will never happen again. You can be sure of that."

"I'm here to make sure of that. I'm an expert in the supernatural and can spot it in any kind of business."

"Are you," I lowered my voice, "supernatural yourself?"

"I once was a renowned stage magician and clairvoyant," he announced proudly.

"But that isn't really supernatural."

"Or is it?" He smiled conspiratorially. "Well then, do you mind if I inspect the premises?"

"Go wild."

He set off down the hallway to the parlor. He studied the room before closing his eyes and holding both index fingers to his temples.

Archibald, in his usual place beneath the fireplace mantel, briefly animated. He studied Mr. Flossman, stuck out his tongue at him, then returned to stone.

"I sense the presence of ghosts in your establishment," Flossman said, opening his eyes.

"Yes." I tried to keep my voice neutral. "We have a few. This place is nearly three hundred years old, and any building this old is likely to have a ghost or two."

"How many do you have?"

"Three, at least."

"Interesting."

He spun on his heel and left the room, never having sensed Archibald. He went down the short hall to the utility room and opened the door. Bella was in the laundry area, putting sheets into a washing machine.

He cleared his throat. "Excuse me, dear. Are you human?"

"I beg your pardon?" Bella asked.

"Are you human or a supernatural creature?"

"I'm just a regular human. Nothing special about me."

"We're all special in one way or another, dear."

He gave her a dramatic bow and returned down the hallway.

Over the years, the utility room had seen its share of supernatural activity, having been attacked by vampires, faeries, and a mob of humans who were pacified with magic. Vampires had been staked and faeries killed there. A demon had also visited our utility room. To my senses, the place reeked of the supernatural. Flossman had detected none of it.

I followed the inspector down the hall and back through the foyer. He passed the storage closet, where Mr. Jubbles had been killed and turned into a vampire, without stopping.

Flossman took his time examining the kitchen, where a faerie had been killed recently, and a vampire was sleeping in a crawlspace behind one of the refrigerators. Flossman did his schtick of closing his eyes and touching his forehead.

After a few minutes, he announced, "Blood has been shed in this kitchen."

By this point, I doubted he had sensed the faerie's demise in here.

"I've cut my finger more than once on the cutting board," I said.

"Hmm. Perhaps that's what it was. Let's move on."

He wandered through the dining and living rooms. Like most

of the inn, magic or some sort of supernatural activity had occurred in these rooms, but apparently not enough for Flossman to detect.

We stepped out into the courtyard.

"This is where the man was murdered by the vampire?" Flossman asked.

"Yes, unfortunately."

The inspector walked over to the fountain, stopping short, and staring at the brick pavers below it. Jerry was on the wall, water gushing from his mouth. He winked at me.

"The murder happened here," Flossman declared.

"No. It happened over there." I pointed to a spot near the outer wall of the inn.

He approached the spot. "There's no blood stain."

"Correct. The vampire didn't spill any blood. He was starving."

Flossman shuddered at the thought. He closed his eyes and did his psychic pantomime. "Yes. It happened here recently. How horrible." He scanned the rest of the courtyard. "Do guests stay in that cottage?"

"No. That's where my husband and I live."

"I see."

He showed no interest in touring the site of many supernatural incidents and marched back into the inn.

"Please show me your registry of the guests currently staying here."

We returned to the foyer, and I pulled up our registration software on the laptop.

"Only three rooms are occupied," I said, pointing to the screen. "Business has been bad, thanks to rumors about supernatural activity here."

I didn't mention that the inn being attacked recently by a

frenzied mob of anti-monster vigilantes didn't help business. An additional kook firing his gun downstairs, and the invasion of the inn by an extremist militia ending in a murder the other night, didn't help either. The guests we had when those events took place left online reviews that were, shall we say, unkind.

"What's this room on the third floor that's blocked off in the registry?" Flossman asked.

"My daughter lives there."

"I need to search for traces of the supernatural in the rooms. Don't worry, I won't go into occupied guest rooms. I can sense the supernatural through their doors."

"I bet you can."

We began with the one-bedroom suite—our only suite—on the ground floor next to the utility room. It hadn't been occupied in ages, ever since I was forced to host a contingent of faeries there (long story). Flossman's psychic powers gave him no clue the Fae had been there.

Flossman wasn't a guy I wanted to share a tiny elevator with, so we took the stairs to the second floor. We went from room to room, him doing his pantomime in the center of each one. At the occupied rooms, he did it while pressing his forehead to their doors.

Flossman didn't find any evidence of the supernatural, even in Mr. Jubbles' recently cleared room. Our resident ghosts were aloof. The Elvis impersonator didn't appear, nor did the murdered nineteenth-century bride.

Ironically, only the ghost of Darren, the previous owner, made an appearance. He walked out of the bathroom of 203 and then passed through the wall. I thought Flossman would have a heart attack.

"Are you okay?"

"Yes. I'm fine." He pressed his palm against his chest. "Never saw a ghost before. Fortunately for you, ghosts are not illegal."

"That's so reassuring."

We were about to wrap things up when Cory ruined everything.

The final vacant room we entered was 204. Its entry door had been propped open, so Cory didn't hear us enter. The door to the bathroom, where Cory was working, had also been propped open, giving us a full view of Cory with his back to us.

The view of his plumber's crack above his belt as he squatted wasn't the worst part. It was the various tools magically hovering in the air, staying within easy reach for him.

Flossman stared at the levitating tools, his eyes blinking in disbelief.

"How-how-how are those tools floating in the air?"

Cory turned around, startled. When he saw Flossman, the tools dropped to the tile floor with a loud clatter.

"Hi," Cory said. "Just fixing a leak."

"Do you mind pulling up the back of your trousers, please?" I asked him.

He stood, flustered, and complied with my request.

"You're a witch, aren't you?" Flossman asked Cory, growing angry.

"Not at all," Cory said with a fake smile. "You must be imagining things."

"Or a warlock, or whatever you call yourself. I can sense the witchcraft in here. Don't you dare deny it!"

"It's just a little-known tradesman's trick," I said. "An illusion. Like you performed when you were a stage magician."

"Don't give me your poppycock! You're an illegal sorcerer, and I shall report you. Your hotel permit is revoked, beginning now. Your current guests must check out, and no more are allowed to stay here."

Flossman pushed past me on his way through the door.

"But this is our home. We can still stay here, correct?" I pleaded.

"If it's within the law, I suppose so."

I watched him scurry to the stairs and disappear from view.

"Oh no," Cory said. "Did I just single-handedly destroy our livelihood?" He looked devastated.

I gave him a quick squeeze. "It would have happened eventually. We have too many enemies now, coming at us from every direction."

"I guess I'll have to find a job. But if I get reported as a witch, there goes my background check."

"You can find work as a plumber. You have the butt for it."

"Do you think we can still rent rooms without a license, off the record?"

"Let me think about it. Finish fixing the leak, and we'll worry about this later."

Bella was waiting for me at the foot of the stairs. "What did the inspector say?" she asked, visibly upset.

"He's suspending our license. But don't worry, Bella, we'll keep you on staff for as long as we can."

"Don't bother. I'm quitting. I'm done with supernaturals and all their craziness. You can mail my last paycheck."

Just like that, she walked out the door. All those years of being like a member of our family meant nothing anymore.

I was stunned. And I was also frozen.

You see, I suddenly found myself in Ehrendil. I hoped Cory had gone back to work, so he wouldn't discover my body left standing beside the staircase like a mannequin.

My astral self was in a room that had obviously been carved

from the interior of a tree trunk. Leighnel burst through the door, his fine-featured face filled with concern.

"Our scouts tell me a detachment of faeries has been spotted near San Marcos—soldiers of the Unseelie Court. This is the closest they've been to the city since their previous invasion attempt."

"Why are you telling me this?" I asked.

He looked surprised. "I thought you'd want to know, so you could alert your army."

"We don't have an army. I mean, the United States has an awesome military, and Florida has its National Guard. But, despite the Great Unmasking, no humans know the Fae exist. No one would take this news seriously. Except for our governor and some of her allies. And they would only sell us out to the Fae."

Leighnel shook his head. "Very sad. Who fought against the Unseelie Court when they threatened your city before?"

"A motley crew of guild members. The leader of the guilds is also on the side of the Fae now."

"Then you must handle this emergency."

"Why aren't the Elves handling it?"

"First, San Marcos is a human city. Second, our king insists on honoring our peace treaty with the Fae. I'm doing my best to disrupt their attempts to harvest phytolucine, but we can't help you stop their invasion."

"I can't stop it," I said, frustrated. "I have the help of two powerful witches, but we can't stop an army. We need to recruit guild members."

"Today, at the very least, you must discover what the Fae soldiers are doing so close to your city. I don't believe they're searching for phytolucine. I think they're up to something else.

You need to find out what it is. If they can operate freely this close to your city, you humans are in trouble."

It was annoying to have my species criticized by another, but he was right.

"Tell me where they are."

When he gave me the location, and I pictured it in my mind, I finally appreciated the gravity of the situation.

"A giant shopping center is going to be built there! Those faeries are defiling our religion of consumerism!"

I didn't know where Sophie was, but I needed her now.

CHAPTER 20

SOPHIE

"Cheating isn't just allowed, it's encouraged," Helga told me as we sat together on a fallen tree trunk.

We were miles from town in what appeared to be an abandoned quarry, surrounded by pine woods and illuminated by a half-moon. The couple hundred or so vampires who made up the Clan of the Eternal Night were scattered around the fighting ring at the center of the quarry, waiting for the Crucible to begin.

I'd never been in the presence of so many vampires before. Two hundred-plus bloodsuckers were a lot of individuals to blend into a small city like San Marcos and the surrounding towns. But our community was the oldest in North America, and since vampires don't die naturally, their population grows, even with rules that limit turning humans into new vampires.

"Why is cheating encouraged?" I asked Helga. "It doesn't seem fair."

"This isn't an athletic competition seeking the best fighter," she explained. "It's seeking the best leader, a fighter as well as a politician. Vampires, just like humans, lie, cheat, and betray their friends. I hate to say it, but we vampires are even more sneaky and manipulative than humans. We need leaders who can survive that."

"How do you decide who wins?"

"If you're pushed or thrown from the ring, you have ten seconds to return. If you don't, you've lost. Some fighters forfeit by voluntarily leaving the ring. If you're destroyed, you've obviously lost. The winner is the only vampire remaining in the ring."

Diego stepped into the ring, which was covered in white sugar sand and surrounded with a low circular wall of limestone cut before the quarry was abandoned over a hundred years ago. He wore tight breeches and was shirtless, his black skin contrasting with the white sand in the moonlight.

He was slim and of medium height, his black hair closely cropped. Despite his unimpressive size, the muscles of his arms and torso were sharply defined and rippled with his every movement.

Two male opponents entered the ring. A squat, muscular vampire with a black beard, and a tall, lean one who had the physique of a ballet dancer. Diego's opponents were both Caucasian with alabaster-white skin.

Helga had explained that Crucibles could include as many as two dozen contestants of any gender. But tonight, only three contestants meant Diego was respected and feared.

"There hasn't been a Crucible for centuries," she said. "Pedro was the leader here, as the first vampire in San Marcos. About a hundred and fifty years later, he was challenged and defeated in a Crucible. But only a few years later, Pedro called for a new Crucible and won. He'd been our duke since then, until Diego destroyed him during the vampire plague and Lethia seized power."

"Who are his opponents tonight?" I asked.

"The vampire with the beard, Mark, really hated Lethia and transferred his hatred to Diego. He claims that Diego's relationship with Lethia proved he is weak. The tall guy, Albert, is your typical slimy politician who has always been vying to be duke."

An elderly vampire, whom I recognized but didn't know, rang a small portable gong. The crowd went silent, and the three vampires circled each other in the ring.

"The contestants can't bring weapons," Helga said. "But the crowd can use or provide them."

"What? That's crazy!"

"If your supporters are passionate enough to interfere, it means you have a mandate to lead. The interference must be reasonable, of course. You can't toss a hand grenade into the ring. The guy who rang the gong is the judge."

My heart thudded with anxiety about Diego.

The wary circling of the contestants ended with lightning-fast moves I could barely follow. The three fought each other with kickboxing moves, biting, and slashing. They wrestled in the sand, punched each other toe to toe, and flew into the air, fighting like birds of prey.

I noticed the other two seemed to be teaming up against Diego. I mentioned this to Helga.

"A common strategy is for the weaker vampires to conspire to work together to defeat the stronger ones," she said. "Then the weaker ones fight each other. It's just like politics, isn't it?"

"I think of politics more as organized bribery than combat."

"For humans, yes. Not vampires."

Diego jumped several feet into the air, kicked Mark in the

head, did a backflip, and kicked Albert in the neck. Both dropped to the sand.

An audience member brandishing a dagger jumped into the ring behind Diego's back, and the crowd buzzed.

"Behind you!" someone shouted.

Diego turned just as the vampire with the knife lunged at him. A kick sent the knife flying over the crowd, and Diego flung the vampire after it.

The crowd roared, laughing and applauding.

Mark had risen to his feet and caught Diego off guard, tackling him. The two wrestled, their moves almost too fast for me to see. Before I knew it, Mark was on top, his hands wrapped around Diego's neck, choking him.

Diego's struggles were faltering. The tall vampire, Albert, kicked him in the head.

"Can vampires die of strangulation?" I asked Helga.

"No. They can't be destroyed that way, but they can lose consciousness."

And that's what was happening. Diego tried bucking his body to get Mark off him, but he was weakening. Albert crouched beside him, holding his shoulders to the ground.

"If you lose consciousness, do you lose the contest?" I asked.

"If one of your opponents tosses you from the ring. Or destroys you."

The crowd gasped. Someone had tossed a sharpened wooden stake into the ring.

Albert picked it up and held it over his head as he walked around the ring, engaging the crowd, which was roaring. Some were protesting, not wanting Diego to be staked. Others egged Albert on.

Diego was barely moving now, with Mark atop him, still

strangling him. Mark saw that Albert had the stake and shifted his body to expose Diego's chest.

Albert approached and placed the sharpened point of the stake on Diego's chest. He laughed and looked at the crowd, holding his other hand with a thumb up, then down.

I broke out in a sweat. I couldn't let Diego be staked like this in front of me. It was barbaric, and, yes, I didn't want to lose him.

If the audience could take part, why couldn't I?

I focused on Albert and sensed his emotions: ambition, hatred, jealousy of Diego, excitement, bloodlust. But he also hated Mark, whom he planned to destroy after Diego.

I quickly cast the spell Orlena had created for me. I increased Albert's hatred of Mark, adding anger and resentment. *Everyone likes Mark better than me*, I made him feel.

I imagined how the crowd would react if Albert surprised them, how the roars would make him feel like a victor.

Pushing these emotions into him, I persuaded him to change his plan.

With dramatic, exaggerated movements, Albert raised the stake above Diego's chest. But instead of plunging it straight downward, he pivoted and thrust it into the center of Mark's back.

Mark screamed. The crowd roared.

And Mark deteriorated into dust that sprinkled upon Diego and the white sand.

Albert relished the crowd's enjoyment of his surprise move. Now, I manipulated his emotions further, making him want to create more suspense and drama, to force the crowd to idolize him.

I don't want to stake Diego. I'll pretend I'm going to do it, then toss the stake aside. It will prove that I'm brave and strong enough to defeat Diego with my bare hands.

He stepped around Diego's prone body, flourishing the stake as if it were a sword. The crowd roared in anticipation.

Meanwhile, I connected with Diego's emotions. His vampire powers were rejuvenating him as he breathed again. He remained on the ground, pretending he was still disabled.

Albert stopped in his tracks and loomed over Diego's body. He raised the stake above his head in both hands, pointing it at Diego, ready to drive it into his chest.

Instead, he flung the stake aside. The crowd went crazy.

While Albert soaked in the crowd's reaction, Diego struck like a snake. Faster than my eyes could register, he jumped onto his feet, grabbed Albert's torso, and tossed him into the crowd.

"Ten . . . nine . . . eight," the referee chanted as Albert pushed through the crowd to return to the ring. Some vampires helped push him through, while others tried to hinder him.

". . . four . . . three . . . two. . . "

Albert jumped down into the ring.

But Diego caught him before his feet landed and tossed him back into the crowd.

Laughter broke out as Albert struggled to return, the referee counting down the seconds.

This time, when Albert jumped back into the ring, he was ready, kicking Diego in the stomach. Diego returned with two roundhouse punches to Albert's head.

He grabbed the stunned vampire and tossed him out of the ring again.

My spell was still active, and I pushed emotions into Albert: compassion toward Diego, respect for him, a feeling of cooperation.

Diego will reward me if I accept him as my new duke.

Albert paused before jumping into the ring. Blood streamed down his face, and he seemed internally conflicted.

The vampires of the Clan will love me because they love Diego.

". . . three . . . two . . ."

Albert raised his hand.

"I concede!" he shouted to the referee.

The crowd erupted with applause and cheers—for Albert as well as Diego.

Helga leaned toward me and whispered, "You used magic, didn't you? I sensed it."

"Say nothing to Diego, please."

The referee rang his gong, then ran over to Diego, seized his arm, and pushed it skyward, calling out, "I present to you Diego, Duke of the Clan of the Eternal Night!"

The crowd roared, both from enjoyment of the spectacle and relief that their wait for a new leader was over. Many poured into the ring to congratulate Diego. Several vampires gave Albert pats on the back as well.

Helga and I got up from our seats on the fallen tree and waited at the edge of the ring for Diego to be free of his admirers. Billy and Eduardo joined us.

"I'm sure glad that ended the way it did," Billy said.

"It wasn't like Albert to behave so gallantly," Eduardo said. "It wasn't like him at all."

Helga looked at me, dying to reveal that I had used magic. I subtly shook my head at her.

Finally, Diego climbed up out of the ring and joined us. We all hugged him, me the longest of all.

"I saw my entire existence flash before my eyes when Albert was about to stake me," Diego said. "I was too weak to escape Mark's stranglehold."

"I think he staked Mark instead to surprise everyone and crank up the drama," said Billy.

"Indeed," Diego replied. "He had been teaming up with Mark to defeat me, so I never expected him to turn on him."

"Are you going to reward him for his decision?" Billy asked.

"Yes. But I'll also watch him for signs of future treachery. Anyway, I don't know about you guys, but I'm famished."

"Shall we go hunting?" Helga asked.

"It's too dangerous in this climate," Diego replied. "Let's go to the cattle ranch outside of town."

"Bovine blood is not a meal befitting the new duke of our Clan."

"It is for a duke committed to keeping his vampires safe."

I took my leave and drove Mom's scooter to my current choice in my rotation of seedy motels. The overnight clerk, working behind bulletproof glass, accepted my cash for the night.

I was in bed, but not asleep, when my phone rang. It was Diego.

"I can't believe you used magic to help me!" he shouted.

"You're welcome."

"You've undermined my victory."

"No," I said patiently. "Spectators are allowed to interfere in the contest. Like the vampire with the knife. And the stake that was thrown into the ring. Right? I only used a bit of empath magic to help Albert change his mind about staking you."

"I didn't need your help."

"You were about to be skewered in the heart. Are you having a tantrum because I'm a woman? Is that what this is all about?"

"No. That is, I am very traditional. Remember, I have been around for five hundred years."

"And you've learned to adapt to changing times."

"You saved me from Lethia, too."

"Friends don't let friends get drained by ex-lovers."

"You're a friend." He said it in a flat, matter-of-fact tone.

"I am." I wished we were more than friends, but I couldn't say that. "The crisis we face now is too big for anyone to go it alone. We must work together and have each other's backs. There's no place for excessive pride or misogyny."

"Hey, that's not fair!"

"If I were a male witch, would you be so upset I helped you with magic?"

He paused. "I believe I would. Being helped by magic undermines my victory. And my place as duke of the Clan."

"I know I'm an outsider, but a Crucible is the worst way to pick a leader."

"The tradition has existed for vampires since the Dark Ages."

"Jeez Louise, that shows you how enlightened it is. You're the best leader of the Clan. You could have been destroyed tonight, and your people would have ended up with a mediocre leader whose only talent is treachery. There are too many adversaries against supernaturals now for us to survive if we have lousy people leading us."

"I see your point."

"How generous of you."

"Listen, Sophie, it's been a long night. I'm in no mood for your sarcasm."

"Got it. So, what are your next steps after consolidating your power?"

"Force the militia from our city. Then, I kill Baldric."

"I thought we were going to wait to kill him."

"You mentioned treachery," Diego said, anger building in his voice. "He's the most treacherous of anyone."

I couldn't argue with that. "Let me know how I can help you fight."

"I will. I still believe you should reveal the governor's secret to the public."

"I'm coming around to doing that. It's scary. Making the announcement must be done properly for maximal effect. Right? I can't let the news outlets quash it. It has to go viral quickly. And I'm afraid the governor and Poxton will still try to kill me to help them shut down the story."

"You have me, and the entire Clan, to protect you."

"Thank you. And congratulations on your victory tonight. You truly deserved it."

"Sleep well."

There was still some sulking in his voice, but hopefully he wasn't too angry with me.

I tried to sleep as it neared dawn. Being unable to return to the inn meant I could keep any hours I liked. It seemed like I would have to adjust my circadian rhythm to keep vampire hours from now on. If I was going to fight alongside them, I'd have to stay awake all night, every night.

However, my ringing phone awoke me from a deep sleep seemingly minutes later. Dirty sunlight seeped through the motel room's cheap curtains, and my phone said it was 7:35 a.m. It was Mom calling.

"Mom, is everything okay?" I asked in a sluggish voice.

"It's the Fae. A scouting party is just outside the city. I don't know if they're looking for phytolucine or doing reconnaissance for their future invasion. I need your battle magic."

"What does this have to do with us?"

"Good question. Meet me at the construction site on the county road as soon as you can."

She ended the call. This was crazy. Why were an innkeeper and her daughter going into battle with the Fae?

I guess I'd find out soon enough.

CHAPTER 21

DARLA

As the population grew in San Marcos, and everywhere else in Florida, cities spread outward like stains. New suburbs appeared outside of older ones. Exurbs popped up even further from the cities.

And we're not talking about pioneers with axes clearing land and building log cabins. This was systematic development on an industrial scale. Giant swathes of farmland and forest in what had once been rural areas were scraped away by giant diesel excavators and turned into generic subdivisions and box-store retail centers surrounded by seas of asphalt parking lots.

Cory drove me past the exurbs outside of San Marcos to a massive wasteland of cleared dirt that awaited construction. On its edges were the remains of a forest that might face a similar fate.

"It's hard to believe people are living out here now," Cory said, parking. "This used to be the boonies. San Marcos was such a tiny city."

"It's still tiny," I replied. "I don't consider these developments part of our city. They're just ticky-tacky sprawl."

"So, we came all the way out here because your Elf friend, Leighnel, said Fae were spotted here?"

"Yes. That's what I said."

"Why aren't the Elves here to stop the Fae?"

"Because the Elves and Fae are not at war. And the Elves want to avoid one at all costs. Leighnel has been monitoring foreign Fae activity because he's concerned about their harvesting of phytolucine. That's how he spotted faeries in the area."

"They're here to harvest phytolucine?"

"No," I said, my tone grim. "He thinks they're an advance party preparing for an invasion. Finally, here's Sophie."

The high-pitched buzz of a motor signaled the arrival of Sophie on my scooter. I was relieved to see she was wearing my helmet.

She parked beside the SUV. We were in a gravel parking lot just off the county road at the edge of the cleared land.

"Yikes!" Sophie exclaimed. "This used to be a forest and a field with cows grazing."

"And it could end up being a battlefield tonight," I said, explaining what I had told Cory about the Fae and how the Elves wouldn't stop them, so it was up to us to do it.

"Why is it up to us?" she asked. "That's not fair."

"Who else is there? The supernatural guilds should be united to fight the Unseelie Court, but Baldric won't allow that because he agreed to deliver San Marcos to the Faerie Queene. The governor will submit to the Fae, too. She also seems to be trying to keep the existence of faeries away from public awareness."

"Yeah, because she's one of them," said Sophie.

"That leaves the police," Cory said. "Will they help us stop the Fae?"

"They will do what they can to protect the city, but they're awfully busy persecuting supernaturals," I said. "Besides, they're a small department. They can't face an army."

"Oh, but we can?" Cory snarked.

"You two have magic. And I have the Goddess. Plus, we're facing a patrol, not an army."

"Where are they?" Sophie asked.

I told her I suspected they were underground. "They're using existing tunnels or building new ones. They usually only come out in the open above ground at night, so if we have a battle, it will be tonight. Today, I want to locate their tunnels and see how much we can mess with them without going underground ourselves."

For us to go into the tunnels would require being shrunk to faerie size, and we didn't have the magic to do that. Nor the inclination. After being held underground, imprisoned by the Fae, I wouldn't go down there again even if a pot of gold awaited me.

"Come with me, family," I said with a trace of bitterness. "We have no guests at the inn to serve. Our new job is fighting faeries."

"And non-supernatural humans," Sophie added.

"Maybe it's time to move to Canada," said Cory.

"That's what Americans always say when politics turn against us here." I began plodding across the cleared dirt. "But evil knows no boundaries."

I looked back to see if they were following me. They were still standing there in the gravel parking lot. I gave them my trademark angry scowl, which made them jump to attention and hurry to catch up.

I asked Cory and Sophie to use whatever magic spells they had that could locate faeries underground. All three of us were naturally sensitive to the presence of the supernatural, such as the magic even everyday faeries had a touch of. But we couldn't depend on this ability to penetrate the earth.

"Harvesting ley lines has taught me how to find magical energy underground," Cory said. "Even if it's faint compared to ley lines."

"I have a spell that heightens my senses," said Sophie. "I'll listen for any work going on down there. Also, my empath senses might alert me to intelligent beings."

"Have at it," I said. "I'm going to draw in as much of the Goddess's power as she'll allow. I'm hoping that will help us."

"Why would faeries be in this specific location?" Sophie asked me before we separated for the search. "Is there something about the destruction of land that attracts them?"

"Leighnel told me only that they were here."

"It could be because of the shopping center that will be built," Cory said. "The Fae could take it over before it's completed and use it to shelter and stage large numbers of their soldiers."

I shuddered at the thought of hundreds or thousands of faeries swarming inside big-box stores.

"There's another possible reason," I said. "There are no trees here."

"Why does that matter?" Cory asked.

"No trees, no roots. The excavators tore the trees from the ground along with most of their roots."

I reminded them about the faeries Leighnel and I had witnessed being killed by tree roots.

"The trees killed the faeries because they were harvesting

phytolucine. The trees were empowered by Danu, and she couldn't have done it if it weren't for me."

"You didn't direct the trees to kill the faeries," Sophie said.

"I had nothing to do with it. My mere presence on earth as Danu's human vessel enabled her to influence the trees."

"Could you make the trees attack if you wanted them to?" Sophie asked.

"I suppose I could when in full goddess mode. If I wanted to witness that horror again."

"Could come in handy, Mom. I'm serious."

"Let's concentrate on searching now. The day is wasting away. If you get any sign of something below you, mark the location with one of these."

I opened my satchel and handed out pencils to Cory and Sophie. I had tied orange plastic strips on them.

"These are the Esperanza Inn logo pencils we put in the guest rooms," Sophie said. "We have a shortage of them."

"We might not need them anymore."

"Mom, don't say that. Our inn has been around since 1736. It survived the American Revolution, the Civil War, lots of civil unrest, and plenty of economic downturns. We'll get through this."

I nodded with a fake smile and marched across the raw earth flattened by, and imprinted with, excavator treads.

We fanned out across the acres of cleared land, working in grid patterns like searchers after an earthquake or bombing, looking for signs of life buried below. We did it for hours under a scorching sun, taking a break only for a lunch of sandwiches Sophie brought back from the nearest deli.

The Goddess had not blessed me with her powers today, but I could sense supernatural activity underground. Sophie and Cory had each left several pencils sticking out of the dirt. We still had much unexplored territory to cover, but the markers my family had left were already telling a story.

The bulk of the markers were clustered near the center of the cleared acreage, where most of the supernatural energy was located. There were also markers leading from the woods to the center, indicating winding tunnels.

"It's freaky to realize there are faeries beneath that land right now," Sophie said, chomping on a sandwich in the back seat of the SUV. We were taking our lunch break in there with the air conditioning running.

"Do you guys have any magic that can attack or disrupt the faeries?" I asked.

"I would need a power boost from ley lines to send any blasting magic through that much earth," Cory said.

"Yeah, I would need them to come out into the open for my attack magic to work," said Sophie. "I have a shockwave spell that might cave in their tunnels, though."

"Good," I said. "Save it for tonight."

"Tonight? We have to be out here tonight?"

"Of course. Did you think we just came here for a picnic?"

After we ate, I forced everyone out from the air conditioning and back out onto the sun-blasted dirt. By the time the sun had set, we'd covered a good portion of the land.

The consensus was that the Fae had tunneled from the surrounding forest to a large underground chamber—a natural cavern or a room they had created themselves. What were they doing in there?

And the amount of energy we detected meant the chamber wasn't filled with soldiers but rather had magic of some sort taking place there.

We ate a light meal of leftover sandwiches after sunset, and I decided it was time to force a confrontation.

Cory drove the SUV out of the parking lot and across the county road, leaving it far enough away that the Fae wouldn't notice it if they surfaced. Unfortunately, this meant it would be more difficult should we need to escape if a skirmish broke out.

"Based on your markers, there are three tunnels leading to the central chamber," I said. "Sophie, use your spell to collapse the tunnels."

"You want to force the faeries out onto the surface?"

"Yes. We need to drive them away from here. And I'd like to know what they've been up to down there."

Cory and I took cover on our stomachs in the dirt, halfway between the parking lot and where we estimated the underground chamber to be. Sophie walked away into the darkness. I could see her faintly in the light of the rising moon, but it was easier to track her via the beam of the flashlight she carried.

I couldn't see the pencil markers from here, but she stopped at three places across the swath of land, spending a few minutes at each one.

My supernatural senses perked up at the presence of magic, and the ground vibrated slightly.

After her third stop, Sophie sprinted across the construction site to join Cory and me.

"Done, done, and done," she whispered.

We waited.

"The faeries down there are getting agitated," Sophie said. "They must have discovered the cave-ins."

"If they come out, you need to capture at least one of them," I whispered. "Use your immobility spell."

We waited some more.

Illuminated by the moonlight, a small mound appeared in the dirt near where we believed the chamber to be. The mound rose in height. It was like an anthill dug from below.

A head popped up. A faerie-sized creature crawled out of the ground and ran toward the tree line. Sophie tensed and magic tingled against my skin.

Another faerie crawled out. Seconds after it began to run, it froze as if having a seizure and dropped to the ground.

"Wait," I whispered.

Two more faeries emerged. When they ran toward the woods, they saw their fallen comrade. Balls of fire soared through the air toward us.

"A sorcerer!" Sophie hissed.

She pulled her sword from its scabbard, and the buzz of energy filled my ears. Purple lightning shot from her sword toward the tiny figures out on the cleared field.

One of them dropped to the ground. But the balls of fire kept coming, landing just in front of us. Cory cursed and stomped out flames that sprang up on his shirtsleeve.

Shooting fireballs was in Cory's wheelhouse. He gave back as good as he got. More faeries climbed to the surface but were quickly felled by Sophie's lightning and Cory's fireballs.

The incoming fireballs from the sorcerer ceased.

We waited for a while, glancing at each other. There was no movement out in the field.

"Let's go interrogate our immobilized faerie," I said. "Spread out when you approach him."

We fanned out, just in case another burst of fireballs came. As we neared the emergency exit the faeries had used, I saw crumpled bodies. One of them wore the red robes of a sorcerer. I relaxed a bit upon seeing him.

The faerie Sophie had enchanted lay on her back, staring at us with terror. Yes, it was a female faerie. I remained silent so I wouldn't interfere with Sophie's interrogation.

But Sophie didn't say anything. She knelt beside the fallen

faerie and put her hand on the monkey-sized creature's shoulder, staying silent while she sensed her captive's emotions.

Finally, Sophie spoke in broken Fae with the aid of a translation amulet the local faerie Gorkee had given her.

The fallen faerie's responses were curt.

Sophie turned to me. "There is something important and highly secret going on underground. This faerie is more afraid of revealing it than of dying. From what I can piece together, there's a laboratory down there where they're creating powerful magic."

"Oh my god," I said. "Are they using phytolucine in the lab?"

"She wouldn't say, of course. But I think so. All I could get from her was that it's a secret weapon. I think the Fae are much further along with their spell to wipe out humans than we believed."

The hum of a car's engine and the crunch of gravel came from the parking area behind us. A searchlight beam swept across the cleared land, stopping when it captured us, blinding me.

"Stop what you're doing," said a male voice on a loudspeaker. "Sheriff's office. Raise your hands and approach my vehicle."

CHAPTER 22

SOPHIE

S tumbling blindly into the searchlight like zombies in an old movie, we approached the patrol car. It was from the St. James County Sheriff's Office. How were we going to explain what we were doing out here? What would the deputy think when he saw the faerie bodies in the dirt?

Because we weren't within San Marcos city limits, we were in the jurisdiction of the county sheriff. I hoped his office wasn't prejudiced against my family like the city police were.

When we reached the car, the deputy searched the cleared land, swinging the searchlight attached to his car beside the side view mirror, back and forth.

I saw no signs of the faeries. The one I had questioned had surely run away into the forest after I released the immobility spell, but what had happened to the dead bodies? Had they been removed already by the survivors?

The deputy turned off the searchlight, stepped toward us from his patrol car, and blinded us again with a flashlight.

"I received reports of fireworks out here," he said. "Were y'all responsible?"

The deputy was a young, gangly fellow with thick-lensed glasses.

"Yes, sir," Cory said. "We're preparing for a big show we'll put on for the Fourth of July. We figured it was safe on this giant piece of cleared land."

"You're trespassing on this land. And you're not supposed to use fireworks except on designated holidays."

"We're so sorry, Deputy," Mom said with exaggerated charm.

"Though the kids in my neighborhood shoot 'em off all the time," the deputy muttered.

I'd left my sword hidden beneath its duffel bag, tucked in a furrow in the dirt, when the searchlight had first appeared. Without it, we looked like a typical middle-class family. A law-abiding one.

"I was just thinking this was empty land, with no risk of starting a fire," Cory said.

"A developer owns it," the deputy replied.

"It was stupid of me. We'll never do it again."

Cory had such a goofy, aw-shucks demeanor, he looked completely harmless.

"Let me see your identification, please."

We each pulled out our driver's licenses and handed them to the deputy. He shined his flashlight on them, glanced at our faces, then took the licenses to his car.

"Please wait here while I run these."

The deputy climbed into his car and turned on the interior light. He typed on his laptop mounted beside his seat and swiped the licenses through a reader attached to the laptop.

I worried a little while we stood there beside his car. We all had sparkling clean records, no arrests or violations for any of us, despite all the supernatural shenanigans we'd been involved with over the years.

But my info was in the Monster Monitor app. I reminded myself that it was a commercial app and had nothing to do with law enforcement. I doubted it would be connected to their database.

The deputy spoke into his radio, then got out of the car, looking anxious. He returned our licenses but asked us to remain where we were.

"We have a few more questions to ask you."

"*We?*" I asked.

"Yes. A team member is joining us."

Backup. He had called for backup. Why? The thought of fleeing crossed my mind, but I quickly squelched it. The news was full of suspects who fled from the cops, and it never ended well for them. It was much safer for us to use the gift of gab and talk our way out of this. Right?

Headlights approached, and another patrol car parked on the other side of us. The deputy who got out was big and mean-looking.

The original deputy walked up to me and grabbed my arms, twisting my body around with my arms behind me. Metal hand-cuffs encircled my wrists and clicked shut. The second deputy stood nearby and glowered, ready to inflict violence on my family or me if we resisted.

"Sophie Grimes," the first deputy said to me. I went by the last name I was baptized with from my father, Mom's first husband. "You're under arrest for threatening a public official."

"What is this about?" Cory demanded.

"What public official?" Mom asked.

"The governor. Ma'am, please step into the car," he said, pushing me into the back seat of the patrol car.

I sat down with my hands cuffed uncomfortably behind me, my mind reeling, my heart racing.

This was real. Baldric truly did tell the governor I knew that she and Senator Poxton were faeries. Not only were they sending the militia after me, but law enforcement too.

I was in deep doo-doo.

And what's with calling me "ma'am" instead of "miss"? I'm not that old. Am I?

Through the rear window, I got a brief glimpse of Mom, her face hysterical, Cory's arms wrapped around her, before we drove away.

WE DROVE ALONG THE ROAD, HEADING FOR THE COUNTY JAIL. And I was trying not to lose my mind. Short mental videos played of what I was expecting for the booking, holding cell, intake, abusive staff, hostile inmates. Mom and Cory would surely call a lawyer right away.

But then the paranoid part of my brain took over.

Why should I expect to be treated like a normal prisoner? I was being arrested because of the damaging information I knew. The governor had sent a paramilitary organization to get me. The trumped-up charge of threatening a public official was meant only to trick law enforcement into arresting me.

The governor would not allow me to be put through the justice system where I could blab my secret to anyone who'd listen. No, they were going to silence me extrajudicially.

After I arrived at the county jail, I'd be "transferred" somewhere. Namely, to an unmarked grave.

I assumed someone from the militia would put the bullets in my head. They were the governor's private, off-the-books, goon squad. Her secret enforcers.

The irony struck me. I used to be an enforcer for the Executive Council of the Supernatural Guilds. At first, I had merely enforced the rules. Then the Council made me use violence, even deadly force, to take out rogue vampires.

I quit that dirty job and would forever bear the stain and shame of it. Now, an enforcer would take *me* out, probably before I even made it through the night.

I had to escape. My magic and my empath powers were my only weapons. Would they be enough?

I had no idea. I had no plan. Which meant I had no hope.

Calm down, girl, and think.

First, I reached out with my empath powers to assess what kind of adversary I had with this deputy.

He was young. Very nervous. He was confident in his skill at arresting perpetrators and delivering them to the jail. But he sensed there was something odd about me and this charge against me. He wondered if I was more dangerous than the warrant for my arrest implied.

Good news for me: he felt insecure that the other deputy wasn't following him to the jail. But why would he? I was handcuffed and locked in the back of the car. All the deputy had to do, he thought, was drive me to the jail and remove me from the car. There were plenty of personnel at the jail to back him up.

I must escape this car en route to the jail. There was no hope for me once I got there.

So, how could I get out of there?

My empath powers were not powerful enough to make the deputy release me. That would be against his best interest and all his instincts. I didn't have magic powerful enough to control someone like a marionette.

The best I could do with his emotions would be to make him feel complacent and trusting of me, so he'd let his guard down and increase my chances of escaping.

Then, if I escaped, I could do the opposite: make him so scared of me that his pursuit would be lackluster. Yes, I would use these emotions on him when the time was right.

Next, the tricky part. How the heck could I stop the car and get out? I was pretty good at sleep and immobility spells, but using them on the deputy would kill us both in a crash. Even if I used a protection spell on myself, I might get hurt.

What else? I could create a smoke-bomb spell, which would force him to pull over, but that would be risky, too. Or I could make him hallucinate something.

I reminded myself to K.I.S.S. Keep It Simple, Sophie.

Calming my racing heart, I focused inwardly, gathering my internal energies. Next, I focused outwardly and drew energy from the elements.

What I did after that was simple, yet powerful. I sent a blast of pure energy into the car's electrical system.

The lights went out, and the engine died. The deputy cursed and pumped the brakes as he steered the car onto the shoulder.

Now was the time to use my sleep spell. With my energies already primed, I cast it upon the deputy. He slumped over in the front seat and began snoring.

Okay, how do I get out of here? I hadn't heard the rear door unlock and there wasn't even a door handle back there, anyway. I sent a powerful blast of sonic energy at the window, and even though it was reinforced glass, the energy weakened it enough to allow my two-footed kicks to shatter and break through the window.

Wait. Those annoying handcuffs had to go. I had an unlocking spell but needed to see the lock in order to cast it. I squirmed on the back seat, trying to get the cuffs into view. Finally, I brought my knees to my chest and, grunting with pain and strain, swung my cuffed hands over my feet.

With the cuffs in front of me, I worked on the unlocking spell.

They clicked open, and I tossed them out the window. Before I climbed out, I decided upon the best use of my empath powers. Even though the deputy was asleep, I could access his emotions through his subconscious mind.

I instilled in him a great fear of embarrassment and shame over my escape. When the sleep spell wore off, I hoped this would lead him to search for me first before he radioed in about my escape.

And just to make things even harder for him, I sent a blast of energy into the radio attached to his vest, disabling it. And his cellphone in his pocket, too. He would have to flag down a passing car after he gave up searching for me.

I climbed out the back window and ran into the nearby woods. Yeah, I was free. It was a great feeling.

But now I was a fugitive. I had more than the militia and Baldric to fear. The entire law enforcement system would look for me.

I had a credit card and cash still in my pocket, which they would have confiscated when I arrived at the jail. And I had my magic. But I really, really wanted Alfie. I needed my sword to be a good fighter.

Against my better judgment, I headed back along the county road to the construction site where I had left Alfie. I doubted Mom and Cory could have taken it while the second deputy was there.

Luckily, my captor hadn't gotten too far from the clearing. Walking along the road at a brisk pace, I returned to the gravel parking area in just over an hour. No cars were around. I paused to make sure no creatures were about, then sprinted across the huge dirt landscape until I reached the center. The bodies of the dead faeries had definitely been removed.

Following the footprints in the dirt, I located the place where Mom, Cory, and I had lain when we ambushed the faeries. It wasn't long before I found my sword where I had left it, hidden beneath my empty duffel bag. What a relief that a deputy—or faerie—hadn't taken it.

Before I walked back to the road, movement caught my eye. I froze.

A faerie was emerging from the hole they'd used to escape from the underground laboratory. He carried a shovel and jogged across the dirt to the line of trees. Another faerie with a shovel followed him.

There was no way I would shoot my magic at them. I couldn't afford someone else to call the sheriff complaining of pyrotechnics at the construction site.

I waited to make sure the coast was clear before I ran back to the road. A faint trace of Fae magic leaked out of the hole from the underground laboratory. I could only assume it was the anti-human spell Mom was talking about. I couldn't tell how it was constructed, but I sensed it was malign.

Despite their deadly encounter with us, the Fae were not abandoning their lab. In fact, they were digging out the tunnels I had collapsed earlier that night.

Mom would have to get the Elves to help with destroying the lab. I was a fugitive and had to look out for myself.

I was miles away from town and doubted I could walk that

far before dawn, but I needed to make it to a more populated area where I wouldn't stand out so much being on foot.

During my long hike, I had plenty of time to think. I decided to go public about the governor and Poxton. My fortunes were at their lowest ebb, and now was the time to take risks.

Little did I know how much worse things could get.

CHAPTER 23

SOPHIE

"Politics Desk," said the gruff male voice answering the phone. "This is Dorkle."

"Hi, my name is Sophie Grimes. I have a news lead for you."

"Yeah?"

"I've learned that Governor Witlessin and Senator Poxton are faeries. They keep it secret because you only see them in human form, but I witnessed—"

BEEP-BEEP-BEEP

Silence.

Okay, maybe it was my delivery. I dumped too much information too quickly. I followed up with an email to the newspaper reporter, one that I knew deep down would never receive a response.

Next, I tried Meghan Whortle, the local reporter and influencer. I considered her an enemy because she had been very active in advancing the Great Unmasking and the hysteria that followed it. She had regularly interviewed the founder of

Mothers Against Monsters. But she'd also never met a conspiracy theory she didn't believe, so I called her.

I was only able to speak with a surly assistant who gave me little hope Meghan would call me back. Even though reporters are supposed to be objective, the impression I received was that pursuing crazy stories that would harm the governor was out of the question.

I went down the list of prominent journalists and social-media influencers, emailing and messaging them. The few responses I got mocked me.

When I contacted the less-prominent, more-sensational people, I received a slightly better reception.

Faeries don't exist, one influencer wrote back.

Everyone believes in vampires and werewolves now. Why not faeries? I replied.

There's been no news about faeries.

That's exactly how the faeries want it.

YOU HAVE BEEN BLOCKED BY THIS USER.

That's the way it went for two days. The governor didn't need to kill me because no one believed me.

I thought of one last route to take. I had wanted to avoid getting involved in politics, but the only person who might believe me had a personal stake in my story being real. The journalists would risk their reputations by following up on my story. This guy, though, was different.

This guy was the governor's opponent in the upcoming election.

Dave Garcia was a mayor trying to unseat Governor Witlessin. He was far behind in the polls, especially after the Great Unmasking and the passage of the Supernatural Criminality Act. In fact, as Election Day loomed, Garcia might be desperate enough to believe me. And he had a team that could do the opposition research to prove my claims.

I called his campaign but was routed to someone who asked me if I wanted to volunteer or donate to the campaign. I said I wanted to donate some dirt, and she hung up on me.

After a few minutes of researching, I found the name of Garcia's campaign manager and her email address.

Your opponent, I wrote, *is leading in the polls because of fear and hate. She is persecuting innocent Floridians who have supernatural abilities or characteristics, falsely claiming they are a threat to normal people. Did you know the governor is a supernatural creature herself? This is more than hypocritical. It's lying to her constituents. Even worse, she's collaborating with supernatural creatures like herself to harm Florida. I have direct knowledge of these claims. Contact me ASAP for details.*

No matter how I composed the email, it made me sound like a crank. Of course it did. My claims were unbelievable. But they were true.

If people could accept that monsters did, in fact, exist, they needed to accept that their leader was a monster. Many leaders throughout history have been metaphorical monsters. Governor Witlessin was a literal one.

Later that day, as I hid in my depressing motel room, I got a response. It was from Joe Romesco, Assistant Campaign Manager.

Please call me to clarify your accusations against the governor.

I immediately typed the number he had supplied.

"Thank you for calling." He had a lilting Caribbean accent. "We're intrigued by your claims, but since they're so explosive, we need to verify them. Do you have any proof?"

"I saw the governor and Senator Poxton in faerie form. They were plotting with an external adversary who plans to attack

Florida and the United States. I don't have any photographs or other documentation."

He was silent for too long.

"You still there?" I asked.

"Yes." He chuckled. "Aren't faeries cute creatures like Tinker Bell?"

"Faeries are part of the folklore of many cultures. Sometimes they're depicted as cute. Often as scary and evil. The real faeries of today are ugly in their natural forms, but they can shift to human form easily and blend into our society. Some are good, many are neutral, and quite a few are evil."

"I'm searching on my computer as we speak," Joe said. "There are plenty of faeries throughout history, but I don't see any recent mentions of them, except in some Scandinavian countries."

"I'll get you evidence they exist. You should know that the governor found out that I discovered her secret and has been trying to have me killed."

"Boy, you never stop with the unbelievable accusations!"

"Let me text you pictures of a friend who's a faerie. We'll go from there. I'm calling you from a burner phone so they can't trace it, but I should switch it for a newer one. If you get a text tonight from an unknown number, it's me."

On the rare occasions I'd seen faeries in their natural forms, it was impossible or impractical to take pictures of them. Some supernatural creatures can't even be captured on camera. But I would try with someone I trusted: Gorkee, an indigenous faerie.

She lived a quiet life in San Marcos, shifting into human form every day to earn a living as a security guard, and was a fierce fighter against the Unseelie Court. Their soldiers had killed her cousin, so her hatred for them was intense.

When I called her, she initially balked at my request.

"I wouldn't want the video of me to get out on the internet," she said.

"It won't. But just in case, we'll put a black box over your eyes so you can't be recognized."

When I explained how important this was, not just for me but for the indigenous faeries, she reluctantly agreed to send me a video.

A video selfie of her transforming from human to faerie form.

I sent it to Joe Romesco. An hour later, he called me.

"I would like to meet with you," he said. "Mayor Garcia's campaign headquarters is in Orlando, but I'm going to be in your area on Thursday. I'll buy you a coffee."

"Sounds good. Remember, I'm a fugitive from the law and from an illegal militia. We have to be discreet. I'll text you a time and location on Thursday."

I spent Wednesday working on organizing the resistance. And jeez Louise, we had a lot of enemies to resist. There were the persecutors of supernaturals, from Mothers Against Monsters to the government itself. There was the governor's private militia, the Boogaloo Brigade. And there was the Unseelie Court, whose army could invade at any moment.

Mom—who couldn't quite absorb what a burner phone was —coordinated with Samson to recruit his fellow members of the Shifters Guild. The Memory Guild, which Mom served as a psychometrist, had very few members who would make decent soldiers, but they had other ways to assist us. I tasked Mom with reaching out to the members of the other guilds.

She also was lobbying the Elves to get them to abandon their neutrality and fight the Fae.

I was in constant touch with Diego. Now that he had consol-idated power as duke of his guild, he had more than two hundred vampires at his disposal, most of whom—except those turned too early or late in life—could fight for the resistance.

All of this had to be done behind Baldric's back. He was a major problem that had to be confronted. Most likely violently.

On Thursday, I bought another burner phone. My cash was running out, but Mom had said she would get more for me.

I called Joe and asked him to meet me at a small, obscure park beside the Route 302 bridge over the Intracoastal Waterway, just after sundown. He was amused by my spy-like behavior. If he only knew how much danger I was in.

When I was arrested at the construction site, Mom and Cory had taken the motor scooter home in the SUV. I successfully "borrowed" it again from the alleyway late Wednesday night, and I used it to get to the meeting place.

The park was merely a green space beside the bridge. It had no features, not even a bench, so it was deserted when I arrived. I stayed in the shadows beneath the bridge span until a sharp whistle went off in my head.

The whistle was from a ward I had cast at the entrance to the tiny dirt parking lot to warn me of intruders. I watched a car park in the lot and a man get out.

He entered the park carrying two coffee cups. He was tall and wore a dark suit. I emerged from the shadows and gave a little wave.

"Sophie? Is that you?" he asked in his musical Caribbean accent.

"Yes. Nice to meet you."

He handed me a cup. "I promised I'd buy you a coffee. Here are a few sweeteners if you use them."

Joe was fairly young, a bit older than I, and of mixed race. He was also cute, with curly black hair.

"There aren't any benches here," I said, "but we can sit on

the grass with a nice view of the salt marshes across the channel."

There was enough moonlight to glisten upon the shallow waters in between the dark mounds of oyster bars revealed by the low tide. We sipped coffee, and I began my story.

"First, you have to understand that there are faeries who have lived among humans since we first showed up here—before Columbus and after."

"Is that what the governor and Poxton are?"

"Exactly. Then there's the Fae of the Unseelie Court, who have arrived here from the land of Faerie and are ruled by the Faerie Queene. They want to conquer human lands. Our local faeries have always sided with humans. Until now. The governor and her cronies want to hand Florida over to the Faerie Queene in return for permission to rule the state like viceroys."

I went on to tell the story of how, when trapped in the Queene's Winter Palace, I ended up witnessing a meeting between the governor, Poxton, and the Queene.

"I saw them in their true faerie bodies," I said. "I wish I could have taken a picture of them. The governor was told by a local faerie who seeks her favor that I know her secret, and she's trying to kill me."

"Good Lord! I think this information is explosive. But I wish we had evidence. I suspect, though, when word gets out, other witnesses will come forward."

"And people will turn against Witlessin and her party. Right? The Supernatural Criminality Act must be overturned, but the state courts are controlled by Witlessin."

"Why are you doing this?" Joe asked, staring at me in the moonlight. "Why put your life in danger?"

"Everyone dear to me is supernatural. Witches, psychics, vampires, shifters—we're all outlaws now. I'm a witch, myself."

"I thought so. I sensed it."

"How? Are you supernatural, too? I sense it in you."

"Have you heard of the baccoo?"

I shook my head no.

"That's what I am, a type of mischievous, impish spirit. Baccoos are from Guyana and Barbados. I've successfully kept my true nature hidden since my parents moved here when I was a child. In this environment, though, I could be unmasked. It'll destroy my career and my life."

The sharp whistle went off in my head. Someone new had set off the ward.

"Quick, hide under the bridge," I whispered to Joe.

A pickup with its headlights turned off rolled into the parking lot. Joe ran beneath the bridge.

Two men got out of the truck. Their militia uniforms were visible in the moonlight.

I had my weapons with me, but I had a better tactic in mind.

Mr. Smeldman, I called out telepathically. *Please come out and save me.*

I added a magical blast of emotions, sending him protective feelings for me—the one who had found him this new home of his under a safer bridge than he'd lived beneath before.

Mr. Smeldman was a troll. Not an internet troll; a big, hulking folkloric troll. And when you have two scary men walking toward you with AR-15s, you want a troll on your side.

And please don't bother the man who's hiding beneath your bridge, I added.

"Looky here," one man drawled. "What's a pretty little thing like her doing out here at night?"

"Good thing we came along to give her a ride," said the other man. "Let's go, sweetheart."

"How did you find me?" I asked.

"Never you mind."

I backed away slowly, but the men were almost close enough to grab me.

Until the deep roar came from under the bridge, followed by Mr. Smeldman himself.

The troll was about ten feet tall and nearly as wide. He wore a canvas tarp like a toga and was covered with dense hair.

"What the—?"

"Shoot him!"

Mr. Smeldman strode quickly to the men and slapped the one who was aiming his assault rifle. The man and his weapon went flying separately through the air and landed in the water. Before the second one could get a shot off, he too was smacked into the water.

The men floated, stunned, moving under the bridge, taken by the current.

"The truck, please," I said aloud to the troll.

He stomped over to the truck. He picked up the vehicle, engine still running, and threw it over his head into the waterway. It moved with the current until it sank beneath the surface.

"Thank you, Mr. Smeldman," I said.

He disappeared under the bridge, and Joe came running out.

"I won't even ask how you convinced the troll to do that."

"You need to get out of town as quickly as you can," I said. "Someone is tracking one or both of us and told those men where to find us."

"Okay. Thanks for the oppo research. I'll be in touch."

"Thanks for the coffee. And, no, *I'll* be in touch with a new phone."

I watched nervously as he drove away, making a U-turn and then driving over the bridge. I started Mom's scooter and drove in the other direction, planning to take a roundabout route to my motel.

The drive seemed like it would never end. It was scary driving at night on the little scooter among the cars that blinded me with their headlights. Every pickup truck made me wary. And there are a lot of pickup trucks in North Florida.

I made it to the motel in one piece, then wasted fifteen minutes lurking in different spots near my room to make sure I hadn't been followed before I went inside. A microwaved meatball sub from a convenience store was my dinner.

While I ate, I checked social media. Already, there were posts repeating allegations about the governor and Poxton, made by "an anonymous witness." Nothing had appeared on the news channels yet; they were more careful about verifying rumors.

But the rumors were flying unimpeded on social media. And just as I was crawling into bed, the internet blew up.

CHAPTER 24

SOPHIE

Joe Romesco, as assistant campaign manager for the governor's opponent, had succeeded in making the dirt about the governor go viral, though I couldn't find any posts directly by Joe or anyone associated with his candidate.

Such is the tantalizing attraction of scandal. The faintest whiff of it attracts social-media users like tomcats to a female in heat. And once that begins, the tyrannical algorithms that rule our online lives take over and tip the world upside down.

I stayed in my motel room, curtains closed, a do-not-disturb sign hanging outside the door, and tracked the mentions of the governor secretly being a faerie as they rapidly multiplied. So far, the mainstream media hadn't yet picked up the story, but it inevitably would.

What annoyed me was how much false information I read in posts or saw in videos. A lot of it was completely made up out of whole cloth.

The most accurate messages stated the governor was a faerie

who fooled us by appearing in human form. It went downhill from there.

The governor had wings she kept hidden beneath her clothes. The governor was an elf, or pixie, or leprechaun. Not just Poxton, but the entire Florida legislature was filled with folkloric creatures and monsters.

Unsurprisingly, everyone seemed to believe that one.

Before long, a conspiracy theory popped up that accused the governor's opponent, Orlando Mayor David Garcia, of being the faerie.

Deep-fake AI videos appeared, depicting both candidates as various monsters, even vampires.

Which reminded me. I texted Diego and told him about being found last night by the militia members. These guys weren't the sharpest tools in the shed, so they must be getting surveillance help from someone, probably a state government agency.

Diego didn't respond, so I returned my attention to the craziness.

Finally, mentions of the scandal showed up on respectable news sites. The content was along the lines of, "Rumors are spreading across the internet that Governor Witlessin is secretly a supernatural creature. The governor's spokesperson dismisses the accusations as absurd."

My TV was on, and I saw an on-air news brief that said the same thing.

As the day wore on, the story was still trending on social media, but it was growing stale because no solid information had emerged.

Until I came across a reporter sticking a microphone into the face of Linda Mung, Garcia's campaign manager and Joe's boss.

"Witnesses have approached us with credible reports that

Governor Witlessin and Senator Poxton are faeries, highly intelligent and dangerous supernatural creatures," she said. "These witnesses are not involved in politics and have no dog in this fight. Our campaign is calling upon the state attorney general to investigate the accusations."

The feeding frenzy regained its energy. That clip showed up everywhere on broadcast and cable news, in podcasts, and in every nook and cranny of the internet.

I chuckled when I came across a story on a public-broadcasting news show that discussed the history of faeries in folklore and whether they might really exist.

Later in the evening came the on-camera quote I'd been waiting for, from Mayor Garcia himself:

"Governor Witlessin's campaign strategy has been to demonize a tiny segment of our population, using fear to trick voters into supporting her. It would make her disturbingly hypocritical if the accusations that she is a supernatural creature were proven to be true."

That clip spread like wildfire, and I went to bed for the first time with a bit of hope that the war against supernaturals might weaken.

WHEN I WOKE UP, DIEGO STILL HADN'T REPLIED TO MY TEXT, but I quickly got swept back up into the news blizzard. Cable talking heads were predicting whether this scandal would affect polling in the governor's race. Pundits dismissed the entire topic as a brouhaha based on nothing.

Meghan Whortle managed to get a scoop. On her daily podcast, she interviewed the friend of a former aide who had once worked for Senator Poxton when he was a state representative.

"Kelly told me she went into his office late one night when she thought Poxton had left for the day," the young woman said. "Kelly said she saw two fiendish creatures sitting on the sofa. They looked like elves or gnomes or little faeries. They were talking in a strange language."

"Oh, my, that sounds horrifying," Whortle said.

"It was. Kelly was so frightened. She said one faerie looked like a shrunken version of Representative Poxton! It even wore a miniature suit like his. And she said the other one looked a lot like Ada Witlessin."

"What happened?"

"They screamed at Kelly like chimpanzees, and she ran out of the office and went straight home. Kelly was fired a week later because she wouldn't sign a non-disclosure agreement. And then. . ."

The young woman broke into tears.

"They killed her!" she said, sobbing.

"What makes you believe she was murdered?" Whortle asked.

"Kelly said she thought she was being followed. The next night, when she was walking to the mailboxes at her apartment complex, a truck ran her over. Who drives fast enough in a parking lot to run someone over? They never found out who did it."

Normally, I would discount this as an unmerited conspiracy theory. But normally I wasn't running from the police and an extremist militia. It was very easy to believe Kelly was run over deliberately to silence her, because the governor and her lackeys wanted me to share the same fate.

Just don't kill me with a truck, please. Anything but a truck.

Meghan Whortle's podcast had thousands of subscribers, but I hoped Kelly's story would reach a larger audience. Legitimate news organizations might be wary of running it if it was mostly hearsay.

Fortunately, social-media users cared nothing about confirming the truth of something before sharing it. I saw more and more links to the podcast episode popping up everywhere.

The hope was that, the more Kelly's and my allegations spread, additional witnesses might appear.

If the story built up enough momentum, maybe, just maybe, it could bring the governor down.

However, I forgot another fact about people nowadays: their attention spans could be measured in milliseconds.

A different big story grabbed everyone's attention. A story that made me want to throw up.

Another vampire had been captured. And certain anonymous vampires had put out the message that if their friend wasn't freed, the militiamen being held hostage would be killed.

Faeries were pushed out of the news by vampires. And if violence broke out, the consequences could be devastating to the supernatural cause. We could forget about a path to equal rights, protections, and the freedom to simply exist.

"That's why you haven't heard from me," Diego said over the phone that night. "We've been in crisis mode."

"Who was abducted? Someone I know?"

"Billy."

"Oh, no. Poor Billy."

"I've instituted strict discipline among our Clan as we prepare to fight the militia, Baldric, and the state. Vampires must limit their movements around town, and every nest must post guards day and night. All human employees must be fully vetted. That's what went wrong."

"What happened?" I asked.

"Billy's nest hired security guards for the daytime hours. One was a spy for the militia, and he let several thugs into the house where they captured Billy."

"Are you searching for him?"

"Of course. But we suspect the militia took Billy far from San Marcos to make it harder for us to rescue him, like we did the last time they took a vampire. It breaks my heart that we haven't been able to find him. Can your magic help?"

"I have spells to find lost possessions, like your favorite hat you dropped somewhere. The only spell I know for locating people needs a sample of their blood."

"Oh, good! We have Billy's blood."

"You do?"

"When you become a member of the Clan of the Eternal Night, you must donate a vial of your blood, which we keep in a sepulcher. Both symbolically and literally, it binds us together by blood, making us a true clan."

I'd never cast the spell before by using the blood of a person who was technically dead, but hey, it was worth a try.

"I don't wish to put you at undue risk by asking you to travel," Diego said, "but the blood must not be removed from the sepulcher. It's located in the Royal Cemetery. Can you meet me there?"

It wasn't too far from my motel. "Yes. I'll meet you in twenty minutes."

"Thank you. Our Clan is filled with rage and worry. I don't want anyone to go rogue and do something stupid."

"What about the hostages you're holding?" I asked. "I think it would be a mistake to kill them."

"Eduardo made those threats without my authorization. I think his threats fell on deaf ears. When the militia abducted Billy, they must have known they were putting their brethren at risk. I believe they've written off the hostages."

"Don't kill them. It would be terrible for our cause."

"Our cause?"

I explained my hopes for the supernatural community. "We can't just think about getting revenge. We need to achieve justice."

"I'm not so sure of that. We vampires have always been treated as evil monsters. The only thing that saved us was being forgotten about and not believed in by humans. And those days are gone."

"My dream is that someday, you won't be stigmatized as monsters."

Diego snickered. "Keep dreaming. I'll see you in twenty minutes."

BEFORE I LEFT, I CHECKED THE NEWS AND SOCIAL MEDIA. THE politicians-are-secret-faeries story was still out there, but it was drowned out by the captured-vampire story. The militia members were repeating the playbook they had used with Mr. Jubbles—posting cruel videos of their captive being tormented.

It made me wonder if the abduction had been ordered by the governor to push her own story out of the news. That theory made sense, because the militia should have been trying to rescue its members, not antagonizing the vampires who held them.

In the end, it didn't matter. We still needed to rescue Billy.

Grabbing my duffel bag of weapons, I slipped out of my motel room and hid in an unlit area at the end of the building, watching to see if anyone was surveilling me. I sensed no magic in the area, so that ruled out faeries. Casting a quick spell to heighten my senses, I listened for conversations by anyone sitting in a parked car. The only sounds were televisions and talking coming from motel rooms.

I started my scooter and headed toward the Royal Cemetery, the oldest one in San Marcos, where the first colonists had been interred. It was a small plot of land near Old Town.

I'd only gone a few blocks on the street leading to Old Town when an oncoming vehicle crossed the center line, turned on its high beams, and came at me head on. It was a huge black pickup truck.

I was going to experience death-by-truck after all.

CHAPTER 25

SOPHIE

I was about to end up like a bug on the windshield of this giant, jacked-up pickup truck.

But some instinct made me turn left into the oncoming traffic lane, instead of right, onto the sidewalk. I just missed getting clipped by the front of the truck. If I had gone off the street onto the sidewalk, the truck would surely have squashed me.

My fate in the wrong lane, where more headlights were coming toward me, was a roll of the dice.

A horn blared, brakes squealed, and I skidded into a parking lot in front of a liquor store and a check-cashing place. Yeah, that was the kind of neighborhood my motel was in.

I hit a pothole and almost lost control of the scooter. An engine roared behind me. I craned my neck and saw the big black truck doing a U-turn on the street to come after me.

I drove into the narrow alley between the liquor store and a vacant building. Behind the liquor store was a private home, and I expected the truck to arrive on that street at any moment. So I went along the rear of the liquor store, passed through the parking lot again, and pulled into the street I had been on before, though now traveling in the opposite direction.

What a clever move, I thought. A couple of left turns would put me on a parallel street I could take to the cemetery.

The rearview mirror on my handlebar filled with the grill of the giant truck. Its engine roared and radiated heat. It was like the hot breath of a grizzly bear on the back of my neck.

The maximum speed of this scooter was around forty miles per hour. I had to get off this street or get run over. There was a driveway just ahead. I turned right—

The truck clipped the rear of the scooter, sending the back wheel sliding sideways. The front wheel bounced off a curb, and the scooter and I went flying over the small lawn of a home turned into an insurance office. We both did a somersault.

I landed in a hedge. The scooter crashed into the front of the house.

The truck screeched to a halt on the street beside us.

My duffel bag was still slung across my back, and I scrambled to get it open and grab a weapon, while casting a protection spell around myself.

A burly, bearded guy jumped down from the passenger door of the monster truck. As I expected, he wore a paramilitary uniform and carried an assault rifle. I couldn't believe he was going to shoot me in public.

A car stuck behind the pickup truck honked its horn. The truck's driver stuck his hand out his window with an obscene gesture. No worries, his passenger would hop back in soon after he took care of business.

The gunman was close enough now to get a clean shot at me through the hedge.

Alfie, though, was out of the duffel bag and the scabbard. And my concentrated energy was reaching its peak.

Purple lightning shot from my sword and struck the militiaman. He yelped and fell backward, landing on his butt, wisps of smoke rising from his shirt.

He aimed at me again, and I released another bolt. It struck him a nanosecond before he pulled the trigger. The bullet shattered the glass of a window above me.

I untangled myself from the hedge and lay flat on the ground behind it for more cover because my protection spell wasn't at full strength. My foe still sat on the ground, looking like he wanted to lie down and take a nap. I helped him do that with another blast from Alfie.

His partner, the driver, had jumped out of the cab to save their assignment that was going sideways. The car behind him honked again. He turned and shot out the car's front tires with a handgun.

While his attention was elsewhere, I hit him with purple lightning. He staggered and fell against the side of his truck.

I'd already used a bunch of energy. To make my protection spell strong enough to stop bullets, I would need too much energy to continue shooting effective lightning bolts. Which would it be—defense or offense?

The first gunman was out cold. His partner was visibly angry and aiming his pistol at me.

I reinforced my protection spell an instant before he fired.

My protection bubble shook as the bullet bounced off it. I reached into my backpack, feeling for the stock of my crossbow.

The driver of the car that had its front tires shot opened his door and got out.

What the heck was he doing?

He screamed an obscenity, produced a gun, and shot the militiaman. Then, he jogged to the pickup truck's cab, climbed in, and drove away.

Only in Florida.

Still lying behind the hedge, I pulled out my phone and texted Diego, telling him I was running late, along with the explanation why. I crawled out of my hiding place and inspected Mom's scooter lying on the ground nearby. It didn't look good.

I slung my duffel bag over my shoulder and walked the rest of the way to the cemetery, police sirens in the distance growing louder.

"My magical energy is a bit depleted at the moment, so please be patient," I said to Diego inside the crypt.

The room, carved out of natural limestone, was barely large enough for the two of us plus a couple of coffins. However, instead of coffins, there was a stone altar with hundreds of cigar-size holes bored into it, a glass vial of blood in each of them. Beside every hole, a name was inscribed in the stone. Flames from a candelabra attached to the wall gave the place a faint, creepy light.

I removed the supplies for the spell from my bag and lit the candles within the tiny magic circle I drew with chalk on the stone floor. Due to the cramped quarters, Diego was inside the circle with me, but that was okay. We'd need his blood too, because of his symbolic family connection with Billy.

I lit the incense in a small pewter bowl. Then came the uncomfortable part: working with blood next to a vampire in a claustrophobic tomb built into the ground.

Diego handed me the vial with Billy's blood. I poured three drops into the incense bowl.

"Your turn," I said.

Diego sliced his thumb with a dagger and squeezed three drops into the bowl. I watched his face carefully to see if the blood aroused him.

Nope. His face was completely impassive.

Next, I chanted the spell's incantation. The flames on the candles placed around the magic circle shot upward as if from a flamethrower. Before they receded, I was overcome by a vision of Billy, tied up inside the shower of a motel room, just like Mr. Jubbles had been.

Now came the tricky part. I forced my will into the magical vision, forcing it to zoom out, rising above Billy, through the ceiling, above the asphalt roof of the motel.

I saw the name on the neon sign: Peach Pit Motel.

I pushed harder, making the vision zoom out further. Below me was a grid of streets in a wooded neighborhood, and as I zoomed out more, I saw industrial areas surrounding it, and, finally, the skyline of a city.

I recognized it as Atlanta, Georgia.

The spell weakened, and the vision faded out. The candles around the circle had fizzled out, too. By the light of the candelabra on the wall, I saw Diego staring at me quizzically.

"He's at a motel called the Peach Pit in Atlanta. He's tied up in a bathroom. I didn't get a room number," I reported. "Should be easy to look the motel up to get an address."

The location would be around a six-hour drive from San Marcos.

"When we get to the motel, we'll use our vampire senses to find which room he's in," Diego said. "Thank you for your help."

I stepped from the magic circle, releasing the last traces of the spell.

"You're welcome. I hope you're able to get Billy back safely."

He opened the rusted iron door, allowing fresh air into the stagnant space. I leaped outside without delay.

After Diego joined me, closed the door, and locked it, I said, "We've been on the defensive for too long. It's time to change the momentum."

"Yes. We're making plans to attack the militia and then take Baldric out. What are the latest developments with the Queene's army?"

"That's how I got arrested." I filled him in on the details of the Fae's underground laboratory, which I hadn't had time to share with him earlier.

"It sounds like they built the lab so close to San Marcos because they plan on casting the spell from there. They can wipe out the humans in the city without even invading it. How are you going to stop them?"

"Mom's trying to convince the Elves to help us. And I'll ask the Gnomes, though they experienced heavy losses when they helped me rescue Mom from the Queene's palace. We might need vampire help, too."

"I would be happy to help Darla, but our Clan is focused on fighting the militia right now. One challenge at a time. Let me call Helga to organize a rescue party for Atlanta, then I'll drive you to your motel."

When we arrived at the motel, I didn't get out of the car right away. It wasn't like I was expecting a kiss or anything. I guess I was just lonely and not eager to hang out in my depressing room, watching videos on social media.

We sat for a while without talking. Diego was surprisingly relaxed. He seemed about to say something that he struggled to pull from within him.

But then his phone buzzed. He looked at it and cursed under his breath.

"What's wrong?" I asked.

"We're too late. They staked Billy. They posted a video of it. That was Helga texting me."

I felt the grief and regret wafting from him.

"I'm sorry, Diego. I'm so sorry."

I put my hand on his upper arm and squeezed gently. He put his hand on mine. As cool as his skin was, it had an energy throbbing beneath it, as if being undead was more vibrant than being alive.

"Thank you," he whispered. He pulled himself from his shock and continued in a louder voice, "I must go now. I'm afraid the guards will kill the hostages in retaliation. I must stop them."

I leaned over and gave him a quick peck on the cheek before I slipped out of the passenger seat.

He burned rubber when he left the parking lot. He definitely wasn't the first person to do that in an establishment like this.

I GUESS IT WAS SICK OF ME, BUT I WENT ONLINE TO LOOK FOR what had happened to Billy. After all, I'd been monitoring all media lately, so you could say it was part of my job. It didn't take long to find it. The militia was responsible for posting it, and it had, indeed, gone viral already.

Videos of people being killed were usually yanked from social-media platforms. This one wasn't, because, I supposed, Billy was considered less than a person. As a supernatural, he was subhuman in the eyes of so many these days.

I will forever carry with me guilt about the vampires I destroyed. For some, it had been necessary to save my life or that of another. The other vampires I'd slain were mandated by my former job as an enforcer.

The staking of Billy, however, was simply cruel, vindictive, and disgusting. It was done out of hatred, to encourage fear and divisiveness.

And it was extra enraging to see it shared on the social-media accounts of politicians—Poxton's among them.

I vowed I wouldn't rest until the militia was driven from our city.

CHAPTER 26

DARLA

"Where do you advertise to reach supernaturals?" I asked Cory as we sat at the tiny dining table in our cottage. We were eating breakfast alone because Sophie wasn't here, and our inn was empty of guests.

Cory looked at me over the top of the newspaper. We're among the few Americans who still read printed newspapers. Who still read the news at all, for that matter.

"Why do you want to advertise to creatures who are now illegal?" he asked.

"To promote the inn. We lost our hotel license, so we can't rent rooms to guests. I interpret that to mean *human* guests. Now that supernaturals are illegal, they need safe places to stay when they travel or are uprooted from their homes. It's a chaotic time for those who are oppressed. We should cater to them."

He scratched his head. "Wouldn't that be illegal?"

"Not any more illegal than hosting human guests—who wouldn't stay in an unlicensed hotel, anyway. We'd be a bed-and-breakfast version of a speakeasy."

"Seems risky."

"Of course it is! But our biggest risk is our business failing and our inn going into foreclosure. Come on, Cory, how long can we sit here with no guests?"

"I haven't mentioned this because I was giving you time to come to terms with our situation. The only thing we can do is sell the inn. Maybe we can buy another one outside of Florida. Or start a different business."

"I simply can't do that." My voice rose. "This place means too much to me. It's a part of who I am."

"We appealed the denial of our license, but I'm not optimistic that will work. It makes no sense to sit around bleeding cash until we're forced to leave."

I sipped my coffee, pretending to mull over what he'd said. However, my mind was already made up. I was only pretending to entertain his proposal.

I kept pushing. "Hasn't it occurred to you that no one would buy this place? It has a reputation of being haunted with supernatural activity going on. We should double down on that reputation by welcoming the supernatural community."

"I admit it might be tough to—"

"At times like these, persecuted creatures need a safe space to gather and have a kinship with others. I have a strong feeling that occupancy will go through the roof! Off the books, of course. I asked about advertising, but the fact is we'll get business just from word of mouth."

"Well, maybe—"

"And San Marcos is on the cusp of war. There's an illegal militia rampaging through town, violating people's rights and terrorizing everyone. And we have the Fae preparing to invade us with magic that might wipe out humans."

"You're not describing a very good business environment," Cory said.

"On the contrary! The city will fill up with supernaturals here to liberate us and beat back the Fae. Where will they sleep? At the Esperanza Inn!"

"Your argument is convincing, but something tells me you've already made up your mind."

I chuckled. "You know me too well. That's why our marriage is so good. And why we make excellent business partners. Such as with our new, repurposed inn."

"What if we're inspected by the DBPR?"

"We'll outwit the inspectors. We're supernatural, after all, with gifts."

"I suppose."

"By the way," I said, "you should learn some spells that will trick inspectors."

"Yes. I'll do that. But seriously, it's not just about getting fined or shut down. We could be arrested for harboring supernaturals."

"The police haven't shown any interest in doing that."

He seemed defeated. "They haven't so far."

"I've already asked Roderick, Archibald, and Pinky to spread the word that we offer good rates and an excellent breakfast. No packaged blood for vampires right now, but I'll work on it."

"Are you sure this is a good idea?"

"I'm sure it's our only option for survival. We might even thrive."

"I'm not changing my sleep schedule to accommodate vampires," Cory said.

"Roderick used to own this place. We'll put him back to work."

"Good luck with that."

DID I EVER MENTION THE ESPERANZA INN OFFERS SPACE FOR meetings and special events? We've had our share of weddings in the courtyard and living room, as well as other celebrations. The Stamp Collecting Society used to meet there once a month, and there was a group of bridge-playing seniors who used the dining room weekly.

All that revenue had been lost to us. But now we had new groups meeting there, such as today. Although this particular group was here for free. Because I was begging them to help me.

Elves, gnomes, and local faeries filled the dining room, sipping tea (which required two hands for the diminutive gnomes) and munching on my famous scones. Pinky served the crowd. She was desperate to regain her lost income after we were shut down.

I was trying to drum up support for an attack on the underground lab built by the Fae of the Unseelie Court. There was even a whiteboard with battle plans sketched on it. Cory stood at the back of the room with his arms folded. He said he was there to lend moral support, but the presentation was up to me.

It wasn't going well.

"As you know," said an elf diplomat, "there's a peace treaty between our Seelie Court and the Unseelie Court."

Leighnel had dragged this bureaucrat to my meeting, because Leighnel had no authority to make promises of support on his own. It sounded like this oily elf he'd brought had no authority either.

"In my opinion, the peace treaty benefits the Unseelie Court, not yours," I said, probably breaching diplomatic protocol.

"They signed it to keep you off the field while they gobble up territory."

The elf frowned. He was one of the few I'd seen with brown, not blond, hair. Of course, he was slender, like Leighnel and all the others.

"If, then, we are to speak frankly," he said, "our treaty with the Fae gives us better relations with them than with humans. The territory you say they're gobbling up is human territory. The ground beneath it, to be exact."

"Beneath forests, too," I replied. "Where they're damaging the tree roots."

He smiled with arrogance. "Trees the humans will inevitably destroy."

He had me there.

"Could you at least ask the king to assign more personnel to assist Leighnel? His work is critically important in preserving the health of forests and monitoring the Fae's harvesting of phytolucine."

The diplomat nodded. "I shall pass along the request. However, I had thought the Goddess Danu would take a more active role in these endeavors."

"I guess she has other priorities."

I turned to Gorkee. "I've relied so much on you, Gorkee, to help me fight the Unseelie Court. Are you still behind me?"

Today, she was in her natural faerie form, small with a head that seemed to me disproportionately large. She had beautiful red hair that made her stunning when in human form.

"After what the Faerie Queene's soldiers did to my family all those years ago, I will always take up arms against them," she promised. "But I can't promise any of the local Fae will join me. Baldric has turned many of them into sympathizers of the Unseelie Court."

"Can you promise me assistance from the Gnomes?"

"I'm afraid that I've only recruited my good friends here." She gestured to three gnomes that sat at her table. "As you know, the Gnomes sacrificed greatly to rescue you from the Queene's palace. Perhaps the right amount of gold could attract more to sign up for this mission."

"I can't afford it," I mumbled.

A major problem that supernaturals faced was the corruption of the Executive Council. Only the guilds had the money to mount an effective defense against the Fae and the humans who persecuted us. And Baldric controlled the purse strings.

I forced myself to be optimistic.

"Thank all of you for your help," I said, smiling at the gnomes and Gorkee. "Our numbers are too small for a direct assault on the laboratory. This time, we won't be battling underground."

I stepped to the whiteboard and drew Xs below the star that represented the underground lab.

"This will be a battle involving magic. What I need from you is to defend my husband while he casts his spell. The Fae soldiers could attack from the woods or from underground."

Gorkee and the three gnomes nodded.

We were doomed, I thought, unless I found more fighters to protect us. Maybe Diego and his vampires, or Samson and some of his shifter friends.

What bothered me most of all was that I didn't know if Sophie would show up. I didn't even know where she was, only that she was okay, according to her encrypted texts.

"May I be so bold as to make a suggestion?" the Elven diplomat asked.

"Please do."

"You must recruit more humans to help you. After all,

humans are the ones the magic the Fae are developing is meant to destroy."

WITH NO HUMAN GUESTS AT THE INN, THE NIGHTLY WINE Hour was no longer a scheduled event. It was simply Cory and me sharing a bottle in the courtyard beside the swimming pool that lay unoccupied, except for a lonely inflatable pink flamingo that drifted about aimlessly.

"Let's have dinner in the inn's kitchen tonight," I said. "There's no one around to disturb us."

We moved to the kitchen in the main building, and I sautéed chicken thighs while Cory made a salad. The small TV I normally watched while making breakfast each morning was tuned to the local news. The anchor mentioned a name that caught my ear, and I turned my attention to the program.

"Colonial Commons, the planned multi-use shopping plaza west of San Marcos, has delayed its grand opening date," the blonde anchor announced. "The developer claims mass walk-offs of workers have put construction way behind schedule. Our Tom Jenkins spoke to the foreman."

A reporter interviewed a guy in a hard hat at the construction site where we had clashed with the faeries. The foreman complained crews were walking off the job, claiming they felt ill.

"There's something about this place that makes me feel restless and anxious to leave," the foreman said.

The reporter, speaking to the camera, said there were no reports of gas leaks or toxic chemicals in the area.

Cory and I looked at each other. His face was drained of color.

"Fae magic," he said.

"Made with phytolucine. It sounds like their spell is complete, or almost so. We've got to stop them quickly."

"Let's drive by the site after dinner. I want to get a feel for the magic."

We hurriedly ate dinner and drove to the construction site. As we neared it, I began to feel nauseous and dizzy.

"Do you feel sick?" I asked.

Cory shook his head. "No, but I feel magic. The Fae sorcerers have been busy since we were last here."

The cleared land looked like a raw wound, just as it had when we were last here. No additional work had been done. The only difference was an office trailer had been delivered, and a tall pile of concrete pipes was stacked near the parking area.

Cory slowed down to pull into the gravel lot, then changed his mind. We crawled past the fields of dirt.

"The magic is so strong," he said through clenched teeth. "I'm not as good as Sophie is at identifying the structure of spells, but I can tell right away it's not human magic. There's something different about it."

"Yeah. It makes me feel ill down to my bones."

"Really? It's not affecting me like that. It's just that, as a witch, I'm overwhelmed by the strength of it."

"Is it meant to kill humans or repel us?" I wondered aloud.

"I don't know. But I don't think the spell has been perfected yet. It's like we're driving past Los Alamos when they were developing the atomic bomb, and you're experiencing the effects of a radiation leak."

"So, it's just me and not you? Is it because I don't have your magic gene?"

"You're a human," he said. "A psychic human with a goddess within you. I'm a witch—a supernatural. I guess the spell is just designed to harm humans."

I'd never considered Cory so different from me until then.

He sped up, and we left the site behind. The unpleasant sensations gradually disappeared.

"We need to shut down this lab," I said. "The Fae may have other ones, but their supply of phytolucine is limited. Leighnel says he's certain of that. We must steal or destroy their supply."

"Is Sophie going to help us?"

"I don't know. She's going to do what she needs to do, which is to survive and stay free."

I had tremendous faith in my daughter, but the odds were stacked against her.

CHAPTER 27

SOPHIE

Days had passed since Billy was staked. The video appeared everywhere online. It was aired on TV, strategically blurred to lessen the horror. Eventually, other viral videos pushed the death video from the public's short attention span.

I didn't hear from Diego during those long, painful days. When he finally returned my calls, I was angry.

"Sorry," he said. "I've been preoccupied with a serious problem."

"Are you going to tell me what it is?"

"The human hostages were killed by the vampires who guarded them. Out of revenge for Billy's destruction."

"Jeez Louise. That's going to be a big problem."

"There is some good news, depending on how you look at it," Diego said. "All three hostages were turned. They're vampires now."

I groaned. "I don't know if that's karma, or an even bigger problem when the humans find out."

"We're trying to make the best of it. Now that they've been

turned into vampires, we're trying to make them loyalists to our cause."

"Good luck. They hated vampires more than anything."

"And now they're vampires themselves. Changing their loyalty is easier than you might think," Diego insisted. "Being turned is a very traumatic experience, and if your parent helps you make the transition, you become extremely attached to them emotionally."

"Parent?"

"Yes. That's what we call a vampire who turns someone. You have all the responsibilities of a parent: keeping your child well fed, healthy, and happy. Then, you must teach your child how to survive in the world. There's so much a new vampire must learn in a very short time. A good parent is something to be thankful for."

"I think I see where this is leading."

"Yes! If we get these new vampires on our side and convince them their militia is filled with hateful ignoramuses who now want to destroy them, they can be a great asset for us. In fact, we're planning to use them to set a trap and lure the entire militia into an ambush of sorts."

"Can you trust the new vampires?"

"We're almost there. When you're a vampire, time is measured in centuries. But when you're first turned, everything changes in minutes and hours. To survive, you must become a totally new person quickly. I'll know when these former humans have fully become vampires in their hearts and minds, as well as their bodies."

"I hope it will happen soon."

"It will, if it hasn't already."

THE HEADLINE APPEARED ONLINE:

Hostage free after daring escape from vampires.

I believed it at first, until Diego told me they had returned one of their newly turned vampires—one whom he said they could fully trust—to the militia in the hope the new vampire would become an undercover agent inside the militia.

I prayed the militia wouldn't discover what their freed comrade had become, or he would be staked immediately.

"There's an abandoned church in the west part of town," Diego told me. "It's the kind of gloomy place where humans would expect vampires to hang out. He'll tell them the other two are safe and will be released if the militia stops attacking us. The humans will ask where we're keeping the two hostages. He'll say at the church. He'll say most of us live there."

"So they'll go there, expecting to rescue the hostages?"

"Yes, and to destroy all the vampires they can find. But we won't be there. We'll be next door in an abandoned school. They could come any night now."

"No, the attack will come during the daytime," I insisted. "Like in *Dracula*, they'll plan on staking sleeping vampires."

"We planned for that, too. We have the Shifter Guild to back us up outside the church. There's a shaded corridor we can use to get from the school into the church, where all the windows are boarded up. If the humans come during the day, it will be dark enough that we can fight those who come inside."

"You sound like you need some magical help."

"Please, Sophie, stay away from this battle. If it doesn't go as planned, it will get chaotic. The militia will open fire, and the police might show up before we're done. There's too much risk that you'll be hurt or arrested."

"I want to fight those inbred losers."

"Please, no. If you're arrested, you won't survive."

I wasn't worried about holding my own in a fight, but I feared getting arrested again. They wouldn't let me get away this time.

"Okay, but I'm worried about you. You'll be waiting there like sitting ducks."

He chuckled. "No, like vipers ready to strike."

IT WAS THE FIRST TIME I'D SEEN MOM IN DAYS. WE HUGGED and all that. There was some crying. Who, me cry? I wasn't crying; she was crying. Okay, we both were crying.

It happened at the very unsentimental location of the dealership where Mom had originally purchased her motor scooter. She'd had it picked up from the site of my accident and gotten it repaired for me.

"I can't express how grateful I am," I told her, wiping away my tears.

"The owner of the insurance office you crashed into thought the rider had been drunk," Mom said. "I told him it had been me, and I'd had a seizure. He sold me a life insurance policy."

"I should probably buy one."

She didn't laugh. In fact, she frowned. "I can't go on living like this."

"This isn't my fault, Mom."

"You've been saying that your entire life, since you broke my vase when you were a toddler."

"I meant what the politicians have done to me. To us."

"I know. Sometimes, I think about moving to another state, even though Florida has always been our home."

"The Great Unmasking is already spreading to other states in the South. We'd have to move to Canada or the UK, where supernaturals can still live in peace and privacy. But that's taking the easy way out. I'm staying. And fighting."

Mom gave a weary smile. "Of course. That's what Cory and I will do: stay, fight, and adjust."

"Adjust?"

"Wait until I tell you about the inn's new business model."

"Uh-oh. Will we finally be profitable?"

"That remains to be seen," Mom said, becoming serious again. "On the subject of fighting, I need to destroy the underground lab we found the other night."

"I'll help you."

"Last time you were there, you got arrested. I'd rather you stay safe, even though I could sure use your magic."

"I understand. Call me if you change your mind."

AFTER SAYING GOODBYE TO MOM, I BUZZED ALONG THROUGH late-morning traffic, returning to the motel. Now that I had the scooter back, I could get around without using a ride-share service, which was too dangerous if you were a supernatural. My car, still parked at the inn, wasn't viable, because the police would pull it over. So, until I could buy or borrow another car, the scooter was the best option.

Several sirens blared nearby, punctuated by the guttural honking of firetrucks. I caught the scent of acrid smoke in the wind. An uneasy feeling filled me, and not simply because sirens meant police were probably close.

Something was wrong. Supernatural forces were in disruption.

I thought about Diego's battle plans, and my unease turned into fear.

Was the church on fire?

I turned around and headed toward the abandoned church, which was across the railroad tracks in an industrial part of the city. Soon, plumes of dark smoke were visible above the buildings.

After crossing the tracks, and a bridge over a creek that led to the bay, I turned onto the street where the church was. I stopped a block away.

Fire trucks, ambulances, and police cars were parked here, but not in front of the church. I quickly saw why.

Several pickup trucks, in two parallel lines a safe distance from the fire, blocked the street on both sides of the church, preventing the emergency vehicles from reaching the building. Men in paramilitary uniforms brandishing assault rifles took cover behind the trucks. I was struck by an emotional wall of defiance and hatred rising from the men.

They had set fire to the church and wouldn't allow it to be extinguished. Fire was one of the few things that could destroy vampires, and the militia wasn't taking any chances.

But had they even tried to enter the church to rescue the remaining hostages? Or did they sacrifice them in their attempt to take out all the vampires they expected to be inside?

I went around the block to see if I could approach the church from the rear, but there was no access.

I returned to the street in front of the church. The building was engulfed in flames, but an updraft carried the fire and most of the smoke upward. Near the line of trucks on my side was a warehouse. A large burly man stood outside an open door watching the fire and the standoff, indifferent to the drifting smoke. I recognized him—Rufus, the Alpha of the Shifter Guild.

I parked the scooter in an alley and hurried over to the shifter.

"Rufus! Is Diego okay?" I had meant to ask about the vampires in general, but look at what slipped out.

He looked at me with surprise. "Sophie, what are you doing here?"

"Diego told me about the plan to lure the militia here. When I saw the fire, I panicked."

"Don't worry," he said. "No one was in the church. We're all in this warehouse, and the vampires are in an abandoned school next to the church. The plan was to wait until the militia breached the doors of the church and then leave our hiding places and attack them. We'd attack from the street while the vampires entered the church through a covered walkway. But we didn't expect this to happen."

"The vampires are still inside the school?"

He nodded. "The hostages are with them. Thank God the fire didn't spread to the school."

"The militia just set the church on fire without going inside?" I asked.

"It looks like it. They believed it was filled with vampires, and I guess the militia thought burning the place down would be safer for them and more of a spectacle. They wanted to make this a huge media event to get publicity and horrify the supernatural community."

"Won't they get arrested for blocking the first responders?"

"My guess is the governor will prevent that from happening."

"If they thought the church was filled with sleeping vampires, they knew two hostages were in there, too."

"Yeah." Rufus shook his head in disgust. "They were okay

with sacrificing them. That's the sort of people we're dealing with. And they call *us* monsters. At least the arsonists got their just deserts."

"What happened?"

"We took care of them." He gave a cruel, wolfish smile. "Too bad we couldn't get them before they started the fire. The rest of these clowns showed up afterward." He gestured at the two lines of trucks.

"I'm sorry it didn't work out," I said.

"What do you mean?"

"Diego hoped to defeat the militia decisively."

Rufus laughed. "Girl, you got here just in time for the show. The militia wanted their fire to be a media circus. Well, that's what they're going to get. Men like that only respect brute force."

"Wait, you're going to attack them in front of the police and everyone?"

"Yep. And in front of the news media and every yahoo with a camera. Do me a favor, though. Please step inside the building. Bullets will fly."

He glanced at his watch and spoke into a handheld radio as I walked past him into the office portion of the warehouse. I looked through an open interior door and saw dozens of men in the empty storage bay. One of them held a rifle. The others began taking off their clothes before shifting. I averted my gaze and stepped back into the office.

Rufus came inside and stepped into the warehouse.

"Go!" he shouted.

The loading doors rolled up.

And an immense pack of wolves raced out of the warehouse into the street, followed closely by giant brown bears.

Yikes!

CHAPTER 28

SOPHIE

The militia members blocking the street had parked their trucks in two rows a block apart, preventing access to the church from either direction. Wearing masks against the haze of smoke and brandishing rifles, they stood inside their cordon, keeping their trucks between them and the first responders.

The wolves simply ran between the police cars and fire engines, then leaped over the militia's trucks. The bears climbed over the vehicles with ease.

I went to the second story of the warehouse to have a better view from an office window. I found the guy who hadn't shifted, aiming his rifle from the window in case he was needed.

It wasn't a fair fight. The wolves and bears jumped on the men and took them down before they even knew what hit them. Raw, primitive fear eclipsed the hatred rising from the men. The snarls of beasts and screams of humans echoed from the fronts of buildings in the street. Scattered gunshots rang from the few militia members who used their weapons before they were incapacitated.

I couldn't tell if any wolves or bears were hit, but if they were, it didn't matter. Their supernatural healing powers meant the wounds were merely painful nuisances.

During the standoff with the militia, the police had sent several cars, but the officers didn't shoot at the shifters at first. I guess they didn't want to risk hitting any militiamen. Or maybe they were stunned at the sight of the giant beasts rampaging in their city.

But now that the militia was getting its butt kicked, the police opened fire. It didn't stop the wolves and bears.

An engine gunned. Somehow, a militiaman had escaped being mauled and was trying to get away in one of the pickup trucks. He had nowhere to go, with the emergency vehicles lined up on one side of him and the other line of trucks blocking the street behind him.

Instead of escaping, he tried to mow down the wolves and bears.

The truck struck a giant grizzly, which roared in pain and caused major damage to the truck. Before the driver could reverse, a black wolf, the largest of them all, leaped up on the hood.

I recognized this wolf as Rufus. He bashed the top of his head into the windshield, shattering it, before plunging through it, jaws open.

The truck rolled slowly backward until it got stuck against the front of a building. Rufus emerged from the cab and shook the blood from his fur. He surveyed the carnage inside the cordon.

The large wolf made a series of short, guttural barks. His pack, including the bears, raced from both bulwarks and returned to the warehouse.

I went downstairs but avoided seeing them shift back into their human forms.

Several motorcycles rumbled to life in the warehouse bay. I stepped out to see all the shifters riding the bikes in twos, exiting through back doors that opened onto an alley.

It was time for me to get out of there as well. The police would arrive at any moment. After I hopped on my scooter, I caught sight of the last in the line of departing motorcycles, so I followed it through a maze of alleys and driveways.

Finally, we emerged on a road several blocks from the church complex. I recognized where I was and made my way toward the motel, worrying about Diego again. I tried calling him with one hand as I drove, and—you guessed it—he didn't answer.

Was he among the vampires in the school beside the church? Did the fire spread into that building too? Were the vampires still there, trapped inside by the sunshine? Firefighters might enter the building and find them.

There was nothing I could do to help them, even with my magic. I needed to be far away from the area and the police, so I wouldn't be arrested.

I tried to calm down by reminding myself that night would come soon, so if they hadn't been discovered, the vampires could escape on foot.

Somehow, though, I found myself circling back to the neighborhood of the church, despite the risk. Ambulances passed me, sirens blaring. When I was a block away, I saw geysers of water rising into the sky and hitting the church steeple as the firefighters could finally do their work.

And I saw something else: four buses—cross-country coaches—leaving the neighborhood. Their windows were tinted too dark for me to see inside. Something told me their passengers were vampires.

I turned around before I got too close to the scene. Then, a limousine with tinted windows passed me, followed by several others. It looked like a funeral procession without a hearse. Or a visit by a head of state.

Nope. I was certain the limos carried the new vampire leader and his inner circle. I followed them.

Along the way, limousines broke from the procession to carry their passengers to various nests in town. I continued trailing the lead vehicle all the way to 14 Granada Street.

The day was fading, but the passengers got out of the limo and entered the restaurant shaded by large black umbrellas. Diego, Helga, and Eduardo were surprised to see me filing into the kitchen behind them.

I couldn't believe how relieved I was to see that Diego was okay.

"Sophie," Diego said, surprised. "Where did you come from?"

"The battle. I stumbled upon it shortly before it happened."

He frowned. "You shouldn't have put yourself at risk like that. You could have been shot. Or arrested."

"I went there only because I saw the church on fire. I was worried about you and the vampires."

"Worried about us? Vampires are quite resilient."

"Not if you're trapped in a building that's burning," I said. "Thank God you weren't in the church, and the school didn't burn."

"I'm happy that you were concerned."

"Of course I was concerned."

The empath in me was picking up an emotion in Diego I hadn't sensed before, at least not strongly enough to notice.

Diego gazed at my face. "Let's take this conversation into the lounge."

We walked past the dark dining room to the bar and lounge

at the front of the building. We remained standing side by side facing the bar, the only light coming from a wine refrigerator because the windows were shuttered against the fading daylight. Neither of us spoke for a while until Diego broke the silence.

"I don't think it's a good idea," he said.

"What isn't a good idea?"

"Falling for a human. I did it once, about a hundred and fifty years ago. It just doesn't work when one partner is immortal and the other one . . . isn't."

"You didn't like watching her grow old in front of you?" I said with more sarcasm than I'd intended.

"I didn't like her dying of cholera." His jaw clenched as he fought against revealing any more emotions.

"I'm sorry. What was her name?"

"Clara. The daughter of a merchant here in San Marcos. She was the light of my life."

She must have been the woman portrayed in a daguerreotype that I'd seen in Diego's apartment. I didn't know what to say.

"Humans have lower mortality rates from disease nowadays." Yikes, that was a weak statement!

"Yes, you do."

"I suppose it's difficult, too, for a human. Falling for a vampire who never ages while your own body fades."

He said nothing. Somehow, we now stood closer to each other than before. How had that happened?

"Besides," I added, "we humans enjoy cooking and eating together. Even though you own a top-rated restaurant, it's not as if we could enjoy an intimate paella together, right?"

"I can still prepare a mean paella." He chuckled.

As we leaned against the bar, our arms accidentally brushed together.

"Yeah," I said. "It's not a good idea to fall for anyone—

human or vampire—during times like these. All the horribleness around us makes us more emotionally vulnerable. More likely to do foolish things."

"Yes. Like this."

It happened so quickly. Our lips were pressed together, and his arms were around me, squeezing me desperately, as if trying to keep my mortal body from fading away.

His lips were warmer than I had imagined, and he had let his inner wall down, leaving his emotions bare to my senses. He felt affection, lust, loneliness, longing—but did he feel love? I wasn't sure.

And just as quickly as we had moved to kiss each other, we broke apart.

I breathed heavily, my heart racing. He smiled, then kissed the top of my head in a fatherly way.

"Please stay safe," he said. "Try not to go out in public. The one thing you can do for me is to stay alive."

I rode the scooter to the motel, oblivious to the sounds of the traffic and the jolts from cobblestones. In fact, I was so preoccupied by my thoughts that I entered my motel room and dropped my bag on the floor before I noticed something wrong.

Baldric was sitting on the bed.

CHAPTER 29

SOPHIE

"How did you get in here?" I asked Baldric before realizing it was a stupid question. He had gotten into my locked room with magic, of course. "Never mind. Let me rephrase that. How did you know I'm staying here? Do you have a tracking spell on me?"

He laughed. "Don't be so daft. Of course I have one. How else did the militia find you more than once? Did you think they put a GPS tracker on your scooter or embedded a chip under your skin? Those goons are great with firearms, but that's about it."

My phone rang, but I ignored it. I was busy casting a protection spell around myself. Baldric surely knew I was doing it.

"I think the militia will be leaving San Marcos," I said. "They haven't had pleasant relations with our resident supernaturals."

"No loss, as far as I'm concerned. But I'm not here to talk about those morons. We have matters to settle, you and I. And don't try any attack magic on me. I'm not in the mood for your paltry spells."

"You want me to make it easier for you to kill me?"

He put his legs on the bed and rested his back on the head-board. I'd always been taught not to put my feet on the bed while wearing shoes, but I suppose faeries were above such etiquette.

"Take your dirty clothes off that chair." He pointed at the battered piece in the corner. "And sit down."

I didn't remove the clothes and sat on them. That'd show him. Why was he there, anyway? To kill me, or propose another agreement that I wouldn't abide by?

"As you surely realize," he said, "the governor and Senator Poxton are aware that you know their secrets. Especially since you went public with your knowledge, Miss 'Anonymous Witness.'"

"They wanted me killed, so why not go public?"

"Indeed. Were you hoping to harm the governor's reelection?"

I nodded.

"Don't get your hopes up. Humans aren't very bright or attentive. The reason I bring this up is the governor and Poxton still want you dead. If I bring them your head—literally or metaphorically—they'll be delighted with me."

I pumped more energy into my protection spell.

He chuckled. "I felt that. You needn't worry. I have no desire to kill you on the governor's orders. Her campaign to persecute supernaturals has been a rousing success, but she's only a craven politician. They're all the same, Fae or human. No, I'd only kill you if it were in my best interest. And it won't be—if you suit my purposes."

Oh, no. Here he comes with a deal with the devil. I tried to sense his emotions, but he had a wall of inscrutability.

I asked, "What are your purposes?"

"We Fae worship the Goddess Danu like humans once did, though we call her by a different name. She is at the top of our pantheon of gods. You wouldn't know it, but I'm a very pious person. I hold the Goddess in the highest esteem and love her dearly."

I didn't like where this was going.

"It pains me that she has not been smiling kindly upon the Fae lately," he continued.

"What do you mean?"

"She is interfering with the Unseelie Court's efforts to harvest a substance found beneath the forest floor. Or I should say it's your mother who is interfering under Danu's orders. Danu and your mother are one and the same, correct?"

I wasn't sure how best to answer that, so I simply nodded.

"The easiest solution would be to eliminate your mother." Baldric smiled at my shocked expression. "Yes, I know. That's a horrible thing to contemplate. I wouldn't want to do that, of course. Especially since it would anger Danu—might even harm Danu, in fact. I want Danu to smile upon her Fae people again."

"Leave my mother out of this," I said.

"How can I? She is interfering with the Faerie Queene's plans."

"Who are you serving, the Faerie Queene or the governor?"

"I told you already, the governor is not worthy of my service." His tone was haughty. "We all know the Faerie Queene will soon rule this state, and your nation, too. I serve the Queene. All the indigenous Fae should serve her, too. Whoever doesn't is a traitor to their people."

"The local faeries have done just fine without a ruler. You guys got along well with the rest of us."

"Oh, in perfect harmony? Ha! That's ridiculous. We've just been biding our time until we could fulfill our destiny as the superior species. But enough of this political talk. I have practical matters I need to resolve with you. You did not honor our agreement to make the guilds loyal to me."

"It was an impossible thing to ask of me," I said with defiance. "The guilds were too far gone. They were through with you. How was I supposed to change that?"

"With your mastery of emotions."

"I only wish I were that powerful."

"Perhaps you will be. Under my wing, of course. When I'm the Queene's viceroy of the southern United States."

"Oh, please."

His eyes narrowed. "You would be well advised to take me seriously. I was going to kill you under the governor's orders and because you didn't honor our agreement. I could break open your silly protection bubble and crush you like an inset with my magic. But I shall not. If you serve my needs, that is."

"How?"

"Keep your mother in check. Spies tell me she is working with the Elves to disrupt the collection of the substance I mentioned before. Danu is inside of her, but your mother is acting with the agency of a human."

"There's no one alive who can keep my mother in check."

Baldric finally smiled. "A daughter always has a way into her mother's heart. And I will watch you."

That was a disturbing notion. "What do you mean?"

"It's like the tracking spell I put on you, but, shall we say, more invasive. And more difficult to cast. I need to place a magical implant in your brain so I can monitor your interactions with your mother. And influence them. If this spell wasn't so difficult, I would have implanted it in the guild leaders instead of relying on your failed empath powers."

"You're not putting anything in my brain!"

OF FEAR AND FAE

"It's not as if you have a choice. I'm simply being considerate by explaining to you what I'm doing. Now, don't act so alarmed. This won't hurt a bit."

Instinctively, I lurched toward my duffel bag, itching to get my hand on my sword's handle.

My bubble, with me in it, went flying across the room and hit the wall hard, knocking a lamp to the floor. I hadn't bothered to anchor my protection spell the way Orlena had taught me.

"Keep it down in there!" yelled a muffled voice from the room next door.

"Don't make this difficult for both of us," Baldric said, his fists plunging through my bubble like it wasn't even there. He grabbed my head in both hands and squeezed it as I lay on my back.

"I'll only control you when you're with your mother," he added through gritted teeth. "I'll leave you alone otherwise. Ow!"

I grabbed him by the family jewels, which are exactly the same on a faerie as on a human. I was not gentle.

Baldric bellowed like an ox and tore my hand away.

With his hands now gripping my wrist, I jerked my torso and headbutted him in the face. He roared and threw me at the wall again. My protection spell had been broken, and my body took the full force of the impact. I slid to the floor.

"I'm telling you, keep it down!" called the guest next door, banging on the wall.

"Help," I mewed, the wind knocked out of my lungs.

Baldric stood above me, panting, keeping a safe distance to the side. A thin runnel of blood oozed from a nostril. His lips were moving as he silently recited a spell's incantation. He pointed at me.

And all my strength disappeared. I lay on the floor, unable to move anything except my diaphragm to breathe. It was the Fae version of an immobility spell.

My muscles were lifeless, but my brain still worked. My inner magical energies were still there, as were my senses and my ability to draw upon elemental energies. I was determined to fight his mind-control spell with every atom of magic I had.

Baldric straddled me and pressed his palms against my temples. He whispered in the Fae language. When he had tutored me, I learned general principles of magic as well as specific Fae spells. They were simple ones, not powerful and complicated like the one he was casting now.

Still, I knew the basic structure of Fae magic, which differed from what most human magic was built upon. I stealthily cast a deconstruction spell to allow me to view the inner workings of his spell.

Yikes. I realized it was more than a spell. Spells use magic to alter an aspect of the material world, whether the change is illusory or actual. But it is always temporary. I suppose you could make a spell last for years, but eventually it will fade, and the material world will return to normal.

Not this spell. Baldric was attempting to alter my brain permanently. It was as if he were adding a computer chip to my central-processing unit. One that he would control. I couldn't allow this.

He was a more powerful magician than I. Attempting to fight back with magical brute force would be futile.

But I had a glimmer of hope. Baldric's spell was based on his intention—the plan of what I would be forced to do for him. And intention stemmed from desire—what he wanted me to do.

There were many kinds of desire, of wanting, of wishing. But they were all based on emotion.

And emotion was my secret weapon.

I opened my senses to read his emotions, to immerse myself in them. He was concentrating too much on the complex spell to notice what I was doing and wall himself off from me.

His spell was an intricate latticework of magic built to respond to his desires and force me to fulfill them. He had told me he wanted me to prevent Mom from interfering in the Fae's harvesting of phytolucine. And he surely wanted to make me serve him in other ways.

To make me fight for him. Or do chores he detested.

Or—omigod—be his lover. This spell would also force me to be his concubine.

Inextricably linked to all his desires was his ego. His narcissism.

He believed he was superior to me, and that was the key to inflicting his will on me.

I was going to turn that on its head.

I cast the spell that Orlena had taught me. I couldn't make him harm himself or do what went against his best interests. But what if his best interest was what I wanted him to do?

I would use his strengths against him like magical jiu jitsu. And his strengths were his powerful ego and self-confidence. My spell pumped emotions and desires into him.

I am superior to Sophie. I have nothing to fear from her. No need to force her to do what I want. What I want, she wants.

I am superior to her, stronger than her, smarter than her. I don't want my will to be planted in her brain like a parasite. I am so much greater than she is, I can absorb her, as if she were a bacterium. Yes, I can absorb her desires so that what I desire, and she desires, are the same.

Making me even stronger.

I sensed I had succeeded in muddling his intentions. He had wanted to make me his robot, but now, he was seeing me as an asset who enhanced him.

He had wanted to put his will into me. But I inflamed his ego to make him want to absorb me into him—into his ego and will. And absorbing me included absorbing the spell he was placing in my brain.

Remember, I couldn't fight his spell head on. What I did was give him the desire to absorb me. With my deconstruction spell, I used that desire to alter the building blocks of his spell. To reverse them and construct them for a new target.

I soon felt the magic he was forcing into me turn in the opposite direction.

He began casting the spell into his own brain—with his desire to absorb me actually directing him and his spell.

I was astounded. I couldn't believe what I was getting away with.

His spell to control me was becoming a spell enabling me to control him, all thanks to me manipulating his emotions.

He didn't fully realize what was happening until he finished casting the spell. When he broke his connection with my mind, his eyes widened with shock.

He no longer had access to my consciousness. He couldn't experience the world through my senses and control my behavior like he had planned.

Instead, he felt my presence in *his* brain.

He screamed with anger and horror, climbing from on top of me to his feet, shaking his head violently, as if that could throw me from his brain and out of his ears.

"What did you do to me?" he shouted, his face stretched with madness. "This is impossible. I'm so much more powerful than you."

"So much more powerful that I'm a part of you now," I said in a hypnotic voice. "What I want, you want. You are so much greater than me, you have no need to resist me. You can do what I want and still be superior to me. Do you understand?"

"No! That's utter nonsense!"

"If a flea makes you itch and want to scratch, does that mean the flea controls you?"

"No, but. . ." He was manic in his confusion.

"Baldric," I said calmly, "I'm just a flea. You have beaten me today. You will leave my room now and never bother me again."

He turned on his heel and stormed out of the room, slamming the door behind him.

"Hey!" came the muffled voice from next door. "Any more noise, and I'm calling the cops!"

I thought about Baldric and shook my head in amazement. Little ol' me with my lesser magic powers defeated a Fae sorcerer. All thanks to my being an empath and mixing it with magic.

The spell that Baldric had accidentally implanted in his own brain made him obey me and leave the room. Could I get him to do my bidding in the future, or would he find a way to disable the spell?

This could be interesting.

CHAPTER 30

DARLA

I felt dizzy, achy, and sick to my stomach as I stood in the dirt of the construction site. The effects of the magic leaking from the Fae's underground lab were unmistakable.

I was the only one feeling sick. Cory said he was unaffected. Did it have something to do with his magic gene?

What bothered me most was Sophie not answering her phone.

"Honey," Cory whispered. "We've all turned our phones off. You should too. The Fae are going to be more active now that the sun is setting, and we can't afford to alert them."

"I was trying to reach Sophie. Having another witch here would give me more confidence," I said, shutting down my phone.

Cory frowned. "You told her she didn't need to come here and put herself at risk. Don't you think I have enough power? I harvested energy from the ley line this afternoon."

"Absolutely." I patted his arm and got a static-electricity shock. "I was needlessly worrying."

The truth was, the worrying was not needless. It was safe to assume a Fae sorcerer was working in the lab, and he or she would have formidable power. And there would be the detachment of workers and soldiers, undoubtedly reinforced by replacements after our recent attack on them.

All we had was Cory's magic to destroy the lab, and bodyguards to protect him from the soldiers. Namely, Gorkee and her three gnomes. We were joined by Samson, who was off duty, and Diego, who had just arrived from a battle in which the extremist militia had been routed. I had even convinced Roderick to come, but I had little faith in his fighting ability and courage.

Interestingly, none of our bodyguards were affected by the Fae's magic. It was designed to repel or kill humans, so I wasn't surprised Gorkee, the gnomes, and the vampires were unaffected. Obviously it didn't work on shifters, either, because Samson felt fine even though he was in human form.

"Is there no place to sit?" Roderick asked me when we arrived at the vast wasteland that had once been a forest.

"Sit?" I replied with maximum scorn. "We're here to fight faeries, not chill out with a mystery novel."

"You know perfectly well I was turned late in life. I have a touch of arthritis that my vampirism hasn't overcome. There is no need to have an attitude with me."

"Sorry. I'm nervous and the Fae magic is making me sick. I feel useless, because I don't have magic like Cory or preternatural strength like you and Diego. And the Goddess has been dormant in me for a long time."

"You, my dear, are our general. Generals command; they don't tear faerie heads off like yours truly."

He was right, though I doubted he had ever killed a faerie. I returned my attention to the battle to come. Cory and I walked across the dirt field, our "bodyguards" surrounding us. We were sensing the underground supernatural energy to determine if the lab remained in the same location it had been in the last time we were here.

I found that many of the pencil markers we had left stuck in the ground were still there. Construction crews had truly been stymied by the effects of the "magic bomb" the faeries were creating.

Our quick check told us the lab was in the same location, bursting with supernatural energy and oozing traces of the anti-human magic. A sorcerer was definitely down there tonight. We detected new tunnels that had been dug to replace the ones Sophie had collapsed, but I didn't care about them. Tonight, our sole purpose was to destroy the lab.

"So, do I just blast the lab?" Cory asked.

I was supposed to be the general, but I couldn't think of any tactic cleverer than simply blowing up the freaking place.

"Yeah. Let's get as far away as we can that's still within the range of your spell."

We retreated toward the gravel parking lot. Our "body-guards" stood in a loose line ahead of us. That night, as we had done before, we had left our cars parked elsewhere to avoid attracting attention.

"Okay, Cory, let her rip."

Cory didn't have the penchant for attack magic that Sophie had. But our battles with the Fae had inspired him to create the magical version of a bunker-buster bomb.

Since he was boosted by extra energy from ley lines, his spell would be powerful enough to penetrate deep underground. A previous version he had tried simply created intense shock waves that mimicked the effects of dynamite or plastic explosives.

He tweaked the spell for this mission, so it would not only

physically destroy the lab and its contents but would also break other magic spells in its blast radius. Sophie had taught him a deconstruction spell he had worked into his blasting spell, making it disrupt the invisible structures of the Fae magic.

"Fire in the hole!" Cory called out, goofily using the clichéd expression from war movies.

The moment he cast the spell, I viscerally felt the vacuum created around him as the immense amounts of magical energy left his body and plunged into the earth fifty yards away.

The earth shook, but no sound of an explosion came from it. My nausea abruptly ended. The supernatural energy we'd felt underground weakened greatly.

But not completely.

"There's movement in the tree line," Diego said.

I followed his gaze across the dirt field to the edge of the remaining forest, about a quarter mile away. Sure enough, faeries were pouring into the field like ants from a disturbed anthill.

"I guess they kept soldiers in reserve," I said.

"I guess," Diego said sarcastically. "We're greatly outnumbered."

"You have a gun," Samson said to me. "Use it."

I had brought our self-defense pistol that we kept in our bedroom closet. After all, this was a battle. But it didn't mean I wanted to shoot any Fae.

He shifted into a wolf. I averted my eyes from the painful process.

"Let's retreat slowly, without turning our backs to them. Maybe they won't follow us into the road."

Our guards stepped backward with Cory and me sticking close to them. The faeries reached us long before we made it to the road. There were dozens in their natural faerie forms, running so quickly I couldn't count them. They carried bows, spears, and swords, not guns like they did when in human form. I figured they hadn't shifted to human because they were attacking gnomes and other supernaturals.

I took a shot with my handgun and didn't appear to hit anyone, which was a remarkable achievement in bad marksmanship. Gorkee and the gnomes loosed arrows at the charging faeries, taking down two.

When the faeries were close enough that we could see their facial features in the moonlight, Samson howled and rushed into their line, tearing it apart. He held a faerie aloft in his jaws and shook him like a chew toy.

Diego jumped into the melee, moving with unbelievable speed. He fought with a combination of martial arts and gruesome butchery. The shifter and the vampire sustained wounds that they simply shrugged off.

Gorkee hacked at the enemy with her sword, the gnomes thrust their spears. The faeries parried them with skill.

Cory remained beside me as we slowly backed away from the faeries, but he was absolutely drained of all energy. Roderick stayed with us, too.

"I'm guarding you two," he said.

"No, thanks," I growled. "Get your butt in there and fight!"

My supernatural friends had stopped the faerie charge and were taking them down, one after another. However, we were still outnumbered. I didn't fire my gun, worried I would accidentally hit my friends.

"Egad, there are more of them coming out of the woods!" Roderick cried.

The tide of battle was going against us. I didn't think it could get any worse.

Until the Fae sorcerer crawled out of an escape hole above

the lab and strode toward us behind the line of Fae soldiers. He appeared to be burned and injured, but he should have been destroyed along with the lab and the spell he had created.

A fireball from the sorcerer whizzed above the melee and landed by my feet, sending sparks hitting me.

Then came another. It hit Roderick in the chest. He shrieked and stumbled backward, falling on his butt. Flames covered his ancient woolen suit and vest. I tossed dirt on the flames while he patted them out.

Being immersed in fire without being able to escape will destroy a vampire. Mild burns, however, are quickly healed by their supernatural healing abilities.

"This is why you should be in hand-to-hand combat like Diego," I said.

Adequately shamed, Roderick walked at hyper speed to the melee and seized a faerie on the outer fringe.

Things were looking pretty dismal. The wolf that was Samson, Diego, Gorkee, and the gnomes were holding their own against the faeries. No one had been seriously wounded. They would have won the skirmish and sent the surviving faeries fleeing, if reinforcements hadn't been approaching from the woods.

Then there was the sorcerer. Cory was too depleted to shoot fireballs back at him, and Sophie wasn't there with her sword. There was only me, with no magic of my own.

Cory grunted as a fireball hit him, and he fell to the ground. I rolled him in the dirt to extinguish the flames. He winced with pain.

I was beyond angry. I needed the Goddess's healing powers *immediately*.

The Fae reinforcements shouted a war cry as they reached their comrades, a sea of vicious munchkins surrounding our troops.

I needed the Goddess's wrath.

Ask, and you, the righteous, shall triumph, her voice sang in my head. *If you receive me willingly, truly, and fully.*

"Yes. I do."

The first thing I felt was the warmth in my solar plexus, pleasant at first, then growing hotter. It spread throughout my abdomen and into my limbs.

My ears buzzed, and the buzzing turned into music in my head, a familiar tune, though an ancient one that I, Darla, had only heard coming from my mouth when I became the Goddess and sang this song.

The Goddess was coming to life within me.

Darla went away, and I became Danu, earth mother, the forgotten goddess who yearned to return to the world she loved and had nurtured.

I knelt beside Cory, still on the ground, my hands gently peeling away the fabric of his clothing and touching his burns. They healed before my eyes as Cory watched, amazed.

My attention moved to the battle raging on only yards away, where our fighters were quickly being overcome by the increased number of faeries. Roderick wasn't much help, remaining at the outer edge of the fighting and picking off victims one by one.

"Cease your hostilities!" I shouted, my voice louder than a trumpet and sounding nothing like Darla's. It was musical and thunder-like at the same time.

All the combatants stopped and stared at me with wonder.

"It is the Goddess," a faerie said in Fae, which I understood perfectly.

"Faeries, return to the forest!" I commanded.

As the Goddess, I had the power to destroy evil organisms that harmed earth's creatures. I could kill diseases, dangerous mutations, and beings from other dimensions.

The Fae were the enemies of Darla and her people, but they were among the earth's creatures. I preferred not to kill them, unless absolutely necessary for the greater good. So, I sang to them the song that filled my head because it brought calm and peace.

The faeries took a few steps away from us. Their officers discussed retreating. Samson, Diego, Roderick, Gorkee, and the gnomes stood there resting and healing their wounds, waiting to see what their foes would do.

The Fae sorcerer ruined everything.

"Why did you stop fighting?" he shouted at them and waved his staff. "Kill these pathetic humans and their supernatural stooges! Kill them now, before I kill all of you!"

The sorcerer sent a fireball whooshing toward me. I batted it away as if it were a beach ball, but the faeries had understood the lesson. They resumed attacking my beleaguered fighters.

The sorcerer was evil and the spell he was developing in its final stages would be devastating to humans. But the spell hadn't killed anyone yet. What the sorcerer had committed, however, was a crime against the forests, stealing the phytolucine they had created.

And I now knew the truth: the trees and plants produced it to repel humans, not harm them. The sorcerer added it to his magic hoping to kill on a mass scale.

The forests will get their vengeance, I, the Goddess, vowed.

And I empowered them with magic.

It happened so quickly that the eyes of faeries and humans could not track and comprehend how the trees moved. One moment, we were in a giant wasteland that used to be a forest and meadow.

The next moment, it was filled with trees. They came from the remaining forest that survived on the edge of the construction site and returned to the land that had once been theirs, sinking their roots back into the soil. It was like a salve that soothed the violated land.

The faeries panicked and scattered throughout the transplanted trees, disappearing from view as they searched for their tunnels. The sorcerer remained on the site, climbing back down into the hole from which he had emerged after Cory had blasted the laboratory.

"Take back what is yours," I said to the trees. "Take the substance that was stolen from you."

A rumbling came from below ground, followed by popping and ripping sounds. The trees were sending their roots into the underground chamber, absorbing the phytolucine. With my Goddess vision, I saw them snake into the half-collapsed space, pushing through piles of dirt and grasping metal canisters that they squeezed and broke open to absorb the substance they had produced naturally.

I heard his screams, but didn't see the sorcerer squeezed and strangled by the roots that completely covered him and filled the chamber.

My vision ended. All was quiet. The warmth fled my body, and I was Darla again.

We stood in a small clearing in the new forest, a space the trees had left for us. Cory, the two vampires, Samson back in human form, Gorkee, and the gnomes looked around with wonder.

"You did this?" Samson asked me.

"Danu did it. The lab has been destroyed, and the phytolucine has been returned to the forest."

"What about the sorcerer?" Cory asked.

"The charitable way to put it is that he is now fertilizer."

Cory grimaced. I guess my answer was not exactly charitable.

"Was this a decisive victory over the Fae?" Diego asked.

"For now," I replied. "They might have other labs and sorcerers who know how to make the potion and create the spell from it. And they certainly have a large army. Let's celebrate for now but be prepared for more war."

That was good enough for me.

EPILOGUE

SOPHIE

"Sophie!" Mom called to me from the kitchen.

I hurried there from the dining room to fetch a fresh basket of warm, buttery goodness.

At the new incarnation of the Esperanza Inn, our scones were still a big hit at breakfast and teatime.

Mom and Pinky continued to whip up wonderful food for our guests, though our guests were a bit different now. Instead of young couples on romantic getaways, families enjoying the historic attractions, or seniors in town to shop for antiques, our new guests were here for business.

We had witches, psychics, shifters, gnomes, elves, dwarves, trolls, ogres, vampires, and more. They were locals as well as refugees who gathered in San Marcos for safety after being run out of smaller communities. And they wanted to push back against our persecution.

Many were also in town to join the rag-tag army that was assembling to defend the city from the Unseelie Court. Their efforts to develop magic to wipe out humans had been temporarily stymied, but the Queene's armies were reported to be on the march to San Marcos.

On a lighter note, I should mention that the vampires were the only creatures who didn't enjoy the scones. They stuck with their usual sustenance, which Roderick was in charge of buying in plastic IV bags, so our guests didn't have to risk hunting humans at night.

That morning, I tried to be chipper as I kept the breakfast buffet going for the ravenous creatures crowding the dining room. But inside, I was mourning.

Other witnesses had come forward who claimed they knew the governor, Senator Poxton, and other cronies were faeries. The claims spread throughout social media, on podcasts, and in random videos. The mainstream media did not cover the allegations other than the few brief mentions of the "rumors" right after I first went public.

There was a lot of buzz, but no one had any photographic proof that our state's top politicians weren't human. Even if there had been such evidence, I doubted it would have mattered.

The governor handily won reelection, along with all members of her party in the legislature whose terms were up.

I assumed my life was still in danger because of what I had seen and heard in the Faerie Queene's Winter Palace. And I still was a wanted criminal. I doubted I was much of a priority for the governor, though. She had many campaign promises to fulfill, and I was little more than a gadfly to her now.

Among her promises was to crack down on supernaturals more forcefully—to "completely cleanse the evil from our state," as she had put it in speeches. Ridding the state of vampires and shifters was her priority, probably because of what they'd done to her militia.

The guilds and I had much work to do to save them and all of us from extinction. If only Diego would reply to my texts and calls, we could plan strategy. And I would know where I stood after our unexpected kiss.

One bit of good news: Orlena was recovering from Baldric's attack. I'd visited her in the hospital just the other day, and she regained consciousness briefly while I was there. The nurse told me they hoped she would recover from the ruptured cerebral aneurysm with little lasting neurological damage.

Another piece of good news: Baldric's reversed spell was still lodged in his brain. Using my empath powers enhanced by magic, I convinced him from afar to resign from his position as president of the Executive Council.

The day after that, I heard the news that he had done so. Pretty cool, right? I looked forward to seeing how far I could take my control over him. Most important, the guilds could elect a new leader and unite to fight for our freedom.

"Sophie!" Mom's voice interrupted my thoughts.

I returned to the kitchen.

"The inspector from the Florida Department of Business and Professional Regulation just showed up and is parking down the street," she said frantically. "He's doing one of his surprise inspections again to make sure we're not operating as an inn. Send the guests upstairs and use your magic to hide any evidence that they're here."

"On it," I replied. It was a tall order, but I had some vision-blocking spells that would work.

"Sorry, but everyone has to hurry upstairs," I announced to

the dining room. "We need to hide you from the DBPR inspector, but you can come back down to finish your breakfast when he leaves."

I opened the French doors to the courtyard. Jerry was stationed at the fountain, water gushing from his mouth. Archibald, perched on the wall beside him, chatted and giggled.

"Get stone-faced, gentlemen. The inspector is here," I told them before closing the door.

"Mr. Flossman! What a pleasure to see you again," Mom said in the foyer.

I cast a spell to hide all the food on the buffet and the half-eaten dishes on the tables. My job was much easier than the acting performance Mom would have to put on.

I rushed upstairs to cast the same spell on the occupied guest rooms. This drill was just one of the hardships we supernaturals had to endure. Things might get even worse. But I was optimistic a day would come when we were no longer oppressed and persecuted.

Remember, our inn was named after the Spanish word for hope.

Never underestimate the power of hope.

PLEASE LEAVE A REVIEW

Dear reader, thank you in advance:
Please give my book a better chance.
Success and sales depend on you,
So kindly post a book review.

WHAT'S NEXT

Book 3 of the Goddess's Daughter: *Of Valor and Vampires*

Life isn't easy now for supernaturals now that we've been unmasked. But we're finally fighting back. Against mobs of vigilantes. Against hate groups. And against a militia commanded by the governor.

At the forefront of our fight are the vampires, the most endangered of all supernaturals. Their leader, Diego, has been in San Marcos since the 1500s. And he's been burning a hole in my heart since, like, forever.

Meanwhile, a Fae army is marching on our city. Their secret ally is our governor, who is willing to sacrifice our city, and the entire state, to gain more power. Our ragtag force of supernaturals is all there is to fight them, but the odds are so stacked against us, we would need divine intervention to prevail.

It turns out I know a goddess. Yeah, my mom.

She's the human vessel of the Goddess Danu, who is gradually taking her over. Am I losing my mother and gaining a goddess?

This should get interesting.

Get swept up by the Goddess's Daughter series (a sequel to the Memory Guild): urban fantasy with magic and monsters, secrets and treachery, a touch of humor, and a slow-burn romance.

Visit your favorite e-retailer or wardparker.com

INTERESTED IN THE BOOKS THAT SPAWNED THE GODDESS'S DAUGHTER?

Check out the Memory Guild Midlife Paranormal Mystery Thrillers

Visit your favorite e-retailer, wardparker.com, or books2read.com/amagictouchmidlifeparanormal

GET A FREE BOOK

GET A FREE E-BOOK

Sign up for my newsletter and get *A Ghostly Touch*, a Memory Guild novella, for free, offered exclusively to my newsletter subscribers. Darla reads the memories of a young woman, murdered in the 1890s, whose ghost begins haunting Darla, looking for justice. As a subscriber, you'll be the first to know about my new releases and lots of free book promotions. The newsletter is delivered only a couple of times a month. No spam at all, and you can unsubscribe at any time.

Visit wardparker.com

ACKNOWLEDGMENTS

I wish to thank my loyal readers, who give me a reason to write more every day. I'm especially grateful to Shelley Holloway and Elizabeth Thurmond for all your editing and proofreading brilliance. To my A Team (you know who you are), thanks for reading and reviewing my ARCs, as well as providing good suggestions. And to my wife, Martha, thank you for your love and moral support.

ABOUT THE AUTHOR

Ward is the author of the Memory Guild midlife paranormal mystery thrillers. The Goddess's Daughter urban fantasy series continues the adventures.

He also writes the Monsters of Jellyfish Beach paranormal mysteries, set in the same world as his Freaky Florida series.

Ward lives in Florida with his wife, several cats, and a demon who wishes to remain anonymous.

Connect with him on Facebook (wardparkerauthor), Book-Bub, Goodreads, Bluesky (wardparker.bsky.social), or Threads (wardparker2223). Check out his books and sign up for his newsletter at wardparker.com.

PARANORMAL BOOKS BY WARD PARKER

Freaky Florida Humorous Paranormal Novels

Snowbirds of Prey
Invasive Species
Fate Is a Witch
Gnome Coming
Going Batty
Dirty Old Manatee
Gazillions of Reptilians

Hangry as Hell (novella)

Books 1-3 Box Set

The Memory Guild Midlife Paranormal Mystery Thrillers

A Magic Touch (also available in audio)

The Psychic Touch (also available in audio)

A Wicked Touch (also available in audio)

A Haunting Touch

The Wizard's Touch

A Witchy Touch

A Faerie's Touch

The Goddess's Touch

The Vampire's Touch

An Angel's Touch

A Ghostly Touch (novella)

Books 1-3 Box Set (also available in audio)

The Goddess's Daughter

(Continuing the Memory Guild Series.)

Of Envy and Empaths

Of Fear and Fae

Of Valor and Vampires

Monsters of Jellyfish Beach Paranormal Mystery Adventures

The Golden Ghouls

Fiends With Benefits

Get Ogre Yourself
My Funny Frankenstein
Werewolf Art Thou?
In Sprite of Herself
Worms of Endearment

www.ingramcontent.com/pod-product-compliance
Lightning Source LLC
Chambersburg PA
CBHW030156200626
46812CB00017B/2179